HOPE'S WAR

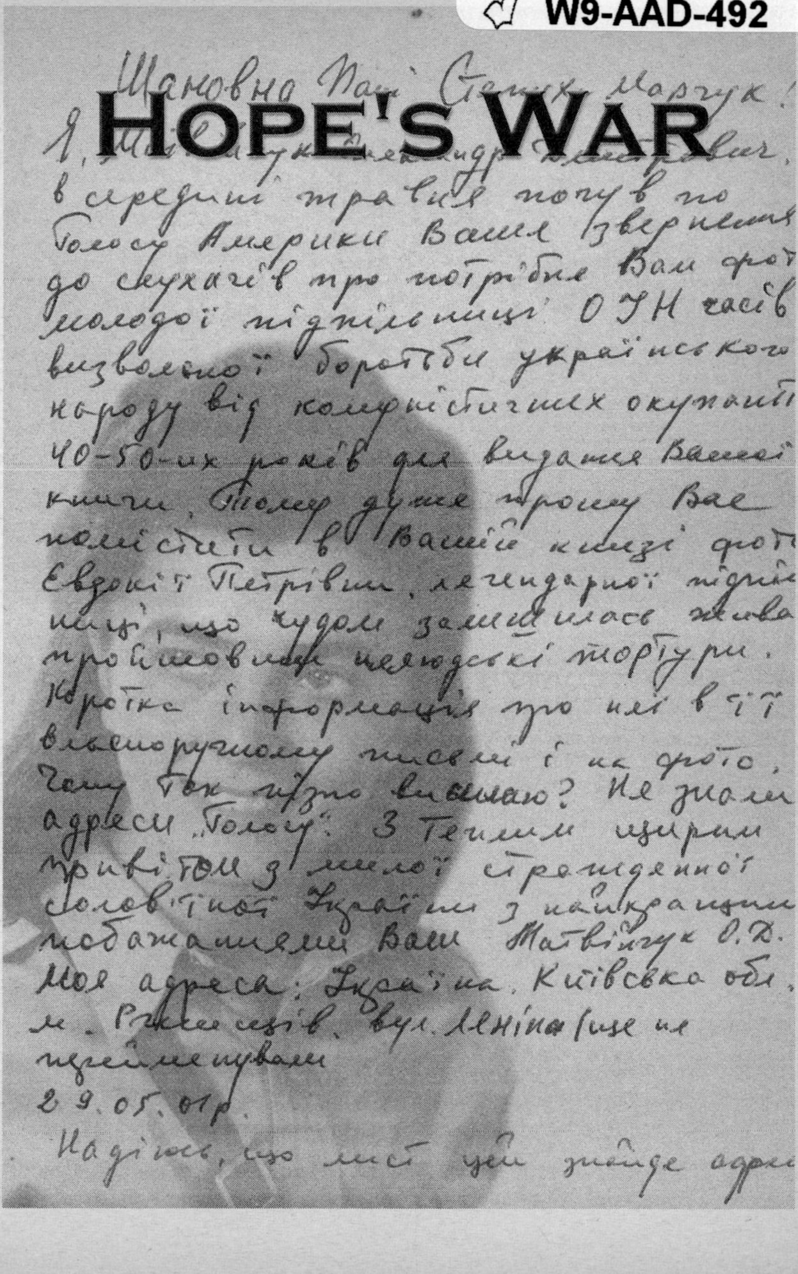

Шановна Пані [illegible] Марчук!
Я, Матвійчук Олександр [illegible],
в середині травня почув по
Голосу Америки Ваше звернення
до слухачів про потрібне Вам фото
молодої підпільниці ОУН часів
визвольної боротьби українського
народу від комуністичних окупантів
40-50-их років для видання Вашої
книги. Тому дуже прошу Вас
помістити в Вашій книзі фото
Євдокії Петрівни, легендарної підпільниці, що чудом залишилась жива
пройшовши нелюдські тортури.
Коротка інформація про неї в її
власноручному письмі і на фото.
Чому так пізно висилаю? Не знали
адреси „Голосу". З теплим щирим
привітом з милої стражденної
солов'їної України з найкращими
побажаннями Вам Матвійчук О.Д.
Моя адреса: Україна. Київська обл.
м. Ржищів. вул. Леніна (ще не
перейменували
29.05.01р.
Надіюсь, що лист цей знайде адре[illegible]

Gentlemen: I am known as a brutal dog. Because of this reason I was appointed as a Reichskommissar of the Ukraine. Our task is to suck from the Ukraine all the goods we can get hold of, without consideration of the feeling or the property of the Ukrainians.

Gentlemen: I am expecting from you the utmost severity towards the native population.

— *Erich Koch's inauguration speech,*
Rovno, September 1941

There are no prisoners of war, there are traitors.

— *Stalin, August 1941*

We are against Russian Communist-Bolshevism and German National-Socialism....[we are] for the equality of all citizens of Ukraine regardless of nationality, in state, public rights and duties, for equal rights, for labor, wages and rest.

— *Ukrainian Insurgent Army,*
September 1944

HOPE'S WAR

MARSHA FORCHUK SKRYPUCH

to Andriana —
best wishes!
MSkrypuch

A BOARDWALK BOOK
A MEMBER OF THE DUNDURN GROUP
TORONTO › OXFORD

Editor: Barry Jowett
Copy Editor: Julian Walker
Design: Bruna Brunelli
Printer: Webcom

Canadian Cataloguing in Publication Data

Skrypuch, Marsha Forchuk, 1954–
    Hope's war

ISBN 1-895681-19-7

    1. World War, 1939–1945—Ukraine—Juvenile fiction.
2. Ukrainian Canadians—Juvenile fiction. I. Title.

PS8587.K79H66 2001   jC813'.54   C2001-902187-9
PZ7.S6284Ho 2001

1   2   3   4   5   05   04   03   02   01

Canada

THE CANADA COUNCIL | LE CONSEIL DES ARTS
   FOR THE ARTS | DU CANADA
   SINCE 1957 | DEPUIS 1957

ONTARIO ARTS COUNCIL
CONSEIL DES ARTS DE L'ONTARIO

We acknowledge the support of the **Canada Council for the Arts** and the **Ontario Arts Council** for our publishing program. We also acknowledge the financial support of the **Government of Canada** through the **Book Publishing Industry Development Program**, **The Association for the Export of Canadian Books**, and the **Government of Ontario** through the **Ontario Book Publishers Tax Credit** program.

Care has been taken to trace the ownership of copyright material used in this book. The author and the publisher welcome any information enabling them to rectify any references or credit in subsequent editions.

J. Kirk Howard, President

Printed and bound in Canada.⊕
Printed on recycled paper.
www.dundurn.com

Dundurn Press
8 Market Street
Suite 200
Toronto, Ontario, Canada
M5E 1M6

Dundurn Press
73 Lime Walk
Headington, Oxford,
England
OX3 7AD

Dundurn Press
2250 Military Road
Tonawanda NY
U.S.A. 14150

CHAPTER 1

KAT BALIUK FELT like a traitor.

She hugged her books to her chest and stepped onto the sidewalk as the bus stopped in front of Cawthra School for the Arts, then she turned and waved faintly to her friends. They were staying on until the next stop: St. Paul's Catholic High School. No one waved back. They were already involved in animated conversations without her. Kat's older sister Genya was also staying on the bus with a group of her friends until the St. Paul's stop, but Genya did turn and wink reassuringly at her little sister just as the bus pulled away.

Kat ran her fingers nervously through her dark blonde hair, hoping that it didn't look as flyaway as it felt. Classes didn't start for another twenty minutes. She looked through her wire-rimmed glasses towards the concrete steps leading into the school and searched the faces of the students loitering there. Not one she could call a friend.

She felt so odd coming to school without a uniform. Last year in grade 9 at St. Paul's, it was a no-brainer getting ready for school, but she must have spent forty-five minutes this morning deciding what to wear. The low-slung cargo pants and midriff-baring tops that the cluster of girls on the bottom step wore were a far cry from grey uniform pants and white blouse. She didn't feel too out of place with the choice that she made for this day: baggy hip-hugging jeans and a T-shirt.

As she walked past the girls, she noticed from the corner of her glasses that they appraised her, discounted her, then continued with their chatter. Probably dance students, she calculated, noticing their tight bodies and hair pulled back into little buns.

There was a group of guys just in front of the school's front doors discussing something with great seriousness. They too looked up for a moment, assessed her, then ignored her. Drama, she figured.

Kat opened her binder, found her timetable and pretended to look up the room number of her first class. Room 113, Visual Arts was already imbedded in her brain. She must have taken that timetable out a hundred times over the summer! But at least she looked occupied.

"Hey there!"

Kat turned, thankful that someone had actually wanted to speak with her. She did her best not to gasp at what stood before her: a Goth in full regalia. Right down to the black lipstick and eyeliner and leather coat held together with hundreds of safety pins. The hair was bright turquoise gelled to bed-head perfection, and the plain silver nose-ring was downright painful to look at.

"Name's Ian, what's yours?" he asked, extending a hand covered with tarnished silver rings.

Kat clasped his outstretched hand limply and introduced herself. She noticed that the girls on the step were watching her and smirking.

"You're from St. Paul's, right?" he asked. "I was there for grade nine last year too."

Kat tried to hold back her surprise. She tried to imagine Ian's head pasted onto a body wearing the white shirt and grey pants, but the image was too absurd.

"I didn't last long," he explained. "They kicked me out one minute into day two when I showed up in a kilt."

"A *kilt*?" exclaimed Kat. "And you're wondering why you got kicked out?" Even the girls at St. Paul's didn't wear the kilts. She would have loved to see the havoc Ian created when he walked through the door. How was it that she had been there the whole year and hadn't even *heard* of this incident? The mind police must've been working overtime on that one.

"You're hardly one to talk," said Ian, smiling.

"What do you mean?"

"You're here for pretty much the same reason that I am."

Kat hadn't thought of it that way, but there was some truth in the statement.

"What's your specialty?" she asked.

"Music," Ian replied.

Just as Kat thought.

Right at that moment, the bell rang so Kat and Ian headed in. "See you around," said Ian.

Kat watched as his turquoise head disappeared down the hallway.

Kat made her way to the end of the hall and then walked down the staircase and past the cafeteria in a sea of other students going in the same direction. Soon room 113 was in front of her and so she pushed the door and walked in.

The actual layout of the art room wasn't that much different from the one at St. Paul's. There were three rows of two-student art tables with stools instead of chairs taking up the main part of the room. Off to one side was a huge supply cupboard, and beside that was an alcove with a table in the middle holding stacks of paper and drawing boards.

The big difference between this art room and the one at St. Paul's could be seen in the paintings that hung on the walls, and in the sculptures that were displayed on shelves. And it wasn't just the quality of the artwork. Obviously, kids going to an art school where you have to audition to get accepted would be talented. It was the subject matter that was the crucial difference. At St. Paul's, there were some subjects that could not be painted or sculpted — or even thought of.

Two girls were already sitting in desks, side by side, close to the front of the room. The dark haired one kept on covering her mouth with her hand to hide her braces as she talked to her blonde friend. Both girls were dressed in dark coloured scoop neck T-shirts, but one had tight black jeans on, and the other was wearing baggy black cargo pants. They turned to look as Kat approached them, and they both smiled.

"You must be Katie," said the girl with braces. "My name's Beth Gupta."

"And I'm Callie Goodfriend," said the blonde.

"My name's Kat, not Katie. How did you know who I was?"

"We don't exactly get new students coming into the program all the time," said Beth, hiding her teeth. "Mrs. O'Connor told us at the end of last year that we were getting an 'exciting new student'." Both the girls giggled. "We heard about what happened at St. Paul's."

Kat smiled uncomfortably.

She didn't really want to talk about what happened at St. Paul's. While that one instance had been a bad experience, she still felt loyal to all her friends there. And it was only a year ago that she had joined with these friends in scoffing at the self-important snobs of Cawthra. There was much tension between Cawthra and St. Paul's, and the fact that their properties backed onto each other didn't make matters any better. St. Paul's students liked to call Cawthra the CGCC — Cawthra Golf and Country Club. It was only for rich kids, after all.

And now here she was, one of Them.

"Well? Are you sitting with us, or what?" asked Beth, pointing to an empty chair behind them.

Kat looked around and noticed that the class was quickly filling up. With a grateful smile to Beth and Callie, Kat sat down behind them. As the other students wandered in and took up seats behind and around her, Kat had a tremor of apprehension. What if she didn't measure up?

She had always been the best student in any art class she had ever taken. But then again, there had never been much competition. Cawthra was different: every single student in this class had been required to undergo the same rigorous audition that she had, and each of them had passed. Not only that, the other students had been here for a full year already, so they were bound to be better. Kat took a deep breath and sighed.

The last person to enter the room was the teacher. Kat already knew from her schedule that his name was Mr. Harding. He was much younger than how she had imagined him. In fact, he was so young looking that in another context, she might have thought he was a senior student. He wore the long sleeves of his white dress shirt rolled up almost to the elbow, revealing muscular arms. The shirttail was tucked haphazardly into a pair of khakis, and although he wore a tie around his neck, it hung loose at an open collar.

He stood at the front of the class and waited, silently, until the murmuring of conversation died down. "It is good to see you all back here," said Mr. Harding. "I am sure that you all spent those glorious summer days holed up in the library researching the Renaissance masters."

Kat gave a gulp, but then realized he was just kidding.

"We have one new student this year, and I would like you to all welcome her," Mr. Harding motioned to Kat. She stood up.

"This is Katreena Balick."

"It's Kat-ar-yn-a. Kat for short," she corrected. "And my last name is B-A-L-I-U-K, pronounced Ball-ook." She could feel the flush of embarrassment heating her cheeks.

"Oh!" said Mr. Harding. "I'll correct that in my files. Welcome, Kat. I think you'll like it here."

"Thank you," she said, then sat down.

Mr. Harding began to pace at the front of the classroom. "For our first lesson, I need a volunteer. Each of you will have to do this at some point, so don't be shy." He surveyed the class. No one raised their hand.

"Callie?"

"That's not exactly volunteering," said Callie, getting up from her desk.

"When I don't get a volunteer, I make a volunteer," said Mr. Harding. The class chuckled at his feeble joke.

"Let's move our desks into a circle," he said. "And you two, Michael and George." Mr. Harding gestured at one teen sitting on the other side of Callie and at another from the back of the room. "Grab the platform from the storage area and drag it into the centre of the class."

After much scraping and pushing, the desks and platform were configured in the way that Mr. Harding wanted. He gestured to Callie.

"Lie down there and pose as if you just got hit by an ice-cream truck," he said, pointing to the platform. The class tittered uncomfortably again.

Callie wrapped her blonde hair into a knot to keep it off her face and then flopped on the platform, her arms and legs splayed out limply. "Like this?" she asked.

"Perfect," said Mr. Harding. "Hold that pose."

"Okay class," said the teacher taking a timer out of his shirt pocket. "You've got two minutes to do a shadow profile of Callie. Use the broad side of a black crayon and start from the middle of the body and work your way out to the edges."

As the timer ticked, the students quickly sketched. With a crayon in her hand and a sheet of paper in front of her, Kat was in her element. Maybe these other students were better than her, but she figured she could hold her own. She smiled with satisfaction as she put in the last touches. Mr. Harding passed behind her, then stopped to study her work. "The feet are inaccurate. Fix that up and it'll do."

Kat felt momentarily crushed, but then she smiled inwardly. She had a feeling that she would be learning a lot in Mr. Harding's class.

CHAPTER 2

THE HOUSE WAS unusually quiet, now that school had started again. Usually Genya or Kataryna would distract him from his unhappy thoughts, but this day had seemed to loom on forever. Once his daughter and son-in-law had left for their respective jobs, and the girls had caught the bus to school, Danylo sat down at the kitchen table with a cup of tea and tried to read the paper, but the words seemed just a blur.

A swirl of lemony steam from the tea drifted to his nostrils, and an image of Danylo's wife filled his mind. Nadiya, or Hope in English, had loved lemon in her tea. And once they had moved to Canada, she would add a little bit of lemon juice to the water when she rinsed her hair. He loved holding her close and burying his face in her hair. In the spring, when the pain of losing her was still too sharp to bear, this memory would have caused him sorrow, but now it comforted him. He breathed in the scent of lemony tea and felt the spirit of Nadiya around him.

He spent the afternoon on his hands and knees in his daughter's garden, digging up potatoes. He preferred his own garden to this tiny one, but with Nadiya's illness and death in the spring, he'd had neither the time nor the heart to plant it. He still found going back to his own house painful. He was thankful that his daughter and son-in-law suggested he live with them for a while, and he was grateful that his daughter had the foresight in the spring to plant this small plot to keep him busy now.

He dug each potato carefully with a trowel, and set each one in the basket. When the basket was full, he set each potato, side by side, out on the window ledge of the summer kitchen and along the stone ledge of the patio to dry out in the sun. When they were dry, he would take each one and gently brush off the dirt with a towel. They stored better if they weren't washed.

He looked down the street for the girls' bus, wondering if this first day of school would be a short one. He was anxious to hear about Kataryna's first day at the new school. After all she had been through, he prayed that this year would be a smooth transition for her.

He did not have the same worries about Genya, or Jenny as her friends called her. Genya always landed on her feet. She was the perfect Ukrainian granddaughter: beautiful in a blonde and blue-eyed way, with a bright smile and easy grace. She was his *malenka ptashka* — his little bird. She was in her last year of high school on the top of the honour roll and had set her sights on studying medicine. Everything seemed to come easily to Genya. He was grateful that she didn't seem to mind moving out of her bedroom and into Kataryna's so that he could live with them for a bit.

Kataryna, on the other hand, always did things the hard way. She was his *zolota zhabka* — or golden frog. And just as the girl in the fairy tale had understood that on the inside the golden frog was a prince, Danylo knew that Kataryna was very special. She was almost blind without her glasses and when she was little, she had broken more pairs than he could count. Teaching her how to ride a bike was like pulling teeth, and he could barely remember her without bruises and scrapes on her skinny legs and arms. Unlike her older sister, Kataryna was inconsistent in school, and she never grew tall. But it was Kataryna who visited the hospice every day when Nadiya was dying. It was Kataryna who sensed intuitively when her presence would be a comfort.

The crunch of gravel in the driveway brought Danylo out of his thoughts. He looked up and saw a ratty blue Volvo pulling up. The passenger door opened and out stepped Genya. "See you later, Karen," she called to the driver of the car, then closed the door and loped up to the back steps of the house.

Before opening the door, Genya peered out into the back yard. "Are you out here, Dido?" she called out in Ukrainian.

"I am here digging potatoes, *malenka ptashka*," called Danylo. He watched as his older granddaughter shaded her eyes from the sun and regarded him from the porch.

"Would you like me to help you finish up?" she asked.

"Thank you, but no," he replied. "I'll be done soon."

"I'll start supper, then," she called back, then went inside.

Not too long after that, the school bus dropped Kataryna off at the corner.

Chapter 3

Kat walked up the steps at the back of the house and noticed the row of drying potatoes along the window ledge. She opened the screen door and walked in, setting her knapsack beside Genya's books, which were stacked neatly on the scrubbed wooden table in the "summer kitchen".

Many of Kat's friends had never seen a summer kitchen before they stepped into hers, and they couldn't really understand its purpose. But it was so much a part of her life that Kat never gave it a second thought. It wasn't much more than an enclosed verandah with a wood stove at one end and a table along the wall. A battered chest freezer was in one corner, and an ancient turquoise Fridgidare was in another. Kat's father had reworked the regular kitchen plumbing so that there was running water and a giant utility sink too. Kat's mother did all her big cooking jobs here. Summer and winter.

She could hear her sister in the regular kitchen clanking pots and pans, but Kat didn't go in. Instead she walked back outside. It was such a lovely day that Kat knew her grandfather would be in the garden. She found him on his hands and knees amidst the potatoes, trowel in one hand, and basket close by. He looked up when he saw her approach.

Kat peeked into the basket and saw that it was almost full. She marvelled at how productive this small city garden had been. A year ago, this had all been lawn.

"It looks like you've got plenty for dinner tonight. Let me help you to your feet."

She extended her hand and grasped Danylo's outstretched one.

"*Oy*," he groaned. "My knees want to stay where they are." He stretched slowly to a standing position and regarded his younger granddaughter with affection.

Kat bent down and picked up the basket with one hand and then looped her other arm around her grandfather's waist. "Let's go in and I'll tell you about the new school," she said.

Kat's nose was greeted with the wonderful aroma of chicken cooking in garlic as they walked into the kitchen. Genya had just finished tearing a head of romaine into a bowl and was mixing up an oil and lemon dressing in a mason jar. Kat's stomach grumbled with hunger.

"You finish up, okay?" said Genya to her younger sister. "I want to get changed." She dried her hands on a tea towel and hurried out of the room.

As she washed and sliced the potatoes, Kat told her grandfather about Cawthra. Danylo's eyes sparkled with interest. "This sounds like the very best place for you, *zolota zhabka*."

"I just hope I don't mess up like last year," said Kat.

"You didn't mess up, *zolota zhabka*," replied Danylo. "St. Paul's wasn't the right school for you."

While Kat appreciated her grandfather's words of support, she couldn't help but feel a small twinge of anxiety. Had she really tried to fit in, after all?

Kat tossed the potato slices with a bit of vegetable oil and then laid them out flat on a cookie sheet and popped them in the oven. "You wash up, and I'll get changed," said Kat, giving her grandfather an affectionate kiss on the cheek as she dashed out of the kitchen and up the stairs.

The door to the bedroom that Kat now shared with her sister was open and the curtains on the bedroom window were pulled back, letting the bright sunlight stream in. Genya had already hung up her grey uniform pants and thrown her white shirt into the laundry hamper. She had changed into her favourite lazing around outfit: a faded pair of plaid boxer shorts and a T-shirt. She was propped up on her bed, doing homework.

"I can't believe you're doing homework already," said Kat in disgust. "Who does homework on the first day, anyway?"

"That's why you struggle and I don't," replied Genya. "If you get everything done as soon as it's assigned, nothing piles up and you get good marks."

Kat felt like gagging. One hour after the first day of the school year, and her sister was already worried about marks? What a warped sense of priorities!

Kat pulled the curtains shut so she could get changed. She took off her pants and top and dumped them on the floor, then pulled on a pair of denim cut-offs and a cotton shirt from another pile on the floor.

"You are a slob," said Genya, gazing at her sister over the edge of her textbook.

Kat frowned at her sister, and then looked around the room that they now shared. Yep, she was a slob. No doubt about it. You could almost draw a line between Genya's half and her half of the room.

When Genya moved in, Kat's bunk beds had to be unstacked and placed side by side, leaving little room for anything else. Even so, Genya's side consisted of a neatly organized chest of drawers and a night stand. No stray papers, books or clothing were visible. Everything had a place and was in its place.

Kat's side of the room looked like a hurricane had swept through. Even though there was a perfectly good laundry hamper set in a neutral zone between the two sides, Kat preferred the pile method. One pile on the floor was for dirty clothes, and another pile was for clothing that was worn, but not yet dirty. Her clean clothing sat in a laundry basket, wrinkled and unsorted, at the foot of her bed. More often than not, Kat just got to the bottom of the clean clothes basket and then piled all the dirty stuff into the basket, washed it, and the whole process started again. It might not look great, but the method worked for her.

Genya tolerated the clothing mess, but she had put her foot down when it came to partly finished art projects strewn on the floor, thumb nailed to the wall, and perched precariously on various flat surfaces. After a few sharp exchanges, Kat had been forced to banish her projects to the basement. She wouldn't have minded so much if Genya had at least let her keep the sculpture that had caused her all the trouble at St. Paul's in their now-shared room. But Genya hated that sculpture most of all.

Kat opened the curtains and peered outside. Her mother's car hadn't pulled up yet. Her father would be home in less than hour. Kat would have a bit of time to gather her thoughts in the solitude of the basement, surrounded by her art before it was time for supper.

CHAPTER 4

THERE WAS A bathroom on the main floor of the house that Danylo shared with his daughter and son-in-law. Danylo stepped inside for a quick shower to wash off the garden dirt and sweat from his afternoon outside. Once he finished, he tied the belt of his terry cloth robe around his waist, then walked out of the bathroom and into the bedroom that had become his temporary refuge.

It wasn't much, but he felt safe here. A dark wood Ikea bookshelf that covered one wall was filled with Genya's old books and videos and cassette tapes. She had moved her current ones into Kataryna's bedroom. Danylo's daughter Orysia had also taken the family photo albums from the bookshelf in the living room and stored them on the shelves in here, rightly assuming that flipping through them would bring her father a measure of comfort. Orysia had also brought in their small collection of Ukrainian books — some novels, but mostly history.

Danylo had initially left most of his own mementoes at the house he had shared for decades with Nadiya, but as the pain of her death was gradually replaced with warm memories of their life together, he began to retrieve mementoes, one by one.

He opened up the top drawer of his dresser and pulled out a yellowed and faded envelope. Inside were the three photographs he had been able to bring from the old country. The oldest was a formal studio portrait taken of his family just before the war. He and his sister, Kataryna, were dressed in their finest dance costumes. In this picture, Danylo was 16 years old, and his sister was 15. The photographer had asked them to smile, but Kataryna had not wanted to. Instead, they both sat solemnly on wooden chairs, staring directly into the eyes of the photographer. Behind them stood their parents, who also gazed solemnly ahead. Danylo's mother wore a white Edwardian blouse, a long strand of amber beads, and a straight dark skirt. His father wore a black suit over a richly embroidered Ukrainian blouse.

As Danylo saw again the fierceness in his sister's gaze, he smiled inwardly. That fighting spirit had caused his sister so much sorrow, yet it was also what made her the heroine that she had become. Perhaps that was one of the reasons that his granddaughter Kataryna was so very special to him: she too had her namesake's fierceness.

The second photo was a rare one of Kataryna during the war. Someone in the Displaced Person's camp had given it to Danylo when they realized he was her brother. This photo brought a sob to Danylo's throat. It showed Kataryna, eyes determined as always, dressed in military gear, weapon in hand. She was the middle of several similarly dressed women, eyeing an unseen commander.

The last photo was the one that was the hardest to look at, yet it brought Danylo bittersweet joy. It had been taken on the day he married Nadiya. In the background, the rough prison-like structures of the Displaced Persons camp were clearly visible. Their fellow DPs had done their utmost to give the occasion a festive appearance. Nadiya wore a simple dress made of white parachute silk. There had been several weddings at the camp and the material had made the rounds. Nadiya's time as a slave labourer in

Germany had left her frail and small, and so the light material hung straight to the ground, no curves to catch it. Every bleak aspect of the photo was negated by the radiant smile that shone from Nadiya's face. The look of hope and anticipation of a happy future was so real that he could almost touch it.

Danylo held the photo to his chest.

A light rap on his door brought Danylo back to the present. "Tato, supper will be on the table in five minutes."

His daughter, Orysia, was home.

Chapter 5

As she walked down the wooden basement steps, Kat could feel the earthen coolness of the room envelop her. She looked at the area she had set up for herself on an old TV tray between the utility sink and the washing machine. It wasn't fancy, but it gave her the solitude that she craved. There was some light streaming in from the four small windows that were just below the ceiling, but the sunlight did nothing to make the room warmer, which on a warm day like today was a bonus. For extra light, she had brought down a floor-standing trilight from the living room, and she used an old wooden folding chair to sit upon.

Her mother had suggested that she set up a place in the summer kitchen, but Kat knew that she would just have to move her stuff whenever canning or dehydrating was being done. Besides, the summer kitchen was as private as a street intersection.

Propped up against the basement wall was an oil painting Kat had done while still in elementary school, a basic head and shoulders portrait of her grade 5 teacher. A series of sketches was scotch-taped to the wall nearby, and showed — mostly — people Kat had sketched as they walked by her as she sat on the lawn in front of her house. Others replicated as accurately as

Kat could the inside of a nearly empty margarine dish. All of the works were stunningly accurate, but looking at them now, Kat cringed in embarrassment. She now recognized them as workmanlike — almost photographically accurate — but with no artistic interpretation.

Kat's later works gave her more pride. Ironically, it was the work she was most proud of that had got her kicked out of St. Paul's. It sat on her father's workbench now, tightly wrapped in a baby blanket, as if even in this dim basement it should not be seen. Kat walked over to it and removed the blanket. As she caressed the contours of her prized work, she remembered how it had all started.

The choice to go to St. Paul's in the first place had been a compromise decision. Kat had gone to St. Sofia's, the Ukrainian Catholic elementary school run through the Catholic school board. There were not enough Orthodox Ukrainians to have their own school, but the Orthodox students who attended St. Sofia's felt very much a part of the school. Aside from the fact that her own mother was the kindergarten teacher, Kat had enjoyed being included in the small close-knit community of less than a hundred students.

She put her foot down however, when her parents had wanted to enrol her in a private Ukrainian high school. Even her perfect older sister Genya had refused to do that. Art was not an option at that school, and Kat couldn't imagine going to a school where she couldn't take art.

One problem with St. Paul's was that Genya was already there, and everyone loved her sister and knew her sister. Kat would have preferred a bit of distance from Genya. It was bad enough that Genya had moved into her bedroom, but spending each and every school day under her sister's glorious shadow was a bit much.

Kat didn't have any other option, though. Her parents wouldn't consider a public high school, and since several of

Kat's friends were going to St. Paul's too, she reluctantly agreed to their choice. At least she could take art.

Aside from art, Religion was mandatory, as were the six other subjects. It had been quite a jolt for her when she started there. Even though she'd been raised Ukrainian Orthodox and was quite familiar with Ukrainian Catholicism because of St. Sofia's, the Roman Catholic tradition was even more different from the religion she was familiar with. She kept on saying things that made the teachers look at her in an odd way — like the day she mentioned in Religion class that she babysat the priest's children.

"Your priest has *children*?" Mrs. Reynaud had asked, her brown eyes peering over half moon tortoiseshell eyeglasses. "He was widowed and then became a priest?"

"No," responded Kat in confusion, "His wife is alive. She works in accounting at the Ford plant."

"You shouldn't lie," said Mrs. Reynaud sternly. "And it's an especially bad sign when one lies in Religion class. About a priest, no less."

Her face flushed hot as she remembered the giggles that rippled through the class.

The next day, Mrs. Reynaud asked her to stay after the bell rang and apologized to her. "I didn't know that Ukrainian Orthodox priests could marry," she explained.

Kat rolled her eyes in disbelief. Even Ukrainian *Catholic* priests could marry. Did this woman live in a cave? And it didn't sit well with her that Mrs. Reynaud had jumped to the conclusion that she had lied. As her grandfather, or Dido, always said, a thief always suspects others of stealing.

That first incident was still fresh in her mind when the second happened. The major Religion assignment of the year was worth 50% of the term mark. Mrs. Reynaud explained that they could use any medium that they wanted.

"A mural, a newspaper that you've written and designed

yourself," she said. "Use your imagination. The theme is the crucifixion and resurrection."

Kat decided to do a papier mâché sculpture.

As the project evolved in her mind, Kat got more and more excited. Kat knew that she and Mrs. Reynaud had got off to a bad start and she wanted to prove to the woman how brilliant she was. Mrs. Reynaud had told them to use their imagination, and imagination was something that Kat had in spades.

Kat pored over the scriptural accounts of the crucifixion, and the image that burned in her mind was of the Virgin Mary at the foot of the Cross, mourning the loss of her son, and feeling the pain of her son. Kat knew how her own mother flinched in pain every time she saw one of her daughters hurt. She remembered how greatly Dido had suffered from the cancer that had killed Baba. Was seeing a loved one in pain worse than experiencing the pain itself? What must it have been like for the mother of God to witness her own child nailed to a cross?

As Kat bent and twisted the wires into shape and then mounted them onto the wooden stand, she felt love and pain and passion tingle through her fingertips and fashion the wire into unexpected shapes. She mixed the paste and tore the paper into thin strips, and as she applied the paper to the wire frame, the form that evolved surprised even her.

Once the rough image was formed, Kat left it to dry for a few days, and then she lovingly shaped it and smoothed it with a fine grit sandpaper, then painted the flesh tones, the blood, and the sky blue of the robe.

Her mother drove her into school on the day it was due because it was too awkward to take on the bus. Kat had the base nestled securely in a box, and the sculpture itself was carefully wrapped in a soft baby blanket.

"Don't I even get to see it before you hand it in?" asked her mother.

"You can see it when I bring it home," said Kat.

It was too unwieldy to fit in her locker, so Kat took it with her to French class and then to art class.

Mr. Patrick, her art teacher, was very curious at what she had been up to. She had already handed in a remarkably realistic clay sculpture, and an excellent pen and ink still life, so he looked forward to seeing her new works. She let him feel the shape through the blanket. "I can feel the head and the shoulders and a flowing robe ..." He looked up at her and winked. "Grade nine Religion is supposed to be the Crucifixion, not the Virgin."

Kat just smiled.

Religion came right after art, and when Kat walked into class, she noticed all sorts of projects sitting on students' desks. Maria had pulled together a last-minute newspaper that looked suspiciously parent-inspired. Another four students had worked together to make an impressively detailed mural showing the seven days leading up to the Resurrection. It was so big that it took up half the length of one wall. Other people had stuck to the tried and true: essays.

Mrs. Reynaud came over to Kat's desk and peered over her tortoise-shell half moons at the covered mound in front of her. "What do we have here?"

Kat could feel her heart beat with anticipation as she unfastened the duct tape that held the baby blanket around her precious creation. As the blanket fell from the sculpture, Kat caressed the back of it lovingly — a flowing blue robe covering the head, shoulders and back of a woman whose arms were outstretched beseechingly.

The outline of the papier mâché sculpture resembled a classic standing, robed saint, but instead of the hands being held together in prayer, they were outstretched wide. A closer look revealed that the sculpture was actually two people, not one.

In the foreground was Christ nailed to a crucifix, but the crucifix itself was the Virgin Mary — an outstretched figure directly behind Christ. The nails in her son's hands pierced her own.

Mary's head was held straight and high in the background, and her son's head was cradled in the crook of her neck, the thorns from his crown piercing the skin of her arm. His bare feet were nailed onto hers, and the wound that pierced his heart pierced right through her chest behind him. Christ wore a ragged loincloth, but Mary was naked with only her son to cover her.

"What have you *done*?" shrilled Mrs. Reynaud. "This is blasphemous." All eyes turned in Kat's direction. There were a few gasps of surprise, then chuckles of laughter, as some of the students realized what the sculpture was. The teacher quickly grabbed the baby blanket from Kat's hands and roughly threw it over the sculpture before more students could see.

"You're coming with me, young Miss. And bring that *thing* with you."

Kat stumbled out of her desk in confusion, feeling her face getting hot with embarrassment. She felt a dozen pair of eyes bore into her back as she gently lifted her precious creation and followed Mrs. Reynaud to the vice-principal's office.

Dr. Sage-Brown was an inch shorter than the shortest student at St. Paul's, but every inch of her was packed with authority. She ushered Kat and Mrs. Reynaud into her office and closed the door.

"What's the problem?" she asked in the manner of someone faced with a myriad of crises on a moment by moment basis.

"See for yourself," said Mrs. Reynaud, lifting the blanket from Kat's creation.

Dr. Sage-Brown suppressed a gasp of shock and delight at what stood before her. Dr. Sage-Brown could see why Mrs. Reynaud was upset with this sculpture, although she herself did not consider this blasphemous. She considered it brilliant.

"Let me deal with this," Dr. Sage-Brown said to Mrs. Reynaud. "Why don't you get back to your class?

Once the door clicked shut behind Mrs. Reynaud, Dr. Sage-Brown locked eyes with Kat. "Surely you knew that such a work would provoke that poor woman?" she asked.

Kat was taken aback. Deep down, she had to admit that she did know the sculpture would create a ripple of excitement, but she hadn't expected Mrs. Reynaud to be so upset. "She told us to use our imagination," said Kat defensively, reaching out and gently caressing the flowing robe of the sculpture. "Once the idea took shape, all I could think of was how wonderful it would be when it was finished. I thought Mrs. Reynaud would have no choice but to find it brilliant."

"Not," said Dr. Sage-Brown, more to herself than to Kat.

The events that followed were blurred. Her parents were consulted. Mr. Patrick was consulted. Mrs. Reynaud was *not* consulted. Kat was given tests and more tests. She talked to school counsellors and the psychologist. They looked at other artwork that she had done, both in and out of class. And Kat soon found herself identified as "exceptionally gifted" in visual arts.

About a month after The Incident, Kat was called back down to the vice-principal's office. "I have good news and bad news for you," said Dr. Sage-Brown, with a hint of a smile. "The bad news is that you will receive a failing grade on your major Religion assignment."

Kat opened her mouth to protest, but Dr. Sage-Brown held up her hand. "Let me finish," she said. "You'll get your credit. Barely."

Kat could feel tears of anger well up in her eyes. She had poured so much passion and energy into her sculpture, yet these people could not see the value in what she had done. She would have done better if she'd just handed in a dull essay. So much for creativity.

"The good news is that, with your parents' permission, I've taken the liberty to contact Cawthra School for the Arts about you," she said. "Your marks have been good, so even with your low Religion mark, you've earned an A average overall, which meets Cawthra's requirement. All you'll need to do is meet with their audition committee, and you should be able to attend Cawthra in the fall."

Kat could barely contain her joy. This was the best possible outcome: not only could she carve a place for herself away from her sister, but she would be taking classes with people who were as passionate about art as she was.

Two weeks after that, Kat had "auditioned" for Cawthra, taking her nine best pieces of art with her, and nervously answering the questions posed by the audition committee.

The door to the basement creaked open and Kat's mother called down. "Come on up, dear! It's supper time."

Kat walked back up the stairs to the kitchen. Her father and mother had both come home from work, and while her grandfather was busy setting the table, her father was changing out of his suit and her mother was putting the food on serving dishes.

Kat reached behind her mother for an oven mitt and grabbed the casserole dish of mixed vegetables. She placed it on the kitchen table and then went back to get the chicken and potatoes and salad. Genya had already poured a glass of milk out for each person and was setting serviettes on the table. Even though the kitchen was small, the daily dance of putting supper out quickly and efficiently went off without a hitch.

As soon as her father came in from changing, they all sat down to eat.

"What a day," said Orysia, Kat's mother, as she speared a piece of chicken and put it on her plate. "I've got twenty-three kids in the morning, and twenty in the afternoon. Sonya in the morning class didn't stop crying until lunch, and then in the afternoon, Matt threw up on me."

Kat rolled her eyes and smiled. "That's a little bit too much information, Mama." As much as her mother complained, Kat knew that she adored her job as a kindergarten teacher at Saint

Sofia's. Had there ever been a first day when someone *didn't* throw up on her?

Walt, Kat's father, silently filled his plate with food and began to eat, listening to the conversation around him. Kat noticed that he looked exhausted. "Is everything all right, Tato?" she asked.

He looked up from his plate and met her eyes. A smile broke out on his face. "It's been a good day, Kataryna."

"What happened?" she asked.

"I finally managed to get Akima Corporation to commit to a twelve month systems purchasing plan," he said.

Walt was the senior sales manager with Mayfair Industrial Supply. He had started out when Kat was just a baby by calling on every machine shop and tool and die shop in the city. As his reliability became apparent, he was gradually promoted. He now only dealt with the largest corporations. A systems purchasing contract with Akima was something her father had been working on for months.

"That is fantastic, Walt," said Orysia. She reached over and squeezed her husband's hand. "We'll be able to put a bit more money aside for when Genya gets into medical school."

Genya looked up at the mention of her name. "That's great news, Tato," she said. "Congratulations on your hard work paying off."

CHAPTER 6

WHEN KAT GOT on the bus for school the next day, her friends from St. Paul's looked up at her and smiled, but no one moved over to give her a place to sit. Flushing pink with embarrassment, she scanned the seats to see if there was anyone else she knew who might make a place for her. The Goth she'd met the day before was sitting in the last seat beside a girl dressed in equally unusual clothing. He smiled encouragingly to her and gestured that there was room beside them. Kat hesitated.

"There's room here," said a voice from one of the seats nearby.

Kat looked over and saw a vaguely familiar face. She was pretty sure it was one of the guys who had helped get the platform into place in her art class the day before.

"Thanks," she said, sitting down. "You're in my visual arts class, right?" she asked.

"That's right. My name's Michael Vincent."

He was an unremarkable looking guy, thought Kat, as she regarded him through the corner of her glasses. A bit on the nerdy side. But it was thoughtful of him to let her sit there and end her embarrassing moment.

At lunch that day, Kat got her food and then walked into the cafeteria looking for a place to sit. Beth and Callie and Michael were sitting together. There were a few other kids from visual arts sitting in the same general area too, although she didn't know all their names yet. She walked up to the table where her three new acquaintances sat. "Is this seat taken?" she asked.

"We were saving it for you," said Callie with a grin.

Kat sighed with relief and set down her tray.

She listened passively to the buzz of conversation and ate her egg salad sandwich. As she chewed she looked around the cafeteria. At St. Paul's it had been harder to notice the cliques because of the uniforms. Here, it was quite apparent.

The tables in the cafeteria were occupied not only according to grade level, but by specialty too. There were a few mixed-specialty tables, most notably the black table. Most students at Cawthra were white and a few were Asian. The handful of black students mingled freely with everyone else during class time, but they seemed to take refuge with each other during lunch.

Another exception was the Goth table, where Kat could see Ian and the girl he'd been on the bus with that morning. Kat knew that Ian was only in grade 10, and the girl couldn't be more than 15, yet they sat with a small group of other Goths who were obviously much older. Kat tried not to stare as she munched on her sandwich and evaluated the girl. She was tiny with fragile Vietnamese features, but half of her head was shaved and the other half had chin-length poker-straight hair dyed blue-black. She wore a sheer powder on her face that made her flawless complexion look unnaturally white, and her lips were carefully penciled and painted a stark blood black. She had drawn thick kohl lines on her upper and lower eyelids à la Cleopatra. Today she had come to school in a skin-tight black leather miniskirt, black net stockings with runs, and heavy hob-nailed boots. Kat considered the whole group a pretty scary bunch, with their pierced noses and eyebrows and ever evolving outrageous hair, but this girl's underlying prettiness made her seem even more grotesque: a parody of sweetness.

Ian looked up and caught her staring at his friend. Embarrassed, Kat quickly looked away. Out of the corner of her glasses, she peaked over again and was startled to see that Ian was getting up from his table and walking towards her. Worse yet, he had the girl in tow.

"Hey there," he said, his turquoise hair gelled stiff above his kohl-blackened eyes. "This is my friend, Lisa. Isn't she beautiful?"

Lisa smiled.

Kat hesitated for a moment, then said, "Hi Lisa, I'm Kat. And this is Michael, Callie and Beth."

As she made the introductions, Kat was embarrassed by the giggling she heard erupting beside her. Callie and Beth were both killing themselves laughing.

"Where did you get that outfit?" asked Beth, her eyes sparkling maliciously above the hand she held in front of her mouth to hide her braces.

"Not the Gap," replied Lisa coolly, giving Beth's outfit the once-over.

Michael had been quiet during this exchange, but he obviously didn't like the cattiness in Beth's question to Lisa. "I think you both look nice," he said lamely.

Kat looked at him and smiled.

CHAPTER 7

HE HAD BEEN standing in the driveway looking down the street when he saw them. Two men had parked in front of his daughter's white wooden house. He thought that they were Jehovah's Witnesses, and unlike the neighbours, Danylo actually answered the door when Jehovah's Witnesses came to call. It was a pleasant opportunity for him to brush up on his English, because with his family and friends, he always spoke Ukrainian.

By the time they reached the front door he had walked through the summer kitchen. He stepped into the regular kitchen and put on the tea kettle and then waited for the doorbell to ring.

They were RCMP officers.

One of the men was tall with red hair and wire-rimmed glasses over a pale freckled face. The other was a few inches shorter, with black hair and bad skin. The redhead handed Danylo a card.

Danylo took it and looked at it. He could read English, but he didn't have his glasses on. He held the card at arm's length, and saw, "Department of Immigration — War Crimes Unit."

What could this possibly mean?

The red haired man pulled out a small tape recorder from his pocket, and the other man clicked open his briefcase and drew out a thick sheaf of papers. With trembling hands, Danylo motioned for them to sit down, and then Danylo's knees gave out and he found himself sitting too.

They asked their questions in the kind of fast English that is difficult to understand. The portions he understood made him uneasy by the way that they asked them. They had to do with a time in his life that Danylo had consciously stopped thinking about. It was so very painful after all. Did these men not realize that?

They asked for details and dates. Where were you on such and such a Wednesday fifty years ago? He answered as best as he could in his slow and precise English. He noticed that the red-haired man turned the tape recorder on sometimes, but then clicked it off at others. The dark-haired man wrote with enthusiasm.

The interview was still going strong two hours later when Kataryna came home. Aside from the unfamiliar car in front of the house, Kat's first clue that something was very wrong was when she walked into the kitchen. The kettle was on a burner turned onto "high" and had boiled dry. She clicked the burner off and slipped on an oven mitt, then gingerly moved the kettle to a cold burner. The kettle was probably ruined.

She stepped into the living room and saw the two men sitting there, one with a tape recorder, the other with a thick sheaf of handwritten notes.

"Who are these men, Dido?" she asked.

The two men stood up. The tape recorder was quickly clicked off.

"It's okay, *zolota zhabka*," responded Danylo in Ukrainian. "These men are asking me about my immigration papers. I can straighten it out right now." He motioned to the men to sit back down.

Kat looked over at the two men. Even though they were in "street clothing", she could tell that they were police officers.

There was something about the cut of their suits and their hair that gave them away.

"Are you charging him with something?" Kat asked.

The officer hesitated for a moment, then answered, "We're trying to determine if he lied to immigration authorities to get into this country."

The explanation seemed absurd to Kat. What could her grandfather have lied about fifty years ago that would be so important now? There was something very wrong going on. She summoned all the courage she could muster and said, "I think you should leave."

Danylo jumped from his chair, "Kataryna, you can't ask them to do that."

But the men had already closed up their briefcases, and were heading towards the door.

"This isn't the end of it," said the dark haired one.

Kat watched the door close behind the two men and then turned to where her grandfather stood. He looked like he was about to crumple upon himself. Although she was more than a head shorter than he was, she wrapped her arms around him and gave him a firm hug. "Sit down," she said. "And tell me what this is all about."

The two sat, side by side on the sofa with Kat's head leaning on her grandfather's shoulder. Danylo had his right hand firmly clasped around a pair of silver rings he wore on a plain chain around his neck. "I don't know, *zolota zhabka*," he said. "They were RCMP. They asked me so many questions that I was getting confused. I think there is some form that I have to fill out."

It seemed odd to Kat that the government would send two Royal Canadian Mounted Police officers over to her house because her grandfather had to fill out a form from fifty years ago. She would have to give this a bit of thought.

Once the supper dishes were cleared from the table, Danylo said that he was tired, and excused himself to Genya's bedroom. He was far from tired: the questions that the officers had asked him had stirred many memories, and none of them were pleasant.

He lay down on the double bed with a soft mattress and flowered comforter and clasped the set of rings that he wore around his neck. Canadians lived such a simple existence. Was there any chance that someone in this world could understand all the things he'd had to deal with in his life?

He held the two silver rings up to his cheek and closed his eyes, a sob escaping from his throat. Memories that he had willed away came rushing back.

The rings were wedding rings. His parents had worn them, and he and his wife had worn them too. His mind flashed back to the first day he had worn the rings on a strap around his neck. He was just a young man when his mother had been killed, and was even younger when his father was shot as a "traitor". Before he buried his mother's body, Danylo pulled the work-worn wedding ring off her finger. He had done the same when he found his father's corpse. He remembered praying for his own death to come soon. Cruelly, God decided to let him live amidst so much death. He vowed that if he lived long enough, he would avenge the deaths of his family and his village. And later, when he learned more, to defend his country.

CHAPTER 8

KAT QUICKLY BEGAN to feel at home at her new school. She did-n't have a lot of friends yet, but she and Callie and Beth and Michael were becoming something of a foursome. As the weeks passed, it was wonderful to be able to talk art with other people who were just as excited by it as she was. Just for this lunch time conversation, it was worth going to Cawthra.

If there was one negative, it was how Beth and Callie treated Ian. Kat couldn't figure it out. Ian looked strange, that was true, but as soon as he opened his mouth, it was obvious he was a nice guy. Why couldn't Callie, and especially Beth, see beyond his make-up and outrageous clothing?

Twice Ian had tried to sit with Kat and her art friends, but both times, Beth was so rude to him that he left.

She figured that Ian must have learned to live with negative reactions, and given his fashion choices — he invited those reactions. He took the same bus route as she did, but even then, they didn't have much to do with each other. The only time they sat together was when both of them happened to be staying late at school and there weren't other students crowding around. Lisa was also on that bus route, and more often than not, she and Ian would sit in serene isolation at the back of the bus.

It was during one of these late rides home that Ian told Kat some exciting news. "I've been chosen to do a piano solo for the Winter Concert."

"Piano?" asked Kat with surprise.

"Yes," said Ian, "And I'm playing Chopin's *Ballade no 1*."

"*Chopin?*"

Ian chuckled. "What were you expecting, Siouxie and the Banshees?"

Indeed, thought Kat.

"Anyway," he continued, "Lisa said she'd help me with the sound and light, but I was wondering if you'd do the set design for me?"

"The piano's in the pit, right?" asked Kat, considering.

"That's right," said Ian. "The piano pit is off to the far left side, and it's raised up a bit more than the orchestra pit."

"How quickly do you have to dismantle your set?"

"Fast," said Ian. "Less than a minute."

The challenge appealed to Kat. What could she do that would be simple, dramatic, and moveable within seconds? She also figured that it should be cheap.

"I'd love to help," she smiled. "Now tell me a bit about this *Ballade* to get my imagination running."

"Instead of telling you about it, why don't I play it for you?" Ian suggested. "Can you come to my house after school tomorrow night?"

"Sure," said Kat.

Kat was surprised the next day to find that Ian's house was only two bus stops past her own. She never saw him except at school, and so had expected him to live much further away.

As they stepped off the bus together, Kat saw Dylan Tomblin walking in the opposite direction on the other side of the street. She had known Dylan from when she was very young. They had gone to the same day camp together for a couple years running, and had even attended the same preschool before that. But Kat had gone to St. Sofia's and Dylan had gone to a public school, so they lost contact.

"Dylan!" she called, flailing her arms.

He turned around and gave a puzzled look at Ian and then at her. All at once, he recognized who she was. His face broke out into a broad grin and he waved back to her, his navy blue and grey football jacket billowing in the wind. Then continued on his journey.

"You know that jerk?" asked Ian.

"He's not a jerk," said Kat. "He was a friend of mine when we were kids."

Ian didn't reply and they walked the rest of the way to his house in silence.

His house was less than ten years old and was much bigger than Kat's family home. The lawn was manicured to perfection and the flowers in the garden were so healthy that they could have been plastic. Kat's grandfather spent hours working on their garden, yet it didn't look as good as this.

Ian led her to the back door and then opened it with his key, quickly scooting in to deactivate the alarm. As soon as the buzzing ended, Ian began to undo his knee-high black Doc Martens.

Kat stepped in behind him and kicked off her shoes. She wrinkled her nose at the faint smell of bleach. The first thing that she noticed was that the kitchen was just as perfect as the lawn and garden. It was so clean that it looked sterile. Kat shuddered. She always equated a perfect house with an empty mind.

"Want something to drink?" Ian asked, opening up the gigantic Sub-Zero refrigerator and pulling out a glass pitcher of orange juice.

"Sure," said Kat, still taking in her surroundings. The white ceramic floor tiles felt chilly through her stockinged feet.

Ian poured them each a glass of juice, then downed his own

in one thirsty gulp. "Have it now," Ian said. "I'm not allowed to have any food or drink in the music room."

"Sure," said Kat again. She took a tentative sip of her juice. It was delicious. Tasted like fresh-squeezed. She drank it all down then handed Ian the empty glass. He rinsed them both and placed them in the dishwasher.

"Follow me," said Ian, and he walked out of the kitchen, through what Kat thought was a living room and through another room that to Kat *also* looked like a living room. Finally, they entered a room that was filled with lemony smelling dark wood, glass, and sunlight.

The floor gleamed of burnished dark oak and a glass-fronted dark oak bookcase soared practically to the ceiling. Not an easy feat, since the ceiling of this room was about a floor-and-a-half up. In the middle of the room was an intricately woven red Oriental carpet. And on top of that was a baby grand piano.

"If you sit over there, you'll get the best acoustics," said Ian, pointing towards a small red brocade-covered antique sofa at the end of the room.

Kat sank into the middle of the sofa and waited with anticipation. Ian, she discovered, was full of surprises.

Ian was still wearing his standard attire: the ragged black leather jacket held together with hundreds of safety pins, plus a black iridescent shirt that glittered like a snake underneath. His pants were tight black leather ripped at the heels, and he still wore a full complement of tarnished silver rings. In addition to his nose ring, he was wearing a single silver earring in the shape of a medieval crucifix. His hair was now a hot pink. Amazing that it didn't just fall out with all the colour changes, Kat thought. His socks, men's designer socks — obviously borrowed from his father's drawer — looked incongruous with the rest of the ensemble.

Ian pulled out the piano bench and then sat down without so much as looking at her. He did a few preliminary hand and finger stretches, then bent over the keyboard, hands hovering, trembling, above. He took a deep breath, and then the hands connected with the ivory keys.

Kat was mesmerized not only by the beautiful melody rising from the piano, but by the appearance of Ian's hands. His fingers seemed lithe and powerful. The ballade began with a gentle melancholy that soon built into a showy intensity. Kat watched Ian's fingers with fascination as they flew across the keyboard. The intensity was almost unbearable after a bit, and Kat tore her gaze away from Ian's fingers to watch his face. She was surprised to see that tears were streaming down his cheeks. Just when she thought she could stand it no more, the music mellowed and became quiet, almost gentle. It almost sounded like a traditional ballad for a minute or so. Then it built up again, trilling, luxuriating in the sheer intricateness of the melody. It became quieter then, and Kat had expected it to end, but instead it began to build up slowly and become more intense.

Kat gripped the brocade cushions with her hands as she could sense the intense anger in the music. She was shocked at the raw emotion that burst forth from the lean fingers. And then when the music became almost overwhelming, the anger diminished and the complexity increased. Now, the music was sheer cold showiness. Ian's face was composed — no tears now.

The rhythm built up again with the same power and intensity, and then, suddenly, it segued into utter abject sorrow. Listening to it made Kat's throat catch in grief. Anger. Grief. A death march. Despair.

Then the ballade ended.

Ian sat with his head down, his hands stretched over the keyboard as if he were calming it, comforting it.

Kat sat on the sofa feeling limp. The music had been so powerful that it was beyond her comprehension. She didn't know why, but it reminded her of her grandfather.

Ian looked up. His eyes were vulnerable. "What do you think?" he asked.

Just at that moment, Kat heard high-heeled clicking on a wooden floor. She looked up and noticed a woman standing a few feet away from the sofa.

"Mom," Ian said, pushing the piano stool back and standing up.

"Hi hon," said the woman. "That was beautiful, although Chopin is so showy." Then she turned and looked at Kat. "And who do we have here?"

Kat stumbled to a standing position and extended her hand. Ian's mother took it and shook it without enthusiasm. As she did, Kat got a good look at the woman. Nothing that she wouldn't have expected, now that she'd seen the house. Manicured, custom suited, expensively frosted hair, face tightly pulled back in a wrinkle-free facade. "Hello, dear," said the woman in a cool voice. "I'm Samantha Smith." She looked Kat up and down. "And you must be one of Ian's *new* friends?"

"*Mom*," said Ian in an indignant voice.

Kat looked over at him and noticed that the bright red of his face clashed with the pink hair.

Mrs. Smith continued, "You should see some of the *people* he's brought home." Her face broke into a sardonic smile. "I mean, if it's possible, they look sillier than he does himself."

"That's enough, Mom," said Ian, walking away from the piano and over to where Kat was standing. "This is my friend, Kat Baliuk, and she's helping me design my set for the winter concert."

One of Mrs. Smith's perfectly waxed eyebrows arched slightly. "Really?" she said. "Well, I'm sure she'll do a fine job."

"Come on, Kat," said Ian, grabbing her hand and pulling her up a dark wood staircase. "We can go over some ideas in the *privacy* of my room." He glared angrily at his mother as he enunciated the words.

Kat followed him upstairs, not sure that she wanted to be going into his bedroom. However, she knew for sure that she didn't want to stay downstairs with Ian's mother, and her own mother wasn't picking her up for another thirty minutes.

Never in her life had she seen a messier room. In fact, how could it even be called a room? More like an archaeological dig. There were piles of papers stacked all over the floor. Some of the papers were yellow with age. Kat could see that some of the piles were old school binders, and others were sheets of handwritten music. And there was a musty, sweaty smell about the place.

There was a floor-to-ceiling bookcase up against one wall, and it was filled with books that must have been Ian's from childhood: Hardy Boys, Goosebumps, the Narnia series, Tolkien. Dog-eared *Mad* magazines were also shoved onto the shelves, as were more sheets of music. Virtually every square inch of wall space was covered with posters — mostly of obscure Goth musical groups that Kat was not at all familiar with. There was also a poster of Chopin at the piano, and another of a vampire.

Kat noticed that in one corner of the floor, it looked like someone had thrown a bunch of trophies into a heap.

"What are those?" asked Kat, pointing at the pile.

"Nothing."

Kat walked over to the trophies and squatted down. She picked each trophy up one by one and examined them. "Most valuable player, 1996," said the plate on one cup, and, "Most valuable player, 1997," on a hockey trophy. There was a hockey trophy of some sort for every year from about grade two to grade eight.

Kat set the last trophy back down in the pile and then stood up, brushing the dust from her knees. "I never would have pegged you as an athlete," she said.

"Me neither," said Ian. "But that wasn't really me anyway — just my parents' idea of who I should be."

Ian picked up a stack of magazines that were heaped on the one chair in the room and placed them on the floor. "Sit here," he said. "And here's a drawing pad so we can come up with some ideas."

Kat quickly sketched the rough dimensions of the stage and then sketched in a piano in the pit. "The piece is dramatic enough," she said. "I think we should go with simplicity in the set."

Ian nodded.

"You're going to wear black, right?" asked Kat.

"Yes," said Ian. "I've got a black tux that I was thinking of wearing without the jacket, and I've got this new coat that I just had made." As he said this, he walked over to his closet and began pulling back hangers. "Here it is."

Ian held out a floor-length black velvet coat.

"Put it on," said Kat.

When Ian put it on, Kat saw that it gave a perfect subtle, yet dramatic touch. The coat was fitted at the top, but wide at the bottom and it was lined with brilliant red satin. He would be able to make a grand entrance in this coat.

"Why did you get that?" asked Kat. "Surely not just for the concert?"

"No," said Ian. "This is my winter coat. Those safety pins holding the seams of my leather coat together make it pretty chilly in the winter."

Kat didn't say anything, but she thought to herself that this coat wasn't going to be all that much warmer.

"If you're wearing black, then the deep maroon curtains on the stage will make you almost invisible," said Kat. "I'd like to see a more neutral colour. I need to find a huge piece of light coloured material that we can drape behind you."

"Something like a painter's drop sheet?" suggested Ian.

"Something like that. Let me think on it," said Kat. "What's Lisa doing for the lighting?"

"I think she's waiting to see what you come up with for the set," said Ian.

Just then the doorbell rang, and Kat knew that it was probably her mother. She ran quickly downstairs behind Ian, but Mrs. Smith had already beaten them to the door and was making small talk with Orysia. Or "Iris" as English people called her.

Kat glanced from Mrs. Smith to her own mother and was startled by the contrast. Ian's mother looked so sleek and cared for, while Kat's mother had a harried look in her eyes that Kat had never seen before. Her navy blue pant suit was crisply ironed, but it looked cheap standing in the doorway of Ian's house. And she looked so small.

Something was the matter. Kat knew it. She had an urge to hug her mother right then and there. She didn't do that though, because she didn't want to show their vulnerability in front of Ian's mother.

"I'll see you tomorrow," called Ian, as Kat and her mother walked down the front steps and towards their car.

As Orysia turned the ignition key and then backed out of the driveway, Kat realized that there were tears welling up in her mother's eyes.

"What has happened?" asked Kat.

"Nothing," said Orysia. "Everything's going to be fine."

Kat knew that everything was, in fact, not fine. She didn't know what was the matter, but something definitely was. During supper that night, her parents barely talked, and her grandfather seemed preoccupied. Was someone sick? Were her parents getting a divorce? Kat wished she knew.

Kat's parents didn't realize that her bedroom heat vent provided her and Genya with a perfect eavesdropping apparatus to the master bedroom. They would blush if they realized that she knew for a fact that they made love each Tuesday and Friday night like clockwork. They also retired to their bedroom to discuss serious matters. And to have arguments.

Kat was already dressed in her favourite flannel nightgown, and she grabbed a pillow from her bed and lay down on the hand-braided rug in front of the heating vent. Genya had walked into the room not long before and was still dressed in her school uniform. She had flopped onto her bed without bothering to get undressed and her eyes were closed. The two girls lay silently as the sounds from the heating vent drifted up.

".... but Vincent and Gray is the best law firm for immigration matters," her mother's voice said.

Immigration matters, thought Kat to herself. So this was something to do with her grandfather? Something to do with the form from fifty years ago?

"They're two hundred dollars an hour," said her father. "And that's *per* lawyer. How could we possibly afford them?"

Kat shook her head in confusion. Why would her parents need to get a team of lawyers for this? What was really going on?

"The others aren't much cheaper," said her mother. "And they're not nearly as good."

"Where will we get the money?" asked her father.

"We'll have to mortgage our house," said Orysia.

What? thought Kat. What are they talking about? What could be so serious and expensive that they had to mortgage their house? Kat knew that they had only finally managed to pay off the mortgage a year before.

"Perhaps your father should sell his house."

"I can't ask him to do that right now. Not so soon after Mama died."

Kat could feel bile rising in her throat. She had to find out what was going on. This was serious. No doubt about it.

"He'll have to sell it eventually, though," said her father. "These cases drag on for years."

"I know," said her mother. "It's going to take up all of our savings, and his too — just to defend him."

Defend him from what? From who? It didn't make sense.

Kat could hear their father pacing below. She could just imagine the expression on his face: scrunched eyebrows, a face slowly turning red, and beads of sweat popping out on his forehead.

"What about Genya's education?" he asked with a choked voice.

Genya's eyes flew open at the mention of her name.

"Let's play it by ear," said her mother. "What choice do we have?"

CHAPTER 9

KAT FOUND IT hard to concentrate at school the next day. During art class, Mr. Harding was still having them do life drawings, and Beth was the current volunteer. Kat propped her sheet of paper on a drawing board and grabbed a pencil to sketch with. What was happening with her grandfather, she wondered. What was it that her parents weren't telling her?

"Are you with us, Ms. Baliuk?" asked Mr. Harding, standing behind her. Kat looked around and realized that the timer had sounded. Everyone else had completed a line sketch, yet she had not even begun. She was too embarrassed to reply, so she just smiled at him weakly.

He looked at her not unkindly and said, "I'll only be marking you on your best sketches, but you should try to do them all."

Kat nodded. She could feel the tears welling up in her throat and she willed herself not to sob.

At lunch, she stood in the cafeteria line with her tray and mechanically grabbed the first things she saw. It wasn't until she sat down with Beth, Callie and Michael that she realized what she had bought: two bowls of Jell-O and a piece of cheese. Strange.

Kat was so involved in her own thoughts that she didn't hear when Beth asked her a question. Kat nearly jumped through the roof when Beth placed a hand on her forearm, "Are you feeling all right?" asked Beth, a concerned look in her eyes.

Kat sighed deeply. "I'm fine."

Callie and Michael had finished their lunch by this time, and they got up to go outside for some fresh air. "You guys coming?" asked Callie.

Kat shook her head. "You go ahead," she said to Beth.

Ian noticed that Kat was sitting by herself, and so he left his friends and walked over.

"Can I sit down?" he asked.

"Sure," said Kat.

"What happened last night?"

Kat's head jerked up suddenly. "What are you talking about?"

"Your mom looked so upset," said Ian. "And now you're acting weird."

"It's nothing," said Kat.

Lisa was watching Ian and Kat from the other table, and Kat noticed her get up and walk over. She flopped down in the chair next to Ian and looped her hand through his arm. "Something going on?" she asked, looking at Ian.

Ian could tell by Kat's expression that the last thing she wanted was to talk about anything serious with Lisa listening in.

"We're talking about the winter concert," said Ian quickly.

Kat saw Ian's mouth move, but she had already retreated into her own thoughts. What was going on with her grandfather? What was it that had happened fifty years ago? She remembered the old photographs that Dido kept in his room. The one of her great-aunt Kataryna was about 50 years old. And the wedding. Baba's parachute silk wedding dress. Did this have sometime to do with the war, Kat wondered?

"Parachutes," said Kat.

"What?" said Ian, looking at her in confusion. "Parachute what?"

"That's the backdrop," said Kat. "For your solo."

Lisa's pale face broke into a delighted smile. "That's brilliant," she said. "It would be a huge piece of shiny material, and it would catch the lighting beautifully, but without taking the attention away from Ian. White would be ideal." As she said this, she bumped him with her shoulder in a possessive way.

"Where would I get a parachute?" asked Ian.

"Ask me tomorrow," said Kat, pasting a weak smile onto her face.

When the bus dropped Kat home after school that afternoon, her grandfather was nowhere to be found. He wasn't in the garden, and he wasn't sitting, brooding, in his favourite chair. The door to Genya's bedroom was closed, and so she gave it a light tap. When no one answered, she opened it a few inches and peeked in. Her grandfather was fast asleep on the top of the comforter. Salt of dried tears etched down the side of his cheeks.

"Dido," she said, gently shaking him by the shoulder.

His eyes jumped open, and he looked startled for a moment, but then he focused on her, standing there.

"Dido," said Kat. "Why don't we go for a walk?"

Danylo sighed with deep sadness and closed his eyes. "I'm tired," he said.

Kat knew that it was more than mere tiredness that made him want to sleep. "Come on," she said. "I've been cooped up in school all day and could really use some fresh air."

Danylo opened his eyes again and looked at her. "Okay," he said. "Why don't we walk to my house and check the garden and get the mail?"

"Great," said Kat.

Kat knew that it would take her grandfather a good ten minutes to get ready. It looked as if he hadn't shaven, and he would want to change into a freshly ironed shirt and trousers.

She looked at her watch and considered. By the time they got back from Dido's house, it would be supper time. She had promised Ian that she'd look into parachutes. Better get a head start now.

Kat opened the phone book to the yellow pages and looked up "parachutes." No parachutes per se, but several parachute clubs and sky diving instructors. It's a start, she thought.

She dialled the first number and got an answering machine. Ditto for the second and third. Finally, on the fourth try, a human voice answered:

"Swoop and Swirl Skydiving, can I help you?" the woman's voice said.

"Um, hi," said Kat. "I've got a weird question ... do you know where I would be able to buy or rent a used parachute?"

"Weird questions are my husband's department," said the woman. "Hold on."

Kat waited, and in a minute, a male voice came on the line, "Yes?"

Kat repeated her question. "Everyone thinks we have a whole basement full of used parachutes," said the man in an amused tone. "Skydivers don't even use that kind of parachute any more."

"What do you mean, 'that kind' of parachute?"

"The big ones with all the material. During the war they were made of white silk. Worth a fortune now."

"Oh," said Kat.

"What about a modern army parachute?" the man offered helpfully.

"Are they huge pieces of material?" asked Kat.

"Yep," said the man. "But they're khaki, not white, and they're not silk anymore."

"Do you have any idea where I would find one of those?" asked Kat.

"You could try an army surplus store," suggested the man.

Excellent idea, thought Kat. Why hadn't she thought of that? "How much do they usually cost?" she asked.

"If you don't need the hardware, you could probably pick one up for about eighty bucks."

"Thanks for your help," said Kat.

She hung up just as her grandfather came out of the bedroom, his face freshly washed and his hair combed. They headed out the door and walked down the street towards her grandfather's house.

The big verandah at the front of the house looked less inviting than it usually did. Danylo hadn't dropped by daily in the last month. Now, more often than not, it was up to Orysia to stop by after work and pick up the mail. Dust and bits of debris had accumulated, giving the house an abandoned look. Kat could imagine her grandmother rolling in the grave at the thought of such a neglected home, so while her grandfather went around to the back yard to check on the garden, Kat decided to grab a broom from the garage and give the verandah a good sweep. She started with the white painted wooden steps and made her way slowly towards the front door, creating a cloud of dust as she went. When she finally got up to the door, she gingerly grabbed the welcome mat and carried it down the steps and to the middle of the lawn to shake it out. She was walking back up the steps to sweep the bit of verandah that had been covered by the mat when she noticed a piece of paper sticking underneath the doorstep. Someone must have put a flyer under the welcome mat. She crouched down and pulled it out from under the doorstep. It wasn't a flyer, but a letter. Kat was about to put it in her pocket to give to her grandfather when she turned the letter over and saw how it was addressed. One word: *murderer.*

Kat was so startled that she dropped it like a hot coal. Just then, her grandfather came around from the back yard. "Did you get the mail, Kataryna?"

Kat quickly picked up the envelope and hid it in her pocket, and then she placed the clean welcome mat back where it belonged. "I was just about to do that," she said, straightening out her legs and standing up. She reached into the homemade wooden mailbox beside the front door and pulled out half a dozen envelopes. She quickly looked through them to see if there were any others like the one she had hidden. There weren't.

"Here Dido," she said, handing him the stack of bills and junk mail.

When they got home, Kat excused herself and hurried to her room. Shutting the door tightly, she opened up the letter with trembling hands. There was a single sheet of stationery and several newspaper clippings which fluttered to the ground as she unfolded the sheet of paper. There was one line scrawled with a shaky hand. It read: *Your turn to pay, old man.*

Kat picked up one of the clippings from the floor. It was a magazine photograph of a man in a dark coloured Nazi police uniform. He was shooting a child. She picked up the other and saw that it was a newspaper article about the thousands of Nazi war criminals that were supposed to be hiding out in Canada.

Was this some nut's idea of a joke? Why was someone sending her grandfather hate mail like this? She had to find out.

Normally, Kat didn't go into her parents' bedroom, but she used the excuse of putting away laundry. The white wash that was still sitting in the dryer contained several of her father's shirts, so she ironed them, and walked into her parents' room to put them in the closet.

It didn't take her long to find what she was looking for. In fact, the whole story was spread out on the cover of her parents' double bed. Kat held the top sheet and read it with shaking hands:

Take notice that the Minister of Citizenship and Immigration intends to make to the Governor in

Council a report within the meaning of section 10 and 18 of the Citizenship Act, R.S.C 1985, c. C-29 and section 19 of the Canadian Citizenship Act R.S.C 1955, c.33 on the grounds that you have been admitted to Canada for permanent residence and have obtained Canadian citizenship by false representations or fraud or by knowingly concealing material circumstances, in that you failed to divulge to Canadian immigration and citizenship officials your collaboration with German authorities and your participating in atrocities against the civilian population during the period 1943-1944, as an auxiliary policeman in German-occupied Ukraine.

And Further take notice that, if the Governor in Council is satisfied, upon the said report, that you have obtained Canadian citizenship by false representation or fraud or by knowingly concealing material circumstances, you will cease to be a Canadian citizen, as of such date as may be fixed by order of the Governor in Council;

Kat dropped the paper back on the bed as if it were dirty. What did this mean? That her beloved grandfather was a war criminal? The paper talked about atrocities committed and collaboration and thirty days to respond. Kat thought she was going to vomit.

She threw the ironed shirts on the bed and ran out of the room. She ran upstairs to her own bedroom and sat on her bed, holding her head in her hands, trying to make sense of it all. Beside her sat the piece of mail that had been sent to her grandfather. Was there someone out there who had reason to believe that her grandfather had done something like what the photo showed? The thought was chilling.

Kat folded the letter and the clippings and put them back into the envelope. She didn't know how to tell her grandfather or her parents about it, but she was afraid to throw it away, so she stuck it between her mattress and box spring.

After she regained her composure, Kat walked back down the steps with slow determination. Her grandfather was in the kitchen, staring into an empty teacup. She sat down in the chair across from him and waited for him to look up and meet her eyes.

"Dido," she said. "Tell me what this is all about."

"What is it that you want to know?" he asked.

"What did you do during the war?"

"I did nothing wrong," he said, his voice cracking with emotion. He got up from his chair and walked out of the kitchen.

Kat sat there, staring at the empty chair.

CHAPTER 10

IN THE SOLITUDE of the Genya's transformed bedroom, Danylo had a jumble of thoughts running through his mind. What person nowadays could understand the kind of choices he had to make in his youth? Movies and television liked to make war seem like a battle between right and wrong, good and bad. But what if both sides were bad? Stalin on one side, and Hitler on the other? What choices did you have then? If he could live that time all over again, his choices would still be the same. The pity was that people now couldn't understand how his was the only noble choice.

Thoughts of the past were quickly washed aside with practical considerations of the current situation. How was he going to afford a lawyer? A trial? He didn't want his daughter and son-in-law to go bankrupt all because of him. Why had the RCMP targeted him after all these years?

Danylo thought of his home a few blocks away. He thought of all the memories it held. He had never been much further than Toronto since he came to Canada. When he and his wife first came, they had lived in a rooming house around Spadina and Queen, and after saving their pennies and dollars for years, they had bought their first home with a garden in the back and a verandah in the front. That home had been on Bathurst

Street, and they had lived there for decades. When they finally moved to Mississauga, it was to be closer to Orysia and Walt and the girls. The quaint tree-lined street had been his refuge, his home, for almost twenty years now. When his wife died, he couldn't bear being there on his own with all the memories. Perhaps he should sell it. But even so, how much money would it fetch? Surely not enough to pay for his court case? And if he did sell it, where would he live? He couldn't possibly camp out in Genya's room forever. That would hardly be fair to her.

Danylo walked over to the dresser and opened the top drawer. Beneath the yellowed envelope was Nadiya's plain wooden jewellery box nestled amidst his socks and underwear. He opened it. Inside was a simple gold Orthodox crucifix on a fine chain that he had given her on their tenth anniversary. There was also a homemade brooch that Orysia had made when she was a child and Nadiya had worn with pride all these years since. A few other homemade mementoes, but nothing in the box of monetary value. Danylo lifted the top tray out to see if there was anything secreted below. Nothing but a small container of prescription medication. These were morphine tablets. His wife would take them when the pain from her cancer became too overwhelming. She didn't like to take them very often because she considered it a moral failing to give in to her pain, and so she had hidden them here so that she wouldn't resort to them easily. Danylo held the pill bottle up to the light and counted how many tablets it contained. More than a dozen. Enough to stop his pain. Should he take them now and save his family all this pain?

He opened the container and shook the pills out into his palm. It would be so easy to take these now, and forget everything. His family would be spared the burden of his court costs. What did he have to live for, after all? But then he looked at his wife's golden crucifix. How could he kill himself? That would be a sin.

The image of Kataryna filled his mind. There were unanswered questions in her eyes. When she had looked at him, their eyes met, and she held his gaze. It was as if she were trying to look into his very soul. To find the truth.

If I kill myself, considered Danylo, my *zolota zhabka* can only assume that I've done something bad. He stared at the pills in the palm of his hand with longing. I can't do it. This burden has been given to me, and I must live it. He put the pills back into their container and snapped the cap back on.

Kat was still sitting, staring at the empty chair when Genya walked in.

"What's up, little sister?" Genya asked, setting her schoolbooks down on the kitchen table and regarding Kat with concern. "You look like you've seen a ghost."

Kat looked up at her older sister. "I have something to show you." And with that, she led Genya to her parents' bedroom and pointed to the correspondence fanned out on the bed.

Genya walked reluctantly over to the bed and picked up the top sheet. "We really shouldn't be in here," she said. "This must be private if they've left it in here."

"It's not exactly hidden," said Kat. "Besides, this concerns us all."

Genya read the top sheet, and when she was done, it fluttered from her hand like a dead bird. "I don't get it," she said.

"Neither do I," said Kat. "I think it's time for a family meeting."

That evening, after dinner was cleared away, Danylo, Walt, Genya and Kat sat back down at the kitchen table. Orysia got the stack of papers from the master bedroom and brought them for all to see.

"You girls have a right to know what's happening," began Walt.

Kat noticed that her father seemed worn down. There was an extra line of worry on his forehead that hadn't been there a month ago, and pockets of shadow were beginning to form under his eyes.

"The problem is," continued Orysia. "That we're not quite sure what's happening yet ourselves. That's why we hadn't told you about this sooner."

"There is a misunderstanding," said Walt. "The government thinks your grandfather committed Nazi crimes during World War II."

Kat frowned.

Genya was silent.

Danylo bowed his head.

Walt flipped through the papers on the table. "We're trying to make sense of this," he said. "We've got to hire a lawyer quickly and get to the bottom of it. When we find out more, we'll tell you, okay?"

CHAPTER 11

KAT FELT RATHER odd walking beside Ian. Yonge and Gerrard was not a place one would normally see Goths; Queen Street West — sure, but Yonge was rapper territory.

A cluster of teens in baggy pants and over-sized running shoes walked past Kat and Ian just as they arrived at the door of Mr. Surplus. Kat expected to hear a ripple of comment as she entered the store with Ian, but the other kids in the store didn't even blink. The store clerks were just as blasé. If anyone stood out here, it was Kat. She looked far too normal.

Kat crinkled her nose at the sharp smell of old cloth. The store was so narrow that if she held both arms straight out at her sides, she could touch the merchandise that was displayed on both walls. And what merchandise it was! Under a glassed counter was an array of army knives and medals. Down the middle aisle was an overstuffed series of shelves topped with combat helmets, gas masks, and officer's caps. In the shelves themselves was a variety of used clothing, cheap T-shirts, and odds and sods of army wear. The racks on either side were stuffed solid with khaki shirts and pants, camouflage gear and the odd traditional uniform. Even the walls were covered with an array of uniforms.

Kat looked around and saw that she was the only one in the whole store that wasn't in some sort of costume. Aside from the two or three rappers, there were kids, adults and sales staff dressed in army fatigues. It was hard to tell the customers from the staff.

"Can I help you?"

Kat turned around with a start. There before her was a man who was almost as short and slight as she was herself. He was wearing camouflage, and his yellow-dyed hair was sprayed hard into a 70s look.

"We're interested in parachutes," said Ian.

The camouflage man smiled brightly, baring a set of crooked teeth in need of a good flossing. "Do you need the hardware or just the material?"

Ian looked to Kat with a question in his eyes.

"We just need the material," she said.

"I think we have one or two in the back," said the man, disappearing through an opening that was barely visible within the racks of clothing. Ian darted in after him and Kat followed.

The sales clerk rooted through the shelves, throwing items on the floor as he continued his search. "I just saw them in here yesterday," said the man. "They couldn't both have sold."

Kat looked in the shelves herself to see if she could identify something that would turn out to be a parachute. It looked like this was a pillow storage area: stacks and stacks of stuffed cloth squares.

"Here's one," the man said, pulling down what looked like a khaki coloured pillow case from one of the top shelves. As it hit the floor, yards of shiny grey-green material spilled out of the case and around Kat's feet. She bent down and picked up an edge of it and pulled. Metres more material came out of the tiny case. It was hard to believe that so much material could be stuffed into such a small package.

"This is nice stuff," said Ian, fingering some of the material himself. "I like this colour better than white."

"So do I," said Kat. "I think this will make a perfect back-drop."

The yellow-haired clerk listened to their conversation with satisfaction. "So I'll ring it up?"

"How much is it?" asked Ian.

"Two hundred dollars," the man replied.

Ian was about to say something, but Kat kicked him in the shin. "I was told that these parachutes were sold for about eighty dollars," she said.

The man looked at her indignantly. "That would have to be a pretty small parachute," he said. "This one is made of 64 pie-wedge shaped panels. The big end of each panel is 30 inches wide and they're sewn together into a huge circle. That's a heck of a lot of material. How big was your eighty dollar one?"

"I don't know," said Kat.

"Could be a 28 panel or something," said the man. "Are you making dresses out of this or what?"

"Stage backdrop," said Ian.

"Well, hold on to this end," said the man, handing a piece of parachute to Ian. "Just stand there."

The clerk held on to another end of parachute and walked out the back storage room and all the way to the front of the store.

"This is fantastic," said Ian.

"I tell you what," said the sales clerk, walking back to where Kat and Ian stood, rolling the parachute material up as he talked. "You buy this right now and I'll give you fifty bucks off."

Kat looked at Ian. She had no idea if a hundred and fifty dollars was within his budget. Did he get money from his parents? Did he have a part-time job?

"You drive a hard deal. Seventy bucks off." The man had obviously misinterpreted their silence as bargaining.

Kat could see a grin trying to break through on Ian's face. "I'll take it," he said.

The man gleefully pushed the mounds of material back into the case. It was amazing that it all fit back in so effortlessly. There were straps on the back of the case like a knapsack, so Ian slung it over his shoulders and the two of them walked up to the front to pay.

There was a glass-topped display case under the cash register, and as Ian waited for the parachute to be rung up, he examined the items in the case.

"Look at this great knife," he said to Kat, pointing to a silver coloured knife with an elaborately tooled handle.

Kat gazed down into the case and examined the knife that Ian had indicated. "It gives me the shivers," she said.

"Why?" asked Ian.

"I just don't like knives," she replied.

Ian turned to the clerk and asked, "This isn't military, is it?"

"No. Someone brought that one in on a trade."

"How much are you selling it for?" Ian asked.

"Thirty dollars."

"I'll take it."

Ian drew out a wallet from his leather pants and opened it. Kat was amazed to see that it was filled with twenties and even a fifty. He counted out enough money to buy the parachute and the knife, and then watched as the clerk carefully wrapped the silver knife in brown paper and then placed it in a plastic bag. Ian stuck the bag into the parachute knapsack, slung it back over his shoulder and headed out the door.

As soon as they got outside, Kat confronted him. "What do you need a knife for?

Ian smiled enigmatically. "I don't need it for anything. I just thought it was a great looking knife. Almost Victorian."

There was so much that Kat didn't know about Ian. It surprised her that he had so much money, and now this knife incident.

CHAPTER 12

WHEN KAT GOT home, she noticed yet another strange car in the driveway. Not a black sedan this time, but a vintage green Porsche. When she walked through the back door, she could hear several voices drifting in from the living room. Both of her parents were there, and a man. The man was saying, "I've printed off some background information for you about the Deschenes Commission and how all of these proceedings got started...."

Kat poked her head into the living room before dashing upstairs to the bedroom. A man in a slightly rumpled suit was perched uncomfortably on the edge of one chair. In his out-stretched hand was a manila file folder filled with a thin sheaf of papers. Her parents were sitting side by side on the sofa, holding hands, and her grandfather was in his favourite rocking chair. Funny that she didn't realize he was even there. He had been that quiet.

Orysia looked up as her daughter dashed by and called to her. "Kat," she said. "Come in here for a moment. I'd like you to meet Mr. Vincent."

Mr. Vincent put the file folder down on the coffee table.

Kat hesitantly stepped into the living room. Mr. Vincent got up from where he was perched and stepped towards her, holding out his hand. Kat assumed this was the Vincent of the Vincent and Grey law firm her parents had argued about. She had expected someone older, someone more ironed. She extended her hand and they exchanged firm handshakes.

"Your mother tells me that you're an art student at Cawthra," Mr. Vincent said.

"Yes," responded Kat.

"My son Michael is there too," said the lawyer.

"What grade?" asked Kat.

"Same as you. In fact, I think you're in the same art class. Mr. Harding's class?"

"Oh, *Michael*," said Kat. "We're in the same class. We even sit together at lunch."

"So I've heard," said Mr. Vincent with a smile.

Kat smiled weakly. She hoped and prayed that Mr. Vincent didn't chat work over dinner every night. All she didn't need was for the kids at school to find out about her grandfather.

She began to walk towards the stairs to her room when Orysia said, "Kataryna, you're welcome to stay here and listen to what Mr. Vincent has to say."

Kat hesitated. She would like to hear, but she thought maybe the lawyer would feel uncomfortable talking about these things in front of her.

"Are you sure?" she asked.

"Yes," said her mother. "Sit right here." She patted a space beside her on the sofa.

"We had thirty days from the date of this notice to respond," Mr. Vincent continued, once Kat had sat down. "Otherwise, Mr. Feschuk would automatically have had his citizenship revoked. On your behalf, I have already responded and we're waiting for a hearing date."

Orysia suppressed a sob.

Kat glanced over at her grandfather. He had an agitated look of frustration on his face.

"What is it that they're saying I did?" he asked.

"I am not quite sure," replied Mr. Vincent. "I am hoping to get the details soon. All I know is that you're being accused of not disclosing your collaboration with the Nazis when you had your immigration interview to come to Canada."

"But how can I disclose collaboration if I didn't collaborate?" asked Danylo angrily. "I fought the Nazis and the Communists."

"The Soviets were our allies," said Mr. Vincent. "Better not mention any of that. Perhaps we can mention about fighting the Nazis though. What I will do now is respond on your behalf for evidence from the prosecution."

That night, after everyone was asleep, Kat was awakened by the sound of pounding rain on the roof. She got up out of bed and stared out at the water streaming down on her window. It reminded her of so many tears. Her mother had done practically nothing but cry since the accusation against Dido. Kat herself felt like she was about to cry at all sorts of unexpected moments. She knew how the sky felt.

The last thing Kat felt like doing was sleeping. Too many things on her mind. She pulled on a housecoat over her long nightshirt and crept downstairs. A mug of warm milk would help her get some needed sleep. She poured some milk into a saucepan and set it on the stove. The action reminded her of her grandmother. Baba had been such a good one to talk to when Kat had something on her mind. How many times had they sat over a hot mug of milk and talked from their hearts?

As the milk warmed, Kat walked into the living room, listening to the rain against the side of the house. It was coming down so hard that there was an earthy mustiness in the air that reminded her of mushrooms. It's *pidpenky* time, Kat thought. And that reminded her of her grandmother too. Baba had loved all kinds of mushrooms, but her favourite were *pidpenky*. When they were plentiful, she would make mushroom soup, mushroom dumplings, mushroom stuffed pastry, and Kat's all-time favourite, *nalisnyky* — thin crepe-like pancakes fried in butter and stuffed with *pidpenky*.

Dido loved *pidpenky* too, although he had an aversion to other mushrooms. In fact, he refused to eat spring mushrooms at all.

It had become something of a ritual for Kat and her grandfather to wait for the perfect fall day to pick *pidpenky*. It had to be before the first frost, but after a heavy rain. Perhaps a day out in the fresh air would do both her and her grandfather some good. Tomorrow was Friday. She'd suggest they go on Saturday.

She noticed that there were still papers scattered about the living room, and she thought she'd clean up a bit while waiting for the milk to heat. On the coffee table, she noticed that the manila file that Mr. Vincent had brought was still sitting there, undisturbed. Hadn't he said that this would give some background information about what was happening to her grandfather? Kat picked up the file and took it with her to the kitchen table. She continued to straighten up the living room, then walked into the kitchen and poured the now steaming milk into a mug. She sat down at the kitchen table with her milk and the file.

It was about a dozen typed sheets. The header said, "Library of Parliament" and "Parliamentary Research Branch" and there was a Government of Canada crest on the top. The title was "Commission of Inquiry on War Criminals." This was the Deschenes Commission report.

She flipped through the pages but the type just swam in front of her eyes. It was too overwhelming to read right now, she decided. Maybe later. She finished the last of her milk and headed back to bed.

CHAPTER 13

THE NEXT MORNING, as Kat and Genya stood waiting for the school bus together, Kat wanted to talk to her sister about what her grandfather was going through, but Genya was not interested.

"If Dido truly cared about us, he would pack his bags and move back to Ukraine," said Genya. "He's obviously done something, and now we're all paying for his past." Genya's face got a bit red as she continued, "We could lose our home because of him. And I probably won't be able to go to medical school."

Kat looked at her sister coldly, "Don't blame the victim."

"If what they say is true, then he's no victim," responded her sister.

"I don't even know what it is they're saying," said Kat hotly. "What is it that he's supposed to have done? And where's the proof?"

Genya glared at her in stony silence. Mercifully, the bus came moments later. Genya sat in the front seat, and her sister walked to the back.

Ian was sitting in the very last row, with Lisa. He looked up at Kat when she walked onto the bus and motioned for her to come and sit with them.

Lisa, for once, did not look too annoyed with the suggestion.

"Ian told me about the parachute," she said. "It sounds perfect."

"It is," said Kat.

"We should practice putting it up," said Lisa. "Can you come to school tomorrow morning?"

"I could stay late tonight," said Kat.

"Can't do that," said Lisa, looping her arm around Ian's elbow proprietarily. "It's Friday. We're going to a party and it's going to take me forever to get ready."

Kat smiled awkwardly. Ian was her friend, but he was Lisa's boyfriend. She'd known that all along, so why did she feel jealous? She tried to imagine what it was that Lisa was planning on doing to herself that would take so long. It had to be a Goth party. Even Lisa's everyday make-up and clothing probably took an hour to assemble. What constituted party wear?

"How about tomorrow, midmorning?" asked Ian. "I'm pretty sure the school's going to be open in case some people need to practice for the concert."

"Can't do it in the morning," said Kat. "And I'll probably be too zonked by the afternoon."

"You're going to a party too?" asked Lisa.

Kat smiled. Wouldn't it be nice to have nothing more serious on her mind than partying, and what to wear to a party? "No," she replied. "I'm getting up at the crack of dawn tomorrow to go mushroom picking with my grandfather."

Kat expected Lisa to laugh at her, but instead, Lisa perked up with interest. "You're kidding," she said. "I do that every spring with my grandparents. We never go in the fall though. Where do you find mushrooms now? We buy dried mushrooms from the Vietnamese store, but there are a couple of days in the spring when we can find this one kind of mushroom that's almost like one of their favourites from back home. And fresh picked mushrooms are so awesome."

"We like them fresh too," said Kat. "But we pick a bunch and dry the rest to use all year round."

"Wow, you dry your own? I'm going to have to tell my grandparents," Lisa said. "They'll be impressed."

Ian looked from Lisa to Kat, and then grimaced. "I can't imagine eating a mushroom that I just picked from the ground. What if it was poisonous?"

Lisa looked over to Kat and they both smiled. It was the classic Canadian response.

"It is something you just *know*," explained Kat.

Lisa nodded.

Kat rolled out of bed the next morning just after dawn. It was an inhuman time to be awake, especially on a Saturday. But *pidpenky* were worth the effort. Kat figured she'd have a shower when she got home, so she quickly splashed cold water on her face and then threw on an old pair of jeans and a flannel shirt and headed down the stairs.

Danylo was already dressed and waiting impatiently at the kitchen table. After all the sadness and uncertainty of late, the thought of picking *pidpenky* seemed like a relief — a refuge — for Danylo. Whenever he held an autumn mushroom and breathed in its wholesome mustiness, it made him think of Nadiya. They had met at the Displaced Persons camp after the war. Nothing as fine as *pidpenky* was served to the DPs, but he and Nadiya had devised a game. As they ate their thin wheat gruel or their onion stew, their stomachs would rumble as they would try to top each other with fantastic tales of *pidpenky* past. Nadiya claimed she could bake them into a pastry; Danylo claimed he could make a *pidpenky* soufflé. Stuffed in a noodle for *borscht*, or thinly sliced and fried in butter, nothing beat *pidpenky* for delicious dreams.

He was sipping a cup of tea with lemon, and on top of Kat's place mat was a cooling cup of tea and a piece of soggy buttered toast that looked like it had been sitting there for awhile.

"Eat up," urged her grandfather.

Kat didn't even bother sitting down. She took a huge bite out of the cold toast and washed it down with a gulp of tea. "I'm ready," she said. They wouldn't be the only ones out this early looking for *pidpenky* so there was no time to waste. Her mother would be delighted if she and Dido actually found some this year.

Cawthra Bush was an old growth forest that backed right onto Cawthra school property, and that's where Kat and Danylo had decided to try this year. Danylo tucked the two canvas bags underneath his arm as he stepped onto the bus. Kat was right behind him, and she noticed with a smile that they had their choice of seats.

Perhaps they wouldn't run into too many people with the same idea after all. Sensible people had decided to stay curled up in their warm beds on this chilly autumn morning. It seemed odd to be taking the Cawthra bus route on a Saturday and especially odd to be taking it with her grandfather.

Kat had not taken a bus ride with her grandfather for almost two years, nor had they gone mushroom picking. Her grandmother's illness had immobilized them all. Danylo chose to sit right behind the bus driver. As Kat sat down beside him, she looked over at his profile and was struck by how worn out he looked. It was as if a light had gone out inside. She could feel tears welling up in her throat. This past year had been so hard on him: first Baba dying, and then this trial.

She remembered the first time he had taken both her and her sister *pidpenky* picking when they were children. Genya didn't enjoy it at all, but then, she wasn't much of a nature lover and hated getting dirty. Kat took to it right away. Aside from the fact that she liked spending time with her grandfather, she had always found great satisfaction in seeing the sparkle in her Baba's eyes when she brought home a big sack of delicious *pidpenky*. With Baba gone and this dreadful accusation against her grandfather, Kat's family needed comfort food more than ever. She also hoped that this adventure would help her grandfather forget his worries, if only for a little while.

When the bus dropped them off in front of the old Cawthra House, there were already several cars parked in the lot. "Not a good sign," said Kat.

"We'll see, *zolota zhabka*," said her grandfather.

They walked past the cars and along the walk at the side of the house until they reached the path that dipped into the ravine and the woods beyond. It was like stepping into another time. The floor of the woods was covered with a deep carpet of autumn leaves and pine needles and the air around them was astonishingly still considering the woods were in a suburban area. Kat filled her lungs with the lovely damp woody smell.

Voices broke the stillness. Two elderly women were crouched down picking through the leaves not a dozen meters away from them.

"Come with me," said Danylo. Then he took Kat by the hand and led her in the opposite direction. Down a path, across a stream, and deep into the woods.

Kat was chilly and her running shoes were already damp, but she agreed with her grandfather. This is how they always did it: they'd find the others and then go in the opposite direction. "There's a mushroom," she said excitedly. Kat reached down and gently squeezed the barrel-shaped stem until it snapped. She had picked their first mushroom of the season.

"Let me check it," said her grandfather.

Kat held it out to him, although she was sure it was a *pidpenok* because of the distinctive brown cap.

Danylo held it up to his nose and breathed in the musty aroma. "Very good," he said approvingly.

Kat opened her bag, and he dropped it in.

Danylo and Kat worked industriously a few dozen meters apart from each other. It really was an excellent day for *pid-*

penky. The best, in fact, that Danylo could remember. After picking more than a dozen clustered under a tree, Danylo stood up and stretched his legs. It was exhausting for him to crouch down and pick the mushrooms, and it was painful to stand back straight again.

He was thankful that Kat was much quicker at this than he was, so they would only take a few hours to fill both bags. As he stretched his back, he spotted another clustering of *pidpenky* a few feet further away so he walked towards them, making sure that Kat was always not too far away.

One time when she was about seven years old, he had lost her in the woods for about a minute. That was one of the longest minutes of his life. He could see her now, squatting amidst a good-sized clustering of mushrooms, methodically picking only the freshest ones. When she was finished in an area, she would stand up quickly. No aches or pains in his granddaughter's joints, that was for sure.

Danylo crouched back down so that he could reach the new clustering of mushrooms. There were quite a few dead leaves in the way, so he picked up a handful and placed it aside. As he reached for another handful, his fingers brushed upon something hard. He looked down and was startled to see a man's black leather shoe. Danylo's heart beat fast at the sight and he clutched his chest. His brain told him that it was just a discarded shoe, but it brought back a rush of horrible memories.

"Kataryna, come here," he called out urgently.

Kat stood up straight and strode quickly over to where her grandfather was. She could see that he was holding his hand to his chest and his face was contorted with pain. "What's the matter?" she asked.

"Help me to my feet," he asked meekly. "I just need to stretch out for a moment."

Kat pulled him to his feet, and then she looked down. A man's shoe. She nudged it with the tip of her running shoe, then bent down and picked it up. "Looks like it's been here awhile," she said, wondering why her grandfather would be so shaken by the sight of a shoe in the forest.

"Put it down," said Danylo.

Kat looked at her grandfather in confusion, but did what he asked. "Maybe we should go home?"

"I'll be fine," he said. "Just let me catch my breath." Kat looped her arm around her grandfather's back and led him over to a fallen log. They both sat down together.

"What's the matter?" she asked.

"That shoe reminded me of something," he said.

"Of what?"

"I can't talk about it," he replied in a husky voice.

It was a cold June morning in 1941. When word came that the Nazis were attacking, the Soviet administration left the area en masse and had taken with them all the food and supplies that they could carry. The locals were left with nothing to eat. And soon, they would be at the complete mercy of the Nazis. His father had gone out to find food days before and still hadn't returned. Danylo knew that if they didn't eat soon, he and his mother would starve. His family's one salvation was that they lived close to the forest. There was a chance that he could sneak into the woods and scavenge wild roots and mushrooms and bring them back before the Nazis arrived. Now that the Soviets were gone, it had to be safer.

In the pre-dawn darkness, Danylo knelt down and blindly felt a beautiful clustering of spring mushrooms behind a rotted log. He carefully placed them one by one in his hand-woven sack and then brushed aside a handful of dead leaves to grope for more mushrooms, but instead, he felt something smooth and firm. He brushed away some more leaves and felt what seemed to be a length of wood covered with cloth. Very odd. A few feet from the rotted log, Danylo felt some more mushrooms and so he picked those and placed them in his sack too, working quickly because the sun was beginning to peek through the tops of the trees. He stood up and brushed the dirt from the knees of his pants, and then bent down to pick up his mushroom sack. What he saw made him cry out in horror. The firm smoothness that he had felt was a handmade shoe, and there was a leg sticking out from it. The corpse of a man lay there, a bullet hole through the neck. Danylo felt the bile rise up his throat when he realized that the man was his father. The first rays of sunlight now mercilessly illuminated the area. His father's body wasn't the only one. There were more than a dozen, all with bullet holes in their necks. Danylo recognized them all. Each one of them had been involved in Ukrainian resistance activities against the Soviets.

Danylo gripped his mushroom sack close to his chest and ran home.

Kat wanted to go home right then, but Danylo wouldn't hear of it. "*Zolota zhabka*," he said, "my sad thoughts will be with me whether we get the *pidpenky* or not, so rather we pick them and I be sad then we don't pick them and I be sad."

Kat couldn't fault his reasoning, but she insisted that her grandfather rest while she finished. It was close to ten by the time she had filled both bags. Instead of waiting for the bus, Kat called home to see if someone could pick them up. Genya answered.

"I'll be right there."

Kat noted her sister's suppressed look of cool disapproval as she pulled up in front of Cawthra House in their mother's car. Kat held her grandfather's elbow and guided him into the passenger seat and then she sat down in the back seat. Once they pulled into the driveway, Kat had barely enough time to get out of the car and help her grandfather out before Genya had put the car in reverse and was backing out of the driveway, spewing gravel as she went.

By the time they got into the house, Danylo was grey with fatigue. He quickly washed and then lay down in his room.

Chapter 14

PREPARING *PIDPENKY* FOR the winter was a time and space-consuming affair. Kat's father had already lit a fire in the wood stove and it had burnt down to a steady dry heat. A few years ago, he had perfected a contraption for drying the *pidpenky*.

Orysia opened her daughter's bag and grinned with delight. "These look excellent, Kataryna!"

"They're exceptional this year," agreed Kat. She opened her grandfather's bag and let some of his mushrooms tumble gently out onto the utility table in the summer kitchen.

It was essential that the mushrooms be processed immediately because if they sat at all, they would go slimy. And they couldn't be washed with water for the same reason. Each one had to be carefully dried and brushed. Kat was tired, but that didn't stop her from grabbing dishtowels and mushroom brushes from the kitchen and pitching in. She and her parents set up a mini factory line to process the mushrooms. Kat blotted one mushroom dry at a time and then handed it to her mother, who would gently whisk away every last remnant of dirt with a small brush. Orysia would then hand the mushroom to Walt, who would break off the stem and set it aside, then thinly slice the cap. The dehydrating contraption he'd come up with consisted of five individual pieces of screen door mesh that had each been framed with wood. He had already covered the first mesh screen with a layer of cheesecloth, and so as each mushroom cap was sliced, he placed the slices side by side on the cheesecloth. When a whole layer was done, cheesecloth would be laid on top and then another mesh frame placed on top.

The warmth from the stove made the summer kitchen a cozy place to work, and Kat delighted in working together with her parents this way. With Danylo asleep, it also gave her the opportunity to talk with her parents about some things that had been on her mind.

"Have either of you read that file Mr. Vincent left?" Kat asked.

Walt nodded, and Orysia answered, "We read it this morning."

Kat reached for another mushroom and carefully blotted every part of it. "What did it say?"

"It was basically a summary of why the issue of Nazi war crimes became hot after 50 years of silence," said Orysia.

"So why did it?" asked Kat.

Walt stopped his slicing for a moment and looked up at his daughter. "You were just a baby when all this happened," he said. "An MP got up in the House of Commons in 1985 and claimed that Joseph Mengele had applied to immigrate to Canada in 1962 and that the government knew his identity at the time but hadn't done anything about it. More than that, some people claimed that Mengele might still be living in Canada."

Kat knew who Joseph Mengele was. He had been one of the most cruel and brutal Nazis of all. As a doctor, he should have been healing the sick, but instead he used his medical skills to do dreadful experiments on humans. The pain and suffering he had caused was infamous. "You're kidding," she said. "How could that have happened?"

"Well, it didn't," replied her mother. "It was an unfounded rumour. Mengele died in South America in 1979 and there is no evidence that he ever tried to enter Canada."

"What's that got to do with this file then?" asked Kat, more confused than when the conversation started.

"The government didn't know it was just a rumour at the time. They decided to set up a commission to investigate and report to the government," explained Orysia. "Also, there were allegations that thousands of other Nazi war criminals were living in Canada."

"That's awful," said Kat. "Didn't the government screen Nazis out?"

"Again," said Walt. "This was just a rumour. When World War II ended, the Cold War began. The government was more concerned with screening out possible Soviet spies and terrorists than former Nazis."

Kat frowned. "I don't understand. They should still have been screening out Nazis."

"I agree," said Orysia. "But thousands of refugees and displaced persons were immigrating all at the same time. It was hard for the immigration officials to do proper screening. There were so many languages to deal with. And the sheer volume of immigrants was something else."

"What does this have to do with Dido?" asked Kat.

"He was one of the many thousand Ukrainian immigrants who came to Canada because their part of Ukraine had been taken over by the Soviet Union."

"He and Baba were Displaced Persons escaping Communism. Dido told me all about that."

"They were escaping both Communism and Nazism," added her father. "The Nazis considered Ukrainians and other Slavs to be sub-human."

"I thought only Jews and Gypsies were considered sub-human by the Nazis," replied Kat.

"Jews and Gypsies were considered even worse than sub-human," said her father. "Where some Slavs were to be kept alive for slave-labour, every last Jew and Gypsy was to be murdered."

A shudder went through Kat that even the warmth of the wood stove couldn't shake. How could one group hate so much? It was utter evil.

"I still don't understand what this has to do with Dido, and what all this has to do with war crimes," said Kat.

By this time Walt had filled up one whole frame with sliced mushroom caps and was working on the second. As he placed the empty frame carefully on top of the one covered with cheesecloth and mushrooms, he continued to explain the situation to his daughter. "The allegation that was made in the 1980s was that amongst those postwar immigrants, there were Nazi war criminals who had snuck in and were being protected by their ethnic communities."

Kat was silent for a moment, considering the scenario as she blotted dry the *pidpenky* one by one. She looked up first to her father and then to her mother, frowning. "Do you think that's possible?" she asked.

"Anything's possible," replied Walt. "But it's not likely. The Nazis were brutal beasts. In the case of the Ukrainian community, I just can't see it."

Her mother nodded in agreement. "If there was a Nazi in our community, he would be drummed out."

"But what you're telling me is that this commission showed that there *were* Nazis hiding out in Canada," argued Kat. "So obviously, someone was protecting them."

Orysia put down her mushroom brush and looked her daughter in the eye. "Actually, hon, that's not what the file says at all."

"Then what does it say?"

"For one, that there are not thousands of Nazi war criminals hiding in Canada. The official list given to the Commission contained 774 names."

"That's still a lot," said Kat.

"But the people on that list were just suspects," continued her mother.

Kat heard a car trunk close in the driveway, and looked out the front door to see that her sister had returned in their mother's car with two huge paper bags filled with groceries.

"Help!" she called from the door step. Walt jumped up and opened the door, taking one of the bags from her and depositing it in the kitchen.

"Did you remember freezer bags?" asked Orysia, standing up from her own work with the mushrooms to give her oldest daughter a hug and to take the other bag from her.

"I've got them," replied Genya.

"We're talking about Dido's case and Mr. Vincent's file," Walt explained to Genya, who could see that another serious conversation was taking place.

Genya pulled off her jacket and draped it over the back of one of the kitchen chairs and then began unpacking the groceries. "I read some of that this morning," she began. "I bet every one of the people on that list did something bad to get there."

Her mother rolled her eyes with impatience. "If you'd read the whole file, Genya, then you know that half the people never lived in Canada, and many on the list weren't even born before World War II. What's the "bad" stuff they were supposed to have done? Have a foreign accent?"

"Maybe a neighbour complained about the music they were playing," suggested Walt, thinking of the music Gen liked to play.

"You are being ridiculous," said Genya. "The government is just trying to root out Nazi war criminals hiding in Canada."

"Then why is it that more than half the people on the list had never even set foot in Canada?" asked her mother.

Kat looked from her sister to her mother and then shook her head in confusion. "That doesn't make sense."

"That's what the Commission thought too."

"Who made up this list, anyway?" asked Kat.

"It was made up by the self-styled Nazi hunter, Sol Littman," explained her father. "And in fact, the whole Commission was set up in response to his false accusations."

"But it doesn't sound like this list was put together with very much thought," said Kat.

"You're right," said Walt. "And in fact, Justice Deschenes himself chastised Littman for his gross exaggerations and for wasting the court's time and money."

"I don't believe it," said Genya. "There are thousands of Nazi war criminals hiding out. I hear it on the news all the time."

"A juicy news story is not necessarily true," continued Orysia hotly. She pointed at the report the lawyer had left for them to read. "Of the 774 cases brought forward to the Commission, only 20 could be substantiated with even surface evidence."

"And those twenty people should be tried," answered Genya. "Just because one is your father, doesn't make it all right."

"That's a low blow," said Orysia. "But I agree with you about criminal court."

"Then what's the problem?" asked Genya. "That's what the Commission recommended. Those twenty were to be charged with war crimes and then tried in a criminal court. They're innocent until proven guilty. That's justice, pure and simple."

"You didn't read the whole report," retorted her mother. "If you did, you'd know that the government couldn't find enough evidence, and the first three charges were dropped because of lack of evidence."

"Then that's the end of it," replied Genya. "If they don't have the evidence, then the case is closed. End of story. I don't know why you're getting so hot under the collar about this."

Kat looked at her big sister in amazement. Could Genya, who was known for her brains, really not understand what was happening? She looked at her mother and saw that she was deeply angry with her older daughter.

"I think you've totally misunderstood what's happening with your grandfather," Orysia said with carefully enunciated words. "The government considered it a 'failure' when they couldn't convict these people. Therefore they changed the law."

"What do you mean?" she asked.

"The remaining people on the list are not being given a criminal trial at all. They are not presumed innocent. On the basis of surface allegations that can't hold up in criminal court, they're being deported instead."

Genya regarded her mother in confusion.

Walt piped in, "They're assuming he's guilty without evidence. They're calling him a war criminal, but this trial that's approaching is not a criminal trial; it's a deportation trial. They're sidestepping the criminality altogether and they're going to deport him because they say that he may have lied during immigration proceedings, and he's got to prove that he didn't lie."

"That's simple," said Genya, pulling more items out of the grocery bags. "All he's got to do is get his original immigration documents from the government archives and what he said during the immigration proceedings will be down there. If he lied, he lied; if he didn't — that will be obvious too."

"But Genya," replied her mother sadly. "The immigration documents were all destroyed by the government. How is he going to prove that he didn't lie?"

CHAPTER 15

DANYLO WAS NOT asleep in his room. He could hear his family arguing about him and it gave him great pain. It cut him to the quick to think that misunderstandings about his past were bringing sorrow to his loved ones now. If only they could see what had happened. If only the government could understand too.

The image of his father's corpse had flashed into his mind unbidden and unwanted that morning. And now a flood of other memories filled his mind.

When World War II started on September 1, 1939, Hitler and Stalin were allies. The Soviets came to his village of Orelets days later, on September 17th, 1939, and the villagers greeted the change with fear and hope. They had lived under oppressive Polish rule for far too long. Ukrainian wasn't to be spoken, and the Ukrainian Orthodox church was suppressed. Ukrainians were not allowed to go to university, and they were blocked from many jobs. Would the Soviets be better?

At first, Ukrainian language schools were opened and Ukrainian culture was allowed to flourish. Many people, including Danylo and his sister Kataryna, had joined the Communist Party.

The first inkling of trouble for Danylo came a month later with the first elections. The slate of candidates consisted of a single name for each position.

"Is this a joke?" Danylo had asked the election commissar after he had stood for hours in the line-up with the rest of the villagers. The line-up extended down the whole main street and ended inside the *chytalnya*, or reading room, in the village square. "Why bother holding an election if you're only allowing one candidate to run for each position?"

The commissar looked up wearily from a sheaf of papers on his makeshift desk. Danylo peered at the list and saw that it appeared to contain the names of each and every villager over the age of eighteen. As each villager "voted", the commissar would take a ruler and a pen and carefully draw a line through their name.

"Don't ask, just vote," said the commissar.

Danylo took the ballot from the commissar's outstretched hand, ripped it in two, and strode out of the building.

That night, Danylo was awakened by a loud banging. His father got up to answer the door, but before he could even get to it, it was smashed open and two Soviet secret police — the NKVD — stepped in. One grabbed Danylo by the hair and dragged him outside. His mother ran after him and tried to beat one of the police with her fists, but he swatted her away as if she were no more than a fly. Danylo's father ran out and grabbed his wife and dragged her back in.

One of the police punched Danylo repeatedly in the face, while the other kicked him in the abdomen. "When we say vote, you vote," they said.

After they left, his parents carried him back inside and his mother washed the blood from his face.

In the newspaper the next morning, the headlines announced, "Communists win overwhelming majority!"

In some ways that first beating was what saved Danylo's life. The next day, Danylo and his sister dug a hiding place deep beneath the barn. The entry was hidden under a pile of manure behind the garden. From then on, Danylo and his family slept in this safe but aromatic refuge each night.

Danylo wasn't the only one to be beaten or dragged off in the middle of the night, and so the initial hope of the villagers for the Soviets was quickly replaced with fear. There were some villagers who profited from the Soviet occupation, however. These were the kind who would denounce their neighbours to get ahead. It was the thugs and the bullies who ruled the day. Starting in September 1939, the NKVD, with local collaborators, rounded up all of the people who had been leaders within the Ukrainian community. They were loaded into cattle cars and shipped off to Siberia. Sometimes, in a fit of efficiency, the newly arrested were simply shot. By April 1940, a new wave of terror had arrived. Vast numbers of people were arrested and shipped off. No one was safe. The NKVD would walk into people's homes at night and arbitrarily arrest whoever they found. The best and the brightest were taken, and had it not been for the Feschuks' hiding place, they too would have been taken away. Then one night, Kataryna mysteriously disappeared.

But as bad as it was, the worst was yet to come. On June 22nd, 1941, the Nazis, who up until that time had been collaborating with the Soviets, suddenly launched a blitzkrieg against the Soviet Union. As the NKVD and Commissars fled, a scorched earth policy was instituted in Soviet Ukraine. The NKVD tried to carry off everything that they could and burn what they couldn't — whole factories, food, machinery, equipment. But that wasn't enough for them. They didn't want to leave people behind who were not staunch Communists, so they arrested even more people. The NKVD would leave tractor engines running all night to muffle the screams of prisoners. As Danylo and his parents huddled in their hiding place, they could only imagine the horrors outside.

And so, as the Soviets slashed and burned and stole and retreated, they evacuated high ranking Communist officials to safety. They also evacuated many professionals whose skills could be of service to Stalin. Left behind to meet the Nazis were the anti-Communist Ukrainians who had somehow managed to survive. Also left behind were the old, the feeble, and the children. They were abandoned by the Soviets without food, without weapons, and without means of protecting themselves.

Danylo and his parents stayed hidden under the barn as long as they could. Even after they ran out of food, they were still afraid to come out. It wasn't until Danylo's mother became ill that he or his father even considered seeking food.

The horror of finding the body of his father amongst so many others that he knew was terrible, but the worst was still to come. When the Nazis arrived, people came out of hiding. Danylo's mother even greeted them with relief. How could the Nazis possibly be worse than the Soviets?

But the Nazis set up administrative offices in the same buildings that had been evacuated by the Soviets. And then they went from house to house and chose people to help them. Of Danylo, they asked that he be an auxiliary policeman, but he refused. They came the next day, and he refused again.

The next night, there was a tapping on their door, and when Danylo answered it, Kataryna stood there. Danylo was astonished to see his sister alive. "How can this be?" Danylo asked in wonder.

"I've joined the OUN — the Organization of Ukrainian Nationalists," explained Kataryna. "When the time is right, we will fight the Nazis, but right now, we must let them think we're working with them."

"I can't work with them," declared Danylo. "They're no better than the Communists."

"You'll do what I say, brother, or I will shoot you myself."

Danylo was taken aback by this talk, but he noticed that as his sister made this statement, she drew a pistol from her jacket and she was pointing it to the dirt floor of the cottage.

"Take the job as an auxiliary policeman," Kataryna ordered. "You and others will infiltrate the Nazi administration to gain weapons and information. When the time is right, you will kill the Nazis and join us in the forests."

Danylo knew better than to argue.

The next day, he was issued an armband, a pistol and two bullets.

As the days passed, a putrid stench began to fill all of the administrative buildings that had been abandoned by the Soviets. Danylo and the other local boys with auxiliary police armbands were ordered to open up the basements of the buildings and locate the source of the stench. The doors had been padlocked from the outside and the locks had to be shot off or sawed through because the keys could not be found. When Danylo opened up the first door, he covered his mouth in horror at the sight that awaited him. Dozens of mutilated bodies were stacked on top of each other, rotting and maggot-ridden. The retreating Soviets had not been content to simply kill the Ukrainian resistance fighters who were left behind: they had tortured them beyond recognition. Although his father was dead, Danylo was thankful that he had merely been shot.

The Nazis saw this horrific tragedy as an opportunity to garner support. They ordered the bodies to be taken out of the dungeons and basements and lined up along the main street. Bodies were also found in the fields. It was hard to imagine how many people had been killed in those last days of Soviet occupation.

The mothers and the wives and the daughters came to identify their sons and husbands and brothers. Men and boys, too young or too old to fight, came to view the bodies too.

Husbands and sons and brothers and lovers and neighbours lay dead and mutilated in a row. The sight was too much to bear.

As the survivors grieved, a black-uniformed SS officer walked up and down the street, viewing the spectacle with satisfaction.

"You know who did this?" he whispered as he passed a grieving woman.

And then he marched out a group of Jews and half a dozen Communists who were too unimportant to have warranted evacuation with their comrades.

"It's these vermin who are to blame," said the officer.

One of the men shook his head fearfully, knowing what the officer was trying to do. "I did nothing," the man protested.

Then the officer turned to Danylo.

"I will leave it to you to punish these murderers."

Danylo stood there in shock. He looked at the mutilated corpses lined up in front of him and he looked at the grieving villagers. And then he looked at the pitiful group of scapegoats.

He knew that if he didn't mete out punishment, an SS officer with a fully loaded gun would be brought in. Plus he would blow his cover. But what could he do?

As he stood there trying to decide, the grieving villagers began to chant, "Kill them! Kill them! Kill them!"

"Get down on the ground," he ordered, pointing his pistol at the group.

The Nazi officer smiled with satisfaction when he saw that his orders were being carried out. He pulled out a gold pocket watch and noted that it was almost time for a nice hot cup of tea. He walked away, leaving the dirty work to the Ukrainian boy.

When Danylo saw through the corner of his eye that the officer was no longer watching him, he pointed his pistol to a tree beyond the people lying on the ground and a single shot rang out. The villagers, stunned by the noise, stopped their chanting. The men lying on the ground groaned in fear of what was to come.

Then Danylo said in a firm voice, "One hundred push-ups, now."

Danylo was startled from his memories by a light tapping at the bedroom door.

"May I come in?" A sliver of Kat's face was peering through a crack in the door.

Danylo took a deep breath to calm himself, and then he grabbed a handkerchief from his pocket and quickly wiped the tears from his face. He did not want Kat to see how sad he was.

"Come in, *zolota zhabka*," he said.

Kat pushed the door open with her shoulder and walked in. She was carrying a tray that held a steaming mug of tea and a grilled cheese sandwich. "I thought you might be hungry," she said. "Besides, you made me breakfast, so I figured I should make you lunch."

A sad smile formed on Danylo's lips. It was so kind of Kataryna to think of him, even though the last thing he wanted to do right now was to eat.

"Thank you," he said. "Set it down and I will eat it in a moment."

CHAPTER 16

MR. VINCENT'S DESK was set in front of a magnificent old-fashioned bay window that looked upon the heavily treed Prince Arthur Street in all its autumn finery. He motioned for Danylo and Orysia to sit down in the deeply cushioned leather chairs that were placed before his desk. After a few pleasantries, he got down to business.

"You're probably wondering what sort of information the government has accumulated against you," Mr. Vincent said, looking at Danylo.

Mr. Vincent opened a thick file on his desk and then pulled out a pair of reading glasses from his pocket. "It says here that the RCMP visited your birth village of Orelets in Volhyn in 1992 and again in 1994 in order to interview the villagers about your activities during the war."

Danylo nodded in acknowledgement. "That's good," he said. "They should talk to people who were there, and would understand what it was like back then."

Mr. Vincent gave Danylo a puzzled look, and then flipped through a few more layers of paper. "Well, Mr. Feschuk, it seems that the RCMP were able to find two people who will testify that you collaborated with the Nazis."

"*What?*" exclaimed Danylo with surprise. "Who? And what did they say I was supposed to have done?"

"One will testify that you threatened local Jews. Another will testify that you collaborated with the imprisonment of Soviet prisoners of war."

"Those are lies," said Danylo.

"And that's what we have to demonstrate," said Mr. Vincent. Orysia asked, "Has the hearing date been set?"

"Yes," said Mr. Vincent. "It will begin on January 11th."

"How many villagers did they contact altogether?" asked Orysia.

"I'm not exactly sure," said Mr. Vincent. "But they would have attempted to interview every single resident who is still alive and who lived there during the war."

"Do they also have a list of residents who will testify in my father's defence?" she asked.

"That wasn't their mandate," Mr. Vincent replied. "They were only interested in the people who would testify against him."

"I would have thought they'd be interested in finding the truth," said Orysia.

Mr. Vincent closed the file in front of him and folded his arms on the desk. "It's not fair," he said. "But we can make it more fair."

"How?" asked Orysia.

"The defence can also interview all of those surviving villagers."

"How do we do that?" asked Orysia.

"We would have to fly to Ukraine with an interpreter to interview them. Then we would have to fly the defence witnesses to Canada."

"Wouldn't that cost a fortune?" asked Danylo.

"It will be expensive," said Mr. Vincent. "But probably worth it."

"How much would this cost?" asked Danylo.

"The defence would have to pay air fare, accommodation, food and incidental expenses for the witnesses who come here to testify," explained Mr. Vincent. "You're looking at about $40,000 if you get six or seven good witnesses."

"Then we've lost before we've begun," said Danylo. "I don't have that kind of money." Indeed, $40,000 was more than Danylo had ever made in a year.

Orysia looked at her father. She knew what he was thinking. She also knew that by mortgaging both their own house and her father's house, they could borrow about $150,000, meaning there would still be $110,000 left for the trial. How would they ever pay it back? Orysia couldn't let herself think of that. Her father was innocent.

"Do you have any idea how much this whole proceeding might cost?" asked Orysia.

"The government spends several million dollars on each one of these cases," said Mr. Vincent. "To forge an adequate defence, you could easily spend one million." Mr. Vincent then looked into Danylo's eyes. "This is not a proceeding to step into lightly."

"But what other choice do I have?" asked Danylo.

"You could leave voluntarily," replied Mr. Vincent.

"But then it will be assumed that I am guilty," said Danylo angrily. "This is crazy."

Even so, Danylo thought to himself, how could he ask his family to take on such a huge burden? How could one man fight the whole government? Yet if he didn't fight, he would be branded a war criminal. Worse yet, his family and community would be reviled. He had no idea what he should do. He looked over at Orysia and was surprised to see a look of cool determination on her face.

Orysia met her father's eyes and nodded slightly. Then she turned to Mr. Vincent and said, "Please make arrangements for an approved translator, yourself, and whomever else should travel to Ukraine. And of course, I will accompany you."

CHAPTER 17

IT WAS A snowy Monday in early December by the time Lisa, Kat and Ian could get together after school to test out different ways to hang the parachute onto the maroon velvet curtains. Preparing for the winter concert was a welcome respite for Kat. Her grandfather's hearing had been set for January 11th, and the winter concert was set for January 25th.

"I love this stuff," said Lisa, crushing the parachute material to her face and breathing in deeply. "After the concert, can I have this? Maybe I can make a dress."

"I don't mind," said Ian. "Unless Kat wants it."

Kat shook her head and smiled. "Not my style."

The parachute was large enough that they could drape it in three huge loose scallops and still have some material to spare. Kat and Lisa practised pinning it up and pulling it down while Ian timed them. Once they got the knack, it took less than a minute each way.

As Kat and Ian and Lisa waited for the late bus, Kat remembered that she had brought something for Lisa. She reached into her knapsack and pulled out a zip-lock bag of what looked like dried animal droppings.

Ian wrinkled his nose in disgust. "What is that?"

But Lisa knew right away. "Are these some of the mushrooms that you dried by yourself?" she asked excitedly.

Kat nodded.

Lisa took the bag and opened it a tiny bit, then breathed in deeply. "Oh, they smell wonderful. My grandmother will be in heaven." She sealed it back up, then gave Kat a big hug. "Thanks."

"If you're interested," said Kat, "come over to my house some time and I'll show you the contraption my father rigged up to dry them in."

"Sounds good," said Lisa.

Kat finished writing her last mid-term exam at noon on the Friday before Christmas. She clicked shut her school locker with a sigh after dumping her books in and grabbing her winter coat out. She had a feeling that she had bombed most of her exams. She had tried to study, truly she had, but the words just swam in front of her. The same thing happened while she was trying to write them. She would read through the questions and her mind would go blank. The worst was today's math exam. If she broke 50%, she'd be lucky.

Kat pulled on her coat and shoved her hands into the pockets. In her rush to catch the bus this morning, she hadn't brought gloves, and it was bitterly cold outside.

Just as she walked out, she saw her bus pull up. There were only two kids boarding, so it left quickly. No time to flag it down. And there wouldn't be another bus for fifteen minutes.

She shoved her hands further into her pockets with a shiver, and walked to the bus shelter.

She thought of all that had happened in the last few months. Her father had been transferred out of the country. Mayfair Industrial had been afraid of the notoriety of Danylo's upcoming hearing, and so they gave her father a choice: He could either work a desk on the inside and receive no commission until the attention died down, or he could break new sales territory for their new office in Oregon. He would get full pay, travel expenses and commission. Kat understood his decision to temporarily relocate. After all, they desperately needed the money. However, she missed her father very much.

Her mother was back from Ukraine, and her father had come back from Oregon for four days over American Thanksgiving. Kat had been looking forward to some normal family time, but instead spent that weekend listening to her parents argue as they took out their frustrations on each other.

Her mother had triumphantly come home from Ukraine with the news that most people in the village would testify favourably towards Dido. The two who refused wouldn't even look her in the eyes; they just walked away in angered silence. Orysia had felt the trip was well worth it. Had she not gone over, the only eyewitness testimony would have come from those two who were the ones who were already testifying for the prosecution.

Kat's father was furious when he found out it would cost upwards of $50,000 to transport and accommodate eleven witnesses for the hearing. "Are you crazy?" he had asked. "You're digging us deep in a hole of debt."

Orysia's eyes stared at her husband coldly.

"Must we have all eleven?" he asked. "Why not just the best five or six?"

Orysia said nothing. She walked away.

There was really no one to talk to about all of this. Kat had drifted away from her friends at St. Paul's, and she didn't feel close enough to either Beth or Callie to confide in them. She wondered how much Michael knew? He treated her no differently at school, and so she assumed that his father had said nothing to him about the upcoming hearing. She knew that Ian suspected something was wrong, but he could never guess the magnitude of what she was going through. Who could?

Just then, she noticed that someone else had entered the bus shelter. She looked up and recognized Dylan, her old acquaintance from day camp. He looked like an overgrown version of the kid he used to be: dark hair buzzed Marine short, a handsome face that still had a bit of childhood pudginess, and friendly chocolate brown eyes. In day camp he'd been a bit on the short and chubby side, but now he was tall and big with muscle, not fat. He wore a navy wool bomber jacket with his school team football logo on it.

He noticed her staring at him so he turned around. "Kat," he said with surprise. "How are you?"

She didn't want to alarm him by saying how she really was, so she just told him she was fine.

"Are you going to Cawthra now?" he asked.

"Yes," she replied. "I switched over from St. Paul's at the beginning of the year."

"There's a lot of freaks at that school," said Dylan. "Be careful."

Kat was surprised at this statement. As far as she was concerned, Cawthra was simply filled with very creative students. If they were freaks, then so was she.

Just then, a black SUV pulled up and the window rolled down. "Hey, there," a familiar voice called.

Kat looked up. It was Ian, his fluorescent yellow hair glinting from the reflection of the snow. "Need a ride?" Ian looked directly at her, and did not even acknowledge that Dylan was standing beside her.

The back door of the SUV opened, and there was Lisa in the back, beckoning her.

With a grin, Kat ran over to the vehicle and hopped in. She waved good-bye to Dylan. "It was nice seeing you again," she called out as she closed the door.

"You should stay away from that creep," said Ian, looking out the window and pointing towards Dylan.

"He's not a creep," said Kat. What was his problem with Dylan, she wondered?

The uncomfortable silence that followed was broken when Lisa said, "Kat, I'd like you to meet my father, Dr. Hung Nguyen."

The driver of the vehicle turned to face Kat in the back seat. Dr. Nguyen extended his hand.

Kat drew one of her freezing hands out of the depths of her pocket and grasped Dr. Nguyen's. She was surprised at its warmth and strength.

"You are Lisa's friend who knows about mushrooms, right?" asked Dr. Nguyen.

Kat smiled. It had never been her claim to fame before. "Yes," she replied. "But probably not as much as you."

Dr. Nguyen grinned, then turned back in his seat to face the steering wheel. "Are you coming to our house, or would you like me to drive you home?" he asked, looking at her through the rearview mirror.

Kat hesitated. Before she could answer, Lisa piped in. "If you're not doing anything, come on over. Ian's coming."

"Sure," said Kat. "That would be fun." She was grateful for the distraction.

Kat looked out the window in silence as Lisa's father drove away from the bus stop. She noticed a few kids walking home, grins on their faces, glad that the holidays had started. A woman crossed in front of the SUV at a busy intersection, her arms loaded down with gift packages. The sight made Kat gulp back sadness. This wasn't exactly going to be a happy holiday for her family.

Lisa's father drove up Cawthra and over the highway and into one of the many new housing developments that had blossomed recently. He turned onto a street with deeply creviced tire tracks of mud and frozen dirt. Lisa's house was a large grey stone mock Tudor on a postage-stamp sized lot. Dr. Nguyen parked in a gravel-covered driveway in front of a two door garage.

When Kat followed the others into the house, she was enveloped in a wonderfully aromatic cooking smell that she couldn't quite identify. It was vaguely familiar. Images of her grandmother fluttered into her mind.

"Come on," said Lisa, unzipping her long boots. "Follow me."

Kat poked her head into the living room and dining room as she passed. Everything was bright, white, and modern. The hallway opened up into a galley style kitchen in the centre of the house. There was an island with a cook top, and on one of the burners was a gigantic stainless steel stock-pot. The lovely aroma was emanating from that.

"My grandmother's making soup," said Lisa, lifting the lid and peering inside. "Can you tell that lemongrass is her favourite seasoning?"

Lisa opened the refrigerator and rooted around until she found three cans of cola. Tossing one to Kat and one to Ian, she gestured for them to follow her into the basement. A corner of the room was finished like a standard rec room with a television, stereo, sofa and chairs, but the rest of it was a huge raised dance floor, with a bar at one end and a small elevated stage and a single screen karaoke system at the other. A glittering mirror-ball was hanging from the ceiling.

"This is bizarre," said Kat. "Your parents must have a lot of parties."

"Not really," said Lisa. "But they sometimes have a few friends over to dance. They love karaoke. My mother won the karaoke system in a contest, so my dad surprised her by building this little stage. Then he put in the lighting system."

Lisa walked over to the stage area and flicked one switch. The lights dimmed; she flicked another and the mirrorball began to rotate slowly. Kat noticed that coloured light was reflecting off the mirrorball and bouncing around the room. Lisa flicked another switch, and her image appeared on the screen behind her.

Ian grinned broadly. "Can I put on a tune?" he asked.

"Take your pick," said Lisa, pointing to a stack of CDs.

Ian flipped through. Most were bubble gum tunes from the 1960s and disco from the 1970s. He pulled out a CD of *Saturday Night Fever*. "This should be good," he said. "What do you think?"

"Sure," Lisa replied with a mischievous smile. "But you've got to perform it."

Lisa popped the disc into the unit and handed Ian the microphone. The screen filled with his image. Along the bottom, the lyrics for "Staying Alive" by the Bee Gees appeared, one line at a time. A bouncing ball keeping time. "Stand right here," she said, pulling him to the centre of the stage.

Kat sat cross-legged in the middle of the dance floor and settled in for the performance. Lisa hopped off the stage and sat beside her on the floor. They clapped to the rhythm of the bouncing ball.

"Well you can tell by the way I use my walk, I'm a woman's man — no time to talk!" Ian wailed.

Kat watched the whole absurd scenario of Ian strutting around like John Travolta . He was really quite good. She had been feeling so depressed all day, but watching Ian do the high camp karaoke rendition had her grinning ear to ear.

CHAPTER 18

SVIAT VECHIR WAS usually one of Kat's favourite days in the whole year. While her friends and their families were putting away the last of the tinsel and starting on their New Year's resolutions, for the Baliuks and others in their community, the festivities were just getting under way. Ukrainian Christmas Eve was celebrated on January 6th, and the meticulous preparation of the traditional twelve meatless dishes started weeks in advance. This year, *Sviat Vechir* fell on a Sunday. Christmas day was on a Monday. It was the first day of school for everyone else, but Genya and Kat would stay home to go to Christmas service with their family. After that, they would have a midday meal of goose and cabbage rolls.

It was a subdued celebration this year for more reason than one. It was bad enough with the deportation hearing just days away. Kat couldn't get that out of her head. But it was also the first year that Kat's grandmother wouldn't be there with them. The year before, Baba had been so ill that the family brought a makeshift *Sviat Vechir* dinner right into her hospice room and had a final family celebration together. At the time, Kat couldn't have imagined a more macabre evening, but this year it was shaping up to be worse.

Not only was Baba gone, but Kat's father wouldn't be there, either. He had been given time off at American Thanksgiving and also between Christmas and New Year's, but Ukrainian Christmas was just another work day to his boss, so Walt flew back to Portland on New Year's Day. Orysia swallowed back her sorrow as she kissed him one last time at the airport. "Get the girls to invite a friend each," Walt had suggested, giving his wife a fierce hug. "The celebration won't seem so desolate then."

Genya opted not to ask anyone. Orysia had noticed that Genya had not brought a single friend home with her since the issue with Danylo had arisen. More often than not, Genya would be out. She had even taken to staying at a friend's house overnight several times a week.

Kat asked Lisa, who was thrilled with the invitation. "Are you going to ask Ian too?" she had inquired.

"Do you think he'd want to come?" asked Kat. She liked Ian and considered him a friend, but she knew that he was Lisa's boyfriend and she didn't want to mess with that.

"I don't know," shrugged Lisa. "Would you like me invite him for you?"

"No," said Kat. "I'll call."

With Danylo's help, Kat and Genya pushed the kitchen table into the living room, moved back all the living room furniture against the wall, and then put in the two extra table leaves, making the kitchen table long enough for even a dozen people. Kat took a freshly ironed table cloth and spread it over the long table top, then set out seven embroidered place mats. Once the newly polished silverware and special china were set out, Kat smiled with satisfaction. Maybe this wouldn't be so bad after all.

Lisa and Ian arrived together around five o'clock. As Kat opened the door to let them in, she noticed the silhouette of a figure in the darkness.

"Is there someone out there with you?" asked Kat, peering out into the darkness, trying to get a good look at the person.

"It's a protester," said Ian, as he stepped through the doorway.

"A what?" she asked alarmed.

"She's got a protest sign she's waving around," said Lisa. "It says 'Nazi lives here.' What's that all about?"

Kat's face paled. Of all the times to choose to picket, why did she choose to come on Christmas Eve? "It's hard to explain," said Kat, closing the door quickly.

Kat hadn't seen Ian since before Christmas break, and the first thing she noticed was that he seemed somehow larger than life. He must have grown an inch, or perhaps filled out a bit. His presence seemed to envelop the room. His hair was freshly dyed a stark black, making him look formidable rather than whimsical. Kat took his coat from him — the satin lined long black coat that he planned on wearing for the concert. As she hung it up in the closet, she couldn't help but catch the distinctive scent of Ian and she filled her lungs with it. She hung Lisa's black leather trench coat up beside it in the closet, feeling a bit jealous that the two coats had arrived together.

Orysia suppressed a gasp when she walked into the living room to greet her guests. Ian had always attracted attention with his flamboyant appearance, but today he looked vaguely threatening to her. Orysia was ashamed of her thoughts. She knew that Ian was a gentle soul. And he had even dressed up for the occasion. He was wearing a white ruffled shirt buttoned high on the collar, and a heavy iron crucifix dangling from a long chain around his neck.

Lisa had also dressed carefully for the evening. No hobnailed boots or ripped net stockings: she wore a simple black jersey dress with a high neck and long sleeves with a hem line that brushed the floor. She was almost nun-like in her simplicity.

They stood awkwardly side by side as Orysia approached them. "*Veselykh Sviat*," she said cheerfully. "That literally means 'happy holy' — but it's how you say happy Ukrainian Christmas Eve."

"Merry Christmas to you too," said Ian and Lisa together.

Just then, the door of Genya's bedroom creaked open and Danylo stepped out. He too had dressed up. He wore the dark grey suit that he had bought for his wife's funeral over a Ukrainian embroidered shirt. In his lapel was a reindeer pin that Kat had bought him the Christmas before.

A smile broke out on his face when he saw that two of Kat's new friends had decided to join them in their celebration. He gave each a bear hug then led them to the sofa that was pushed up against the wall to make room for the table.

Then he walked into the kitchen and gestured to the three cooking females to come out to the living room. "Let us gather around the table for the *kutya*."

Danylo carried a crystal bowl filled with *kutya* — a mixture of poppy seeds, honey, wheat and walnuts — and set it at the head of the table. Orysia placed a stack of small dessert bowls beside it. When they all found a spot around the table, there was still one empty. Danylo placed one spoonful of the mixture in each of the bowls, and Orysia set one in front of each person, and also one in front of the empty spot.

Lisa and Ian looked towards Kat to see what they should do. Everyone remained standing, and then Danylo took a small bit of the *kutya* on his spoon and held it in front of him. Everyone else did the same. "May God protect us this coming year, and may it be full of health and happiness for all," said Danylo. Then he ate his spoonful of *kutya*. Everyone else did the same.

"Now the fast is broken and we can eat," said Danylo to Ian and Lisa.

Orysia and her daughters went back into the kitchen to continue preparing the twelve course meatless feast, and Danylo got a container of grape juice from the fridge and took it into the living room with him. Filling three wine glasses from the table, he handed one each to Lisa and Ian, and kept one for himself. "A toast to friendship," he said.

They clinked their glasses and sipped.

"The candle hasn't been lit," said Danylo more to himself than to his guests. He opened the front curtains slightly and set down a single candle holder. "This light is to help travelers find their way home," he explained.

As he lit it with a match, he looked out the window and noticed a figure in the darkness. He squinted, trying to make sense of what he saw, but then he saw the outline of the placard and understood what it was.

"You will see that there are only six of us here, yet there are seven place settings on the table," Danylo said to Lisa and Ian who were sitting quietly side by side. "That place setting is for our departed loved ones. But it is also for the wandering stranger."

With that, Danylo set down his wine glass of grape juice and opened up the front door. He walked down the front steps of the house and out towards the sidewalk to where the lone protester stood. It was an elderly woman. She stared back at him with surprise and disdain.

"Madam," said Danylo. "I would like to invite you into our house for dinner."

The woman lowered her placard and stared at him with incredulity. "You expect me to accept your offer? You, a war criminal? And you, who just let two punk neo-Nazis into your house?"

Danylo sighed deeply. Each of her words cut him to the quick. "I am offering you my hospitality on a cold night," he said gently.

The woman spat on the ground in front of him and walked away.

CHAPTER 19

WHEN KAT CAME downstairs on Ukrainian Christmas morning, the first thing she did was to peek through the front curtains. The protester was gone, thank goodness.

Her mother, still in her housecoat, was already up and busy preparing the goose. It would roast while they were at church for *Sluzhba Bozha*. Kat could never understand why they didn't just have leftover meatless cabbage rolls, perogies, *borscht* and *nalysniky* from the evening before for their midday meal. There were tons of leftovers. But her mother was a stickler for tradition, so in spite of all the leftovers, fresh meat-filled cabbage rolls and roast goose was served on *Rizdvo* — Christmas day.

Kat poured herself a glass of water, not wanting to have food before Divine Liturgy, and then she helped her mother. Danylo and Genya were still getting ready by the time the goose and cabbage rolls were in the oven.

While her mother got dressed for church, Kat opened the front door and retrieved both the *Globe & Mail* and the *Toronto Star* from the mailbox. She didn't even glance at the headlines as she carried the papers into the kitchen and deposited them on the table. But then a word on the front page of the *Star* caught her attention. The word was "Nazi". Kat unfolded the front page and her heart stopped. The headline was: Local man accused of Nazi crimes.

Below the headline was a large colour photo of her grandfather at the front step of their house. The top of Kat's own head was clearly visible behind him. Kat felt as if the wind had been knocked out of her. She quickly sat down on a kitchen chair and gulped for air. This can't be happening, but then again, why not? The hearing was at the end of the week. She tried to scan the article, but the words swam before her eyes. How and when had this photo been taken? Her grandfather was wearing his suit and Ukrainian blouse, and the reindeer pin was clearly visible on his lapel. It looked like it had been taken last night. How did they get such a close shot without them knowing, Kat wondered? Perhaps someone was watching them now? The thought made her shudder.

She threw the paper down on the table and flipped through the *Globe*. On A6 she stopped. A small news item caught her eye: Nazi war criminal hearing set for January 11th.

Kat willed herself to be calm and then read every word in the article. The bile rose in her throat. As far as the press saw it, her grandfather wasn't "accused"; he was guilty.

While she was still pondering the article, her mother walked out of her bedroom, dressed for church and looking happier than Kat had seen her for awhile. But when Orysia saw the expression on her daughter's face, her smile crumpled into concern. "What has happened?" she asked.

"Dido made front page of the *Star*, page 6 in the *Globe*."

She held out the papers, but Orysia shook her head.

"I don't want to see it," said Orysia. "I can tell by your face that I don't want to see it."

Just then, Genya came down the stairs, and Danylo came out of his room at almost the exact same moment.

"What is the problem?" asked Genya, looking from her sister to her mother.

Kat picked up the front section of the *Star* and held it up. "This is what's the matter," replied Kat.

"Great," said Genya. "Just what we need. We're going to be living our life in a fishbowl." As she said this, she gave her grandfather a hostile glance. "And Merry Christmas to you too."

Danylo stood there, stunned. He didn't know what he was more upset about: the articles in the newspapers, or Genya's reaction. He reached out and grabbed the newspaper from Kat's hand and held it at arm's length, trying to get it into focus. "It calls me a Nazi," he said with bewilderment. "I fought the Nazis."

"Ignore it," said Orysia. "Let us put this behind us and go to church. It's Christmas Day." And with that, Orysia grabbed her car keys and marched out the front door.

Kat was following close on her mother's heels, but no sooner was Orysia outside than she came back in, almost bumping into Kat. There were tears spilling down her cheeks. "My God. I can't take this." She sat limply down on the sofa. "Go and see what they've done."

Someone had taken what looked like blood and had splattered the white wood of the house with it. There was a huge black swastika spray bombed beneath the red spatters.

"I'm calling the police," said Genya, striding into the kitchen and grabbing the phone.

Danylo walked up to Orysia and put her head on his shoulder, just as he used to do when she was a child and needed comforting. Instinctively, he patted her back, and she hugged him fiercely.

Genya stepped back into the living room, the phone still in her hand. "The police are coming right over to photograph the damage."

Orysia raised her head from Danylo's shoulder and looked at Genya with dismay. "But we'll miss church."

"Actually, Mama, they asked us to wait until they get here. We'll be late, but they will send a couple of plain clothes officers into the cathedral to keep an eye on things while we're there."

"They said that?" asked her mother in awe.

"This is a hate crime," replied Genya. "They take it seriously."

Kat was amazed at her sister's cold command of the situation. Did nothing ruffle her?

It wasn't long before two officers pulled into the driveway in a patrol car. One was a black woman with hair buzzed short, and the other was an older man with a paunch. He carried a camera and an evidence kit.

The woman got out a pad of paper and asked questions, while the man took photos of the graffiti from a number of different angles. Once he had finished taking photos, he took a small plastic spatula out of the evidence kit and scraped some of the red paint or blood off the house. He placed both the spatula and the sample into a plastic bag from the kit, and then he sealed and labelled it.

"This is nasty business," said the woman officer, still scribbling in her notepad. "But I guess it's not surprising, given the circumstances."

Kat bristled, "My grandfather is innocent until proven guilty."

"I know that," said the woman, arching one brow and looking Kat in the eye. "But you are a magnet right now."

Kat nodded.

"Is this the only hate incident you've experienced?" asked the officer.

Kat's eyebrows creased in confusion for a moment, and then she said, "Does stuff sent in the mail count as a hate incident?"

"Absolutely," said the woman. "Has your grandfather received hate mail?"

Danylo, who was listening to this exchange, answered for Kat. "No," he said. "I have received nothing suspicious in the mail."

"Actually, Dido, you have," said Kat. And then she looked at the officer. "Hold on a minute and I'll get it."

She loped up the stairs to her bedroom, and retrieved the envelope and clippings that she had hidden under her mattress. When she brought it down and showed it to the police officer, Danylo's cheeks reddened with anger.

"When did that arrive?" he asked.

"A while ago," admitted Kat. "I didn't want to upset you."

The officer had an evidence bag ready. "Drop it in," she said. "It's too bad that you didn't report this immediately," she said to Kat. "We would have had a much better chance of getting finger prints off it if you hadn't handled it so much."

Kat hung her head. "I'm sorry," she said.

"If you get something else, call us immediately."

"Okay," said Kat.

The woman reached into her pocket and drew out a card. "Keep this handy," she said. "The reporters and photographers shouldn't be allowed on your private property. Ditto for protesters." The officer pointed to the sidewalk, "Anything past there is public, though, so we can't stop people from gawking as long as that's all they're doing."

They both got into the patrol car once the photos were taken. "We'll swing by this way a bit more regularly until things simmer down," said the woman. "The plain clothes should be at your church by now."

"Let's go," said Orysia, looking at her watch. "We've missed half the service already."

Danylo followed her out of the house, but paused when he got outside. He stared at the horrible graffiti on his daughter's house. "How can we leave with those marks still on our house?" said Danylo. "It shames me to have my daughter's house defaced like this."

"It is not you who should feel ashamed," said Orysia.

Bathurst Street was so jammed with cars in front of St. Volodymyr Cathedral that Orysia could barely get her car through, let alone find a parking spot. She dropped off Danylo and Kat at the steps, and then she and Genya drove around the block to find a parking spot. Miraculously, they found one.

Kat and Danylo stood in the chilly air while they waited for the other two. They could hear the singing of the people inside. "Are you sure you don't want to step in out of the cold?" asked Kat.

"No," said Danylo. "I don't know how I can even face all the people inside. They probably have seen the papers this morning."

"Dido," said Kat. "Those are your friends in there. They know who you are."

Danylo was silent.

The aroma of wool coats and liturgical incense greeted Kat's nose as she opened the doors of the cathedral and stepped inside. It was no larger than a regular church, but the sumptuous interior set it apart. Light streamed in through the stained glass windows and reflected off the massive crystal chandelier and lit up the gold leaf paintings on the walls. The cathedral was so packed that people were standing behind the pews at the back, and even out into the entryway. A couple of people turned to see who was coming in so late, and then there was a ripple of low whispers. In a wave, people moved, making room for Danylo and his family. Silent hugs and hands squeezed, and then Danylo and his family were ushered to a space in the pews.

Usually after the liturgy on Christmas day, people would hurry home. Christmas day was spent with family. But one of Danylo's old country friends grasped him firmly by the elbow and led him downstairs to the church hall. Puzzled, Orysia, Genya and Kat followed.

A cluster of people formed around Danylo, a buffer almost, thought Kat, from the real world. Some of Kat's friends from St. Paul's were there, and a couple of girls she'd lost touch with since graduating from St. Sofia's elementary school. There were also elderly people who Kat recognized as her grandparents' friends, and also their sons and daughters, who were her parents' friends.

When her grandmother was alive, she had been involved in the women's auxiliary, making perogies and cabbage rolls as bazaar fund-raisers with the other women. Kat watched as Lidia Krawchuk, who had been a dear friend of Baba's and was the current women's auxiliary president, stepped forward and grasped her mother's hand.

"In some ways I am glad that Nadiya is dead so that she doesn't have to suffer through this," said Mrs. Krawchuk. "That they could do this to a man who lost his family in World War II, and who fought bravely for Ukraine is a crime in itself."

Kat looked around and saw that others were nodding in agreement.

"We will do what we can to help," said the woman.

Orysia's eyes welled up with tears of gratitude. She wrapped her arms around the woman's shoulders and kissed her on the cheek.

Then Father Petrenko came down the steps. Kat noticed that he had replaced his sumptuous Christmas vestments of gold and white with a simple black cossack. In one arm he held a collection basket. "Danylo," the priest said, extending his hand. "I am thankful that you are here today. May your faith bring you comfort."

Danylo bowed his head.

"When I read the papers this morning, I was angered. What a shameful thing to print on the day of Christ's birth," continued the priest. "My father fought beside you in Ukraine," he continued. "God knows the truth."

Then Father Petrenko held up the basket. "We took a collection for you," he said. "This isn't much, but I hope it helps."

Kat looked over at her grandfather and saw that he had a brave smile on his face, but tears of gratitude were welling in his eyes. Orysia's demeanour was similar. What surprised Kat was her sister's expression. Genya, who was the epitome of cool control, had one of Danylo's hands clasped firmly in hers. Her mask of calm was betrayed by a trickle of tears down one cheek.

Chapter 20

It was well past noon when they got home, and the goose was roasted, but no one felt much like eating.

Kat and Danylo took some rags and a big pail of sudsy water to try to clean the front of the house. Whatever the red was, it wasn't permanent. It came off of the house without leaving a stain. The same could not be said for the huge black swastika. Danylo tried scrubbing it first with the soapy water and a bristled brush, his hands raw in the winter cold. When that didn't work, he tried paint solvent, but that just smeared it. He ended up painting over it with some leftover white paint that had been stored in the basement.

While they were still cleaning up, Kat noticed that the lone protester had come back. The woman seemed surprised to see Kat and her grandfather outside of their house. She looked at them both coldly and then continued to pace up and down the sidewalk.

Kat felt a mix of conflicting emotions as she watched the woman. Her first thought was one of anger. Had this woman purposely chosen to start her campaign on a Ukrainian religious holiday, wondered Kat indignantly. The papers had done the same. It was like salt in a wound.

Kat wanted to explain to her that this whole thing was a mistake. Didn't the woman realize that her grandfather was a suspect, not a criminal? Kat stepped towards the woman, but Danylo clasped her by the shoulder, holding her still. "Leave her be," he said.

When they got inside, Genya and Orysia had set the table, so Danylo and Kat quickly washed up and sat down at the table.

The mood was sombre. Orysia picked at her food, and Genya kept on glancing up at her grandfather. Finally, she put her fork down and said, "I think it's time for you to tell us what this is all about."

Danylo regarded his older granddaughter with sadness, but he remained silent.

"Why are they targeting you?" she persisted. "There has to be a reason."

Danylo sighed and then met her eyes. "There were bad police," he said. "But some of us were there for another reason."

With that, he walked into his bedroom and closed the door tight.

CHAPTER 21

KAT DIDN'T GO to school the next day. She told her mother she wasn't feeling well. Orysia suspected that her younger daughter didn't have the heart to face the world, so she didn't push it.

That night, long after the lights were out, and her sister was fast asleep in the other bed, Kat was still wide awake. Kat thought of the letter and clippings she had given to the police. In her mind's eye, she could see clearly the photo of a uniformed man shooting a child. It was a chilling image. The mere thought of such cruelty made tears well up in her throat. What would she do if she found out that her grandfather had actually done such a thing? It just couldn't be. Her mind couldn't get around such a thought.

Kat also wondered what people outside of her own community were thinking about all of this? Would she ever be able to show her face at school again? Genya was as calm and cool as ever. She was angry at the disturbance in her life, but that was about it. She went to school on the day after Ukrainian Christmas as if nothing had happened.

Kat was finally drifting off when she heard a smacking sound on her bedroom window. Was this another graffiti artist's idea of a joke? Who was out there? She looked over to her sister to see if she had heard the noise, but Genya was sound asleep.

Kat pulled the covers closer around her and tried to do the same, but she was startled by another loud smack at her window. This was too much! What did people think this was? A circus? Surely the protesters could at least let them sleep in peace at night. Kat pulled her bedroom curtains back in a fury and raised her window. She stuck her head out and was about to yell angrily down at the insensitive clod who wouldn't leave her alone when she saw a familiar splash of purple hair. Actually, it wasn't all that familiar. Ian had been pink and turquoise and black. She hadn't seen his hair purple yet, but who else could it be?

"What are you doing down there?" she called.

The purple hair moved, and suddenly Kat could see Ian's face beneath it.

"I was worried about you," he called up in a loud whisper. "All the stuff in the papers, and then you didn't come to school."

"Stay right there," whispered Kat. "I'm coming down.

Kat pulled a pair of baggy overalls over her bare legs, tucked in the oversize T-shirt that doubled as a nightgown and hurried down the stairs. She didn't want to wake up the household, so instead of inviting Ian in, she shoved her feet into her winter boots, grabbed her coat, and slipped silently out the front door.

Kat shivered in the wintry air as she and Ian walked down the street to the park at the end. It was at this park that her grandfather had pushed her on a swing when she was little. She remembered the time when she found a five dollar bill in the sandbox. She had begged her grandfather with tears in her eyes to mail it to the poor children of Chernobyl. As soon as they got home that day, she watched him laboriously address an envelope in English. She stuck her bill in, and he added a five of his own for good measure, and then she licked the envelope shut.

The park looked menacing now in the dark. The silhouette of bare trees looked like giant claws stretching out towards them. A new set of climbers had been installed just the summer before and someone had cleared it of snow. Kat climbed up and sat at the top of the slide, Ian sat down beside her.

The words tumbled out in a mad rush as Kat tried to explain all that had been happening in her life. As she spoke, she was gripped by a violent case of the shakes. Her whole body was like a quivering mass of Jell-O. She didn't know whether it was from the cold or from nerves.

Ian took off his meticulously safety-pinned leather jacket and wrapped it around her shoulders, his arm lingered protectively against her back. The jacket was imbedded with the musky scent of Ian. It wasn't exactly pleasant, but she found it oddly comforting.

"You're going to freeze," said Kat, grateful for the coat, but worried about her friend.

"I'll be okay if we sit close," said Ian.

Kat leaned into him.

"So that's why the protester was there," he said. "Why didn't you tell me all of this before?"

Kat smiled bitterly. "It's not really a good conversation starter," she said. "I mean, what did you want me to say? 'How are you doing today, and oh by the way, my grandfather might be a Nazi war criminal?'"

"You've got a point," said Ian. "So what happens now?"

Kat explained that her parents had already hired Michael's father, and that his first court appearance was on Friday. "But the accusations are so vague that it's hard to make a defence."

"Are you coming back to school tomorrow?"

"I don't know," said Kat. "How are the kids reacting to it?"

"It's not been a big deal. I mean, not a lot people pay attention to the news," said Ian. "The ones who heard about it are curious, but I don't think you've got to be worried about being lynched or anything like that."

"Thanks for that comforting thought," said Kat dryly.

"It's strange that the government would revoke citizenship and deport," said Ian.

"Unfair would be a better word," said Kat.

"No," said Ian. "What I mean is, it's like saying there are two classes of citizens in Canada: those who are born here and those who immigrated. I'd think a whole lot of immigrants would worry about who was going to be next on the government's hit list."

Kat hadn't thought of it that way. She had been so caught up in the drama that had engulfed her own family that she hadn't looked at the bigger picture.

"For example," continued Ian. "Look at Lisa. Her parents came over as Vietnamese boat kids. They escaped the Communists too."

"I didn't know that," replied Kat.

"Someone from the old country could just as easily accuse her parents or grandparents of something, and on the basis fabricated evidence, they could lose their Canadian citizenship too."

A chilling thought. It seemed odd that that a country that prided itself on human rights would do something like this.

Suddenly, a set of headlights beamed on. There was a patrol car parked right in front of them at the edge of the park. Two officers bearing flashlights got out and walked over to Kat and Ian. The officers were both male, and neither was all that old.

"Care to explain what the two of you are doing out here in the middle of the night?" one of the officers asked.

"Just talking," replied Ian.

The officer looked at Ian from the top of his purple hair to the bottom of his knee length black boots and suppressed a grimace. "There's been some trouble in the area," said the cop.

"What kind of trouble?" asked Ian.

"Hate crime. You know anything about it?"

"I do," said Kat.

The officer looked at her sharply.

"It was at my house," she explained. "Swastika, animal blood."

"Gross," said Ian, looking over at Kat incredulously. "What kind of a nut-case would do something like that?"

The officer took another look at Ian's outfit and just smiled. "There are all sorts out there," he said. "You two should be getting home — it's a school night, after all."

"We will," Kat promised.

With that, the officers walked back to their car and drove off.

Ian and Kat walked back down the street towards her house in silence. Kat was still shivering slightly, so Ian had insisted that she keep wearing the jacket even though the frigid air easily flowed through the open seams.

"You must be frozen solid," she said. "Come in, and I'll get my mom to drive you home."

But when they got right up to the front lawn, there was a sudden shuffling sound and a metallic clank. Kat saw a pair of running shoes and a dark jacket brush past her. Ian bolted after the figure. She heard what sounded like cloth ripping, someone falling and then a few choice curses.

"He got away," said Ian, getting up and brushing snow away from his leather pants. "But at least I did a number on his jacket."

"Did you recognize him?"

"No. But he was taller than me. And he had dark hair."

When they got all the way up to the house, Kat could see that he had been in the midst of spray bombing another swasti-ka. So far, it looked like a giant black plus sign. There was also a plastic margarine dish. Ian nudged it with the edge of his boot. "It's filled with something sloshy," he said.

"Probably the animal blood," sighed Kat.

"Ick."

"This guy must have seen the police car go by and figured he was safe for a while," said Kat, walking up the front steps. "Come in and get warm. I'll call the cops."

"Sure," said Ian.

Kat felt oddly detached about the hate incident. It was as if it weren't real. The first time it had happened she had been horrified and afraid. Now she was numb. It also felt odd to her that the first time she had Ian into her house without Lisa was as a result of something like this. Her house was so tiny compared to his, but she figured the police might want to talk to him. And it wasn't until just now that she noticed all the clutter. Newspapers were still flipped open to pertinent pages and strewn out on the table. The sofa looked worn, and there were a couple of dirty mugs and dishes left sitting on the coffee table in the living room. Her mother usually picked things up just before going to bed, but tonight she hadn't.

Ian seemed not to notice the mess and just followed Kat into the kitchen where she made the call. As she was on hold with the police, she heard a bedroom door open and close. A few moments later, her bathrobed grandfather, squinting from the kitchen light, stood in the doorway.

"This is an odd time to be entertaining, *zolota zhabka*," said Danylo. Kat noticed that his eyes sparkled in recognition when he saw Ian.

Just then, an officer came on the line. Danylo listened in alarm to Kat's report. "And my friend Ian and I actually interrupted the guy in the midst of doing it," she said.

"We'll be right over."

By the time Kat had hung up the phone, the whole household was awake. Orysia was dressed in a long pyjama top and she had thrown a terry cloth robe over it, but her feet were bare. Genya came down, heard what was happening, and went back upstairs to sleep.

The same two policemen who had encountered Kat and Ian in the park were the ones who arrived at the door. Kat noticed their barely concealed scepticism as Ian described running after the culprit. After the interview, she and Ian led them outside and showed them the half-painted swastika and the margarine dish of blood. Inwardly, she was thankful that neither she nor Ian had touched anything with their hands. She could just see them accusing her or Ian of doing this! One of the officers gingerly placed the container of animal blood in an evidence bag, then put in on the floor in the passenger side of the patrol car. He then turned to Ian and said, "We'll give you a lift home, son." He opened the back door of the cruiser.

As they pulled out of the driveway, Ian called out to Kat, "See you at school tomorrow, okay?"

As they drove off, Kat realized with a start that she still had Ian's jacket over her shoulders.

CHAPTER 22

KAT'S HEART BEAT rapidly when she saw the school bus pull up at her stop the next morning. She noticed Michael sitting in one of the seats, but the space beside him was full. None of the other kids even glanced at her as she stepped in and walked down the aisle. This was actually normal — studied indifference. She was about to sit down in one of the empty seats near the front when she glanced at the back and saw that Ian and Lisa were there. She was angry at herself for feeling a twinge of jealousy. Kat saw Ian look up at her. He motioned with his eyes for her to come and sit with him and Lisa. She noticed that Lisa had also looked up and was gesturing encouragingly too. She wanted to be close to Ian because she knew he was her friend. Also, she had his leather jacket neatly folded in her knapsack. She gave them both a faint smile, then walked down to the back and sat down with them.

It felt odd walking into art class that day. Kat expected her classmates to ogle her curiously, but that didn't happen. When she sat in her usual spot behind Michael, he turned about and gave Kat a self-conscious grin.

"How are you holding up?" he asked.

So he knew.

As if he could read her thoughts, Michael said, "Nah, my Dad doesn't talk shop at home. I put two and two together when I read yesterday's paper."

Kat nodded in acknowledgement. Beth, who had been doodling on a blank sheet of paper on her desk, looked up, a frown creasing her brow. "What are you guys talking about?"

The comment surprised Kat. Didn't everyone here *know* what had happened to her grandfather? What was she supposed to say to Beth?

Michael saved her by quickly replying, "Kat's grandfather needs some immigration papers filed, and my Dad's looking after it."

"Oh," said Beth, not remotely interested. "And that was in the paper? Boy, this is a boring town."

If only, thought Kat.

Beth's lackadaisical attitude contrasted greatly with Mr. Harding's when he walked into class a few moments later. Kat noticed that he scanned the room, saw her sitting there, and immediately locked eyes with her. The stare made her blush, and so she looked down at her notebook.

They were working on detailed pencil sketches of an object. Kat's object of choice was her left running shoe. It was an emotional relief to be able to concentrate on replicating every stitch, every fabric crease of her old Nike. It was sheer pleasure to be involved in an activity that involved the skill of her hands, but left her mind free to wander.

"It's good to see you back at school, Kat," Mr. Harding said. He was standing right behind her.

Kat was so startled that she nearly fell off her stool. She had been so engrossed with her work that she hadn't seen through the corner of her eye when Mr. Harding crept beside her.

"Come see me after class, Kat," said Mr. Harding.

When the bell rang at the end of the class, Kat lagged behind and watched as her classmates filed out. Mr. Harding was sitting at his desk, sorting through papers. Kat stood polite-ly before him, waiting for him to look up. She hoped he would-n't be too long; any moment now, students for the next period would start filing in.

Mr. Harding looked up at her and smiled. "Thanks for stay-ing," he said. "I wanted to talk to you alone for a moment." He shuffled some papers on his desk and then said, "I know about your grandfather's upcoming hearing."

Kat nodded. She'd figured that one out.

Mr. Harding propped his elbows up on his desk and held his hands together as if he were praying. "I want you to know that I don't hold it against you because of what your grandfa-ther did," he said.

Kat could feel her heart pound in her chest. She had done nothing wrong. And as far as she knew, neither had her grand-father. Yet Mr. Harding wasn't going to hold it against her? This was so confusing.

"And I want you to know," continued Mr. Harding, "that if you fall behind in some of your assignments, don't worry. These are unusual circumstances."

Kat nodded. He was being so nice, but it somehow didn't feel nice. She was afraid to say anything in case a sob escaped her throat.

"Please realize that my door is open," said Mr. Harding. "If you start to run into difficulties with your school work, come to me before too much of it slips away. We'll work something out."

Kat blurted out a "thank you," then swallowed back a rush of tears. She ran out of the room.

Michael's locker was just a few doors down from Mr. Harding's class. As Kat rushed out of the room, she noticed out of the corner of her glasses that Michael had taken his blue win-ter coat from his locker and was regarding her with worry. She rushed past him without even acknowledging his presence and headed for the exit.

CHAPTER 23

WHEN SHE STEPPED off the bus at the end of her street, Kat noticed that there was a buzz of activity in the direction of her house. She clutched her books to her chest and walked down the sidewalk. A TV van was parked in front of the house, and another was idling across the street.

The protester was in front of the house, marching with her sign. Kat slowly walked toward her house, her eyes cast down. Perhaps the woman wouldn't notice her if she darted through the neighbour's backyard and hopped the fence? No, Kat decided. I've done nothing wrong. I'll walk to my own house.

She walked right past the vans and the protester and looked directly into the woman's face. What she saw was a pain so deep that it made Kat gasp. She quickly turned and ran down the driveway and flung herself through the back door.

No sooner did she get in than she realized that the phone was ringing. Within seconds of her stepping in, there was someone knocking on the front door. Was it the protester? She picked the phone up first, but all she heard was a click. As soon as she put it back on its cradle, it began to ring again. She picked it up again, and this time a man's voice blasted obscenities at her. Kat quickly hung it up. It again started to ring. This time she ignored it.

She put down her books and headed through the kitchen and into the living room to answer the front door. As she did so, she noticed that Genya's bedroom door was closed tightly. She assumed that her grandfather was in there. Had he tried to answer the phone too?

Kat was drawn to the insistent rap at the door. She opened it and was surprised to see a television reporter decked out in a hot pink mini skirt and jacket and a full face of stage make-up. She shoved a microphone at Kat. "I'm speaking now with a family member of Nazi war criminal, Danylo Feschuk."

Kat tried to close the front door, but it wouldn't budge. She looked down and saw that the woman had firmly wedged her foot with its hot pink pump between the door and the frame. Kat looked up and saw a camera man standing a few feet behind the reporter and realized with horror that she was probably part of a live action news report.

"May I get your name, please," asked the reporter.

"Kat, Kat Baliuk ..."

"Danylo Feschuk is your grandfather?"

"Yes."

"What do you think about your grandfather and his crimes during the war?" asked the reporter.

"I ... I ..."

Just then, Kat felt a firm hand on her arm. She looked over her shoulder and saw her grandfather standing there, a look of deep pain in his eyes. "Kataryna, please get away from the door," he said.

Kat stepped behind her grandfather just as a flurry of activity burst on her front lawn. Several cameras flashed and two more reporters crowded in behind the pink woman. Where had they all come from?

"Please leave my granddaughter alone," said Danylo in a firm voice. "I would appreciate it if you would all go home."

With that, he tried to shut the door, but the reporter still had her foot wedged in with determination.

"Just one statement," said the woman.

"My statement is that I am innocent. You people are too young to know what it was like. Now please go."

Danylo gently pushed the woman away from the door and managed to close it. He quickly chained and double locked it. Kat pulled back a corner of the curtains on the front window and peered out to see if the reporters were going to leave. She was amazed to see that there were now two news vans parked out front. How had they got there so fast? They must have been on stake-out.

The lone protester was still there too, staring angrily at Kat's peephole in the window.

Kat was about to put the curtain down when she saw her mother's car turn down the street. Kat's first instinct was to call her on her cell phone and tell her to keep on going. But the phone was still ringing, and the reporters had already spotted her anyway. Kat watched as Orysia parked in the driveway and got out of the car. She was immediately swarmed by the horde of reporters.

"No comment," Orysia shouted as she hurried up to the back door, reporters barely a step behind. Kat ran to the door and pulled her mother in, shutting the bolt behind her.

Instinctively, Orysia walked to the ringing phone and picked it up. Her face went ashen. She left the phone off the hook.

"How is it that all these reporters suddenly know about this?" asked Kat.

"The hearing is the day after tomorrow," said her mother. "That's public information."

The reporters stayed out in the front yard for several more hours, accosting Genya when she got home too.

When Genya stepped inside, she noticed that the phone was off the hook and without thinking, put it back in its cradle. It rang almost instantly. When she picked it up, she was treated to an earful.

"That's it," she said, hanging up hard on the caller, and then leaving the receiver off the cradle. "Mama, can I borrow your cell phone?"

Orysia rooted around in her purse, then handed her daughter her cell phone. Genya made a few quick phone calls and then clicked it shut and handed it back to her mother. "We'll have an unlisted number by tomorrow morning. Also, I have informed the police that we have trespassers."

Kat marvelled at her sister. So efficient.

The story was aired on the six o'clock news on Global, CityTV and CBC. It was also aired every hour on the hour on a number of radio stations.

The CBC news began with a full face view of her grandfather through the kitchen window from that very morning as he was making tea and toast. Given the angle, it had to have been taken with a long range lens from the neighbour's roof. Over this picture, the announcer said, "Proceedings to deport Nazi war criminal Danylo Feschuk will get under way in Toronto on Friday. The 78-year-old Mississauga grandfather has been accused of lying to immigration authorities about his Nazi past. Feschuk has been identified as one of the notorious Ukrainian police who were known to have committed atrocities in World War II Ukraine."

The image then changed to a shot of her grandfather's house.

"Here is the Mapleview home where the retired auto worker lived for the last two decades until the death of his wife this past summer. While he still owns this house, he is currently living in with his daughter and son-in-law on Devon Road."

An image of Kat's house came into focus, complete with protester in front and reporters all around.

"None of the family members would talk to the press about the serious charges against Mr. Feschuk...."

Now a shot of Kat trying to shut the door on the pink reporter, and then a shot of her mother getting out of the car.

"Neighbours describe Feschuk as a quiet and friendly man who wouldn't hurt a fly."

An image flickered of a reporter talking to Mrs. Wentworth, who had lived beside her grandparents for as long as she could remember.

"But David Green of the Centre for Human Tolerance has another view."

A man in a business suit sat behind a desk with his hands folded in front of him. "The Canadian government shamefully let in Nazis in the 1950s while at the same time they were barring the immigration of Jews who had escaped the Holocaust. I am glad to see that the government is finally taking action to track down and prosecute the thousands of Nazi war criminals who are living in our midst."

The last image Kat saw before the commercial break was David Green's eyes staring out, seemingly meeting her own.

CHAPTER 24

IT WAS THURSDAY, January 10th. Danylo's hearing started the next day. Orysia had told her daughters that she did not want them to attend. "It's a school day," she said. "And neither of you can afford to lose a day."

That was painfully true. In order to qualify for the tuition scholarship, Genya had to maintain an average in the 90s, yet with all the upheaval in her life, her marks had plummeted. She was floundering in Math with a bare A, and was only making Bs in her other courses. At the rate she was going, she wouldn't get into the university of her choice, let alone get a scholarship.

For Kat, it was even worse. When her report card arrived in the mail the day before, she was shocked to discover that she had failed every subject but Art. And she had a sneaking feeling that the only reason she wasn't failing Art was because Mr. Harding had felt sorry for her.

Kat decided that the time had come to take matters into her own hands.

Dr. Bradley had an open door policy when it came to students. Her office had glass walls and was situated in front of the administration offices. Students passed by all day long and gazed in unconsciously, watching as their principal went from phone call to phone call and parent meeting to staff meeting to student meeting. Kat got to school early on the day before Danylo's trial. So early, in fact, that she beat Dr. Bradley, who liked to pride herself on her early-bird habits.

Kat sat down in front of the glass door and placed her knapsack beside her. She pulled out a drinking box from her pocket and sipped on it patiently, waiting for the principal to arrive.

Kat was so caught up in her thoughts that Dr. Bradley was upon her before she even noticed. "Come in," said Dr. Bradley, who was carrying a take-out cup of coffee in one hand and a bulging brief case in the other.

Kat scrambled to her feet and offered to hold Dr. Bradley's coffee while the principal rooted through her coat pockets for the key to the office. "Success!" she said, pulling out a key laden chain, selecting one and opening the door with it.

Kat followed her into the office and set Dr. Bradley's coffee down on the desk.

"Make yourself comfortable," said Dr. Bradley, motioning with her hand for Kat to sit at one of the two chairs positioned in front of her cluttered desk.

Kat didn't take her coat off and didn't put down her knapsack. She perched on the edge of the chair furthest from the desk and hugged her knapsack to her chest.

Dr. Bradley had removed her own coat by this time and was sitting in her wooden swivel chair on the other side of the desk. "You are a bundle of nerves," she said, taking in Kat's demeanour. "You've been through the loop, haven't you?"

Kat nodded, but still didn't say anything. She was afraid that if she started, she would begin to cry. And where do you start with a problem like this, anyway?

Dr. Bradley sensed Kat's difficulty, so she began the conversation with what little she knew about it. "I'd read the newspaper reports," said Dr. Bradley, "but I didn't realize Mr.

Feschuk was your grandfather until I saw the television news last night."

Kat just sat and nodded, clutching her knapsack to her chest.

"Let's just see your transcripts," said Dr. Bradley. She took her desktop computer out of sleep mode and entered Kat's name into the system. "Whoa," said Dr. Bradley when Kat's current course standings appeared on the screen. "When you plunge, you plunge deep, girl."

Kat's shoulders hunched in resignation.

"The hearing starts tomorrow?" Dr. Bradley asked.

"Yes," Kat managed weakly.

"I think you should go. You would be a great moral support for your grandfather."

"My mother doesn't want me to go," said Kat forlornly.

Dr. Bradley arched her eyebrows. "She obviously hasn't seen your report card. You'd be better off to start fresh again next year than to try and salvage these marks."

Kat nodded in agreement. "I haven't had the heart to show her yet, what with all that's been happening."

"I can understand that," said Dr. Bradley. "Why don't I give your parents a call and we'll have a meeting?" suggested Dr. Bradley. "I think the best thing for you right now would be to attend your grandfather's hearing. You can't possibly concentrate on school work in your condition."

"Will I lose my year?" asked Kat.

"Most likely," said Dr. Bradley. "But I'll save you a spot for next year. You are a brilliant student and this is a bona fide family crisis."

For the first time in a long time, Kat felt a sense of relief. Her hunched shoulders relaxed just a little bit, and she slowly let out the breath that she hadn't even realized she had been holding.

Dr. Bradley got up from her chair and walked around to where Kat sat. She crouched down beside her and wrapped her arms around her shoulders. "It may not feel like it now," said Dr. Bradley, "but this too shall pass."

Kat walked out of the school just as the early bus arrived. Michael was the first to step off, and he was concentrating on something so hard that he almost walked right into Kat. He did a double take when he recognized her. "Are you okay?"

Kat explained that she was dropping some courses and would be attending the hearing.

"I don't blame you," said Michael. "I'd do the same thing in your position. You're not dropping art class, though, are you?"

"I wish I didn't have to," said Kat with resignation. "That's the only subject I'm not failing."

"I figured as much," said Michael. "Mr. Harding asked me about the case once, then mentioned what a talented student you were."

"Mr. Harding asked you about the case?" The thought gave Kat the creeps. Why was Mr. Harding so interested in this? She remembered her own conversation with him, and how uncomfortable it had made her feel.

"I couldn't tell him anything even if I wanted to," said Michael. "And I don't want to."

Kat nodded. It relieved her to know that.

"I can take notes for you in art so that you don't get too far behind."

"That would be great," said Kat. "Give me a call when you have a chance and we can go over stuff together."

Michael shifted from one foot to the other and his face flushed pink. "I ... I don't have your phone number," he said. "It's unlisted."

"But your father has it," said Kat.

"Client privilege," said Michael.

"Right," said Kat. "I forgot. Give me your hand."

Michael stretched out his hand and she wrote her new phone number on his palm in ballpoint pen. "Now just don't wash your hand," she said, smiling.

When Kat got home, it was midmorning and the reporters had again begun to accumulate. At least now they knew better than to trespass. Why didn't they just leave? What is it that they're trying to see? Maybe they thought they could catch her grandfather unearthing an old Nazi uniform and trying it on, she thought giddily. Didn't that happen in some movie?

Danylo still hadn't come out of his room by lunchtime, and she knew he had eaten no breakfast. Neither had she, for that matter. There was a frozen batch of *vushky* with *pidpenky* in the freezer from *Sviat Vecher*, Kat took out a dozen of the mush-room-stuffed noodles and re-zipped the package. Then she got a Tupperware container of leftover *borscht* from the fridge. She warmed the soup and defrosted the noodles and combined them in a pot on the stove. When it was steaming hot, she tapped on her grandfather's door.

"Leave me alone."

In normal times, that's just what Kat would have done, but these were not normal times. She remembered how depressed her grandmother got when her cancer recurred. She'd do exactly the same thing: lock herself in the room and mope. Well, Kat didn't take it then, and she wasn't about to take it now. She tapped on the door again.

"Go away, I said."

"No," said Kat. "Either you open this door, or I do."

"Don't be a pill," grumbled her grandfather.

With that, Kat opened the door. Her grandfather was sitting on the edge of the bed, going through the items in her late grandmother's jewellery box. All sorts of homemade knick-knacks were spread across the comforter.

"I made some soup," she said.

"What kind, *zolota zhabka*?" asked her grandfather.

This was a good sign, thought Kat. "*Borscht.*"

"With *vushky*?" he asked, his eyes lighting with interest.

"Yes," said Kat. "With quite a few *vushky.*"

"Well, I wouldn't want it to go to waste," her grandfather considered. "Perhaps I'll help you eat it."

Kat smiled to herself, thankful that she had been able to think of something her grandfather couldn't turn down.

CHAPTER 25

THE HEARING WAS being held in the Canada Life building in downtown Toronto and it started at 9 am sharp on January 11th. Kat and her mother and grandfather arrived forty-five minutes early and parked in the underground garage, then took the elevator to the fifth floor. As the elevator doors opened, Kat was dismayed to find that there were about a dozen people already waiting in the hallway outside the courtroom. Kat slipped one hand into her mother's and the other into her grandfather's, and then the three of them strode down the hallway with self-conscious determination to the huge double doors marked 5106. Kat let go of her mother's hand, then reached out to pull on the handle. The door was locked.

She turned around and faced the people. She noticed that most had been staring at her grandfather, but they quickly looked away when they saw that she was looking at them.

Danylo gripped her hand tightly, and when she looked at his face, she saw that his lips were a thin white line. She was afraid that he might collapse from the anxiety of the whole thing. She looked around to see if there was some place she could take him so he could sit down. There were three benches, but they were already filled. Guiding her grandfather by the elbow to the nearest bench, Kat looked down at the middle-aged man sitting closest to the end and asked, "Would you mind getting up so that my grandfather can sit?"

The man stared at her incredulously. "You want me to give up my seat for *him*? I don't think so."

A hush filled the hallway, and the onlookers regarded Kat, Orysia and Danylo. A vaguely familiar man's voice piped up. "Please sit here."

Kat looked gratefully over to where the voice came from, and was surprised to see Hung Nguyen, Lisa's father. Dr. Nguyen was already standing, and he motioned graciously to the bare spot on the bench that he had just vacated.

Danylo sat down gratefully.

"Thank you for coming," said Kat. She introduced Dr. Nguyen to her mother.

"And there are two people that I would like you to meet," said Dr. Nguyen, gesturing towards an elderly Vietnamese couple sitting on the bench next to Danylo. "These are my parents. When I told them about this hearing, they insisted on coming."

"That's wonderful, thank you," said Orysia. "But why are you so interested?"

"We're naturalized Canadians too," he explained. "This deportation law could just as easily be applied to us."

Orysia looked confused.

"We escaped the Communists in Vietnam. They considered us traitors because we fought against them. I have heard of stories being fabricated for vengeance. The Canadian government could just as easily deport us if they took that evidence as truth."

Just then, there was a clicking sound, and the huge double oak doors to the courtroom opened up from the inside. A woman in a blue suit stood there, keys in hand. "Come in," she said in a quiet voice.

The people who had been waiting stretched their legs, gathered their things, and walked in briskly, wanting to get good seats. Kat and her family and the Nguyens waited behind.

The blue-suited woman gestured towards Danylo. "I'll show you where to sit," she said, not unkindly.

Kat surveyed the room as they walked in. It reminded her of church. There were two rows of chairs on the right, then an aisle, and then five rows of chairs on the left. Kat noticed that all of the people who had been waiting in the hallway had already seated themselves on the left side, and that the blue-suited woman was ushering Danylo, Orysia and herself to the front of the right side.

Why were there only two rows on the right side, wondered Kat. Was there an assumption that the accused would have less supporters? In this case, it turned out to be true, and Kat was glad that the Nguyens had decided to attend.

Kat turned her attention to the front of the courtroom. The judge's bench was on a platform that was raised two levels from the ground. Mounted behind him on a soft green cloth was the Canadian coat of arms, looking cold and majestic. Beside it was a Canadian flag on a gold-coloured flagpole with a gold maple leaf on top. Directly in front of the judge's bench and one level lower sat two women at a shared bench. One was dressed in a black robe, and the other wore street clothing. Both had their eyes cast down and were reviewing notes in front of them.

A few feet in front and to the left and right of the women were two podiums with microphones. There was a wooden table attached to each podium, and then another wooden table behind. The tables were covered with stacks of books and bound notes and pens and paper. Kat recognized Mr. Vincent sitting at the table in front of her. He was wearing a black robe that made him look something like a priest. Beside him were two other lawyers: one a silver-haired woman, and the other, a man about the same age as Mr. Vincent. They too were wearing the antiquated black robes.

Kat looked over towards the other long table. There were three black-robed lawyers sitting over there. Kat noticed one, a young woman, who was appraising Danylo with cold superiority. What does she know that I don't, wondered Kat. She gave her grandfather's hand a reassuring squeeze.

Kat looked behind her and to the left to get a better look at the people who sat there. She saw the man who had refused to give up his seat to her grandfather. About ten unfamiliar people sat in the seats around him — elderly women with permed white hair and oversized eyeglasses, and men who were shrivelled and old. There was one familiar face: the lone protester.

A woman entered the courtroom and sat beside the protester. She was not much older than Kat. Her dark brown hair was pulled away from her face and was fastened with a clip. She grabbed the older woman's hand and squeezed it, then looked up and met Kat's gaze.

Kat stared back unflinching, then turned her attention to who was sitting on her grandfather's side. The Nguyens were directly behind her, Dr. Nguyen's mother tipped her head slightly in acknowledgement as Kat caught her eye. Kat's heart sank when she looked beyond the Nguyens and saw only empty seats behind. Were none of Danylo's friends coming to support him?

But just then, the blue-suited woman ushered in some more people. Kat recognized three elderly couples from the church. A few steps behind them was a middle-aged blonde woman in a business suit. She was accompanied by a younger man who also wore a suit. Kat recognized them as the president and vice-president of the local Ukrainian Canadian Congress. She breathed a sigh of relief. Their presence would give her grandfather moral support. Odd, Kat noted, her glance darting from one side of the courtroom to the other. These men and women looked so much like the ones on the other side that they could all have been siblings. But it was more than an aisle that held them apart.

"All rise," said a woman's voice.

Kat rose with everyone else, then watched as a door opened up below the flag and a man in a black robe with a gold mantle walked into the room. The antiquated court garb made Kat think of the Inquisition.

"You may be seated," said the judge in a monotone voice as he took his place behind the raised bench. He perched a pair of black-framed reading glasses on the end of his nose and read from a paper in front of him.

Kat's head swam as the judge began to speak. Much of it didn't make sense to her, but some was very familiar. Her grandfather was being accused of "obtaining Canadian citizenship by false representation" because he had "failed to divulge collaboration with German authorities" and that he had "participated in atrocities against the civilian population during the period 1941-1943 as an auxiliary policeman in German-occupied Ukraine."

The judge then said that he would ask both the plaintiff and the defendant to state their positions. The plaintiff was asked to begin.

Mrs. Caine, the young woman lawyer from across the aisle rose and addressed the judge.

"Your honour, we will prove to this court that Danylo Feschuk, the man sitting opposite, voluntarily collaborated with the German army between 1941 and 1943 when he worked as an auxiliary police officer in the village of Orelets in the administrative province of Volhyn, which is in the northwest corner of present-day Ukraine. We will further prove to you that he committed atrocities on civilians during his time as an auxiliary police officer. Further, we will prove that he did not disclose these atrocities to immigration authorities when he applied to become a Canadian citizen. If he had done so, he would not have been granted citizenship. Mr. Feschuk deserves a much harsher penalty than mere revocation of citizenship, but unfortunately, this is the only avenue of redress open to us at this time."

The young woman sat down, and then Mr. Vincent rose.

"Your honour, the defence does not dispute the fact that Danylo Feschuk was an auxiliary police officer for the Germans between 1941 and 1943. The defence further states that Mr. Feschuk had no reason to hide his role as an auxiliary police-man, because citizenship would not have been denied him for that reason. In addition, there is no evidence that he commit-ted atrocities. We will demonstrate that his role as an auxiliary police officer did not constitute collaboration with the Nazis. Indeed, we will show that while his superiors may have believed he was collaborating with them, he was in reality working with the resistance, as thousands of other auxiliary police through-out Volhyn were doing. Mr. Feschuk had nothing to hide from immigration authorities when he came to Canada, and there-fore he had no reason to lie."

The next hour or two was taken up with minutiae that Kat really couldn't follow. In her mind hung a single word: atroci-ties. Of what was her grandfather being accused? How would she still be able to love him if she found out that he had com-mitted atrocities?

Mercifully, a lunch break was called. As Kat and her family slowly walked towards the double oak door in a daze, Mr. Vincent caught up with them. Kat noted that he had removed his black robe and was wearing a normal grey wool suit. "The cafeteria in the basement has decent food," he said. "And it's not too expen-sive." He motioned to them to follow him down the elevator. The supporters from the church and the Nguyens were close behind.

Kat happened to get a spot in the cafeteria line-up just behind the young woman lawyer who presented the case against her grandfather. She had removed her black robe too, and Kat found her much less threatening in her cream coloured jacket and trousers. The woman grabbed a carton of milk and then a tossed salad from behind the Plexiglas door. "Stay clear of the noodle soup," she said to Kat pleasantly. "It's vile."

Kat smiled back at her. How odd that this woman could be so nice. It must all be in a day's work for her to tear apart and impoverish families. Kat grabbed some red Jell-O and a carton of orange juice for herself. She didn't really feel like eating: she was just going through the motions.

When she sat down across from her mother and beside her grandfather, she noticed that the Nguyens and the other supporters were all sitting within a hands-breadth of Danylo. Kat found that comforting.

She looked across the table at her mother and saw dark circles under her eyes. Those hadn't been there six months ago. This case had certainly taken its toll on her. Kat hadn't really looked closely at her mother for some time, and so she noticed other changes too. She must have lost some weight. Her cheeks had a hollow appearance to them and there was a furrow of worry between her eyebrows. Her gaze met Kat's. There was something new there too, realized Kat. Her eyes used to have a look of soft contented kindness in them, but this was now replaced with a steel blue glint of determination. The change sent a shiver through Kat. It was if this woman sitting across from her was no longer her mother, but some sort of warrior queen. As if she knew what her daughter was thinking, she suddenly winked, and that motherly softness fleetingly returned.

"What is the order of the proceedings?" Kat asked her mother.

"The first part is the hardest," explained Orysia. "The plaintiff goes first, so that means they dish out all the bad stuff they have on your grandfather."

Kat dipped her spoon into her red Jell-O. "Then what?"

"Then we tell our side."

Kat pondered that. It would be good to get the bad stuff over at the beginning, she figured, but what would they say? She almost didn't want to know.

Kat looked over at Danylo. He was staring into a Styrofoam bowl of noodle soup. Kat watched as he put one spoonful into his mouth and slowly swallowed. Then he pushed it away. Kat noticed that his face was still pale and that his hands trembled. "Have some Jell-O," she said, offering him her spoon.

"I can't eat," he said. "I just want to get this over with."

Don't we all, thought Kat.

The hearing resumed with a historical expert called by the plaintiff. Professor Chris Gillin had travelled from Britain to testify at Danylo's hearing. He was tall and slim and clean-shaven. Kat estimated his age to be no more than forty.

Professor Gillin was considered an expert on National Socialist Germany and the Holocaust. He had written four books on the subject, including one called *Ordinary Soldiers*, a book about the Order Police in Nazi Germany.

He described how and why the Germans initiated the auxiliary police programs. In July 1941, barely a month after their invasion of Soviet territory, the Germans realized that they lacked the manpower to administer all the villages and towns throughout the vast region. Units of local police or *Schutzmannschaften* were chosen, and the Security Police were in charge of them. These men were not issued uniforms. Instead, they wore old Soviet or German uniforms and were identified by a special armband.

The men and their families were given food, plus the men were supposed to be paid on a daily basis. If not enough volunteers could be generated through incentives alone, the Security Police could recruit from the prisoner-of-war camps.

As Professor Gillin read from his notes, Kat flinched as he listed each killing.

"The participation of Ukrainian auxiliary police in killings of Jews can occasionally be documented." he said. "I have a report from one German officer that states, 'On September 19 and 20, 1942, a Jewish action was carried out in the village of Domachevko by the SD Sonderkommando, with the help of a squadron of Gendarmerie and the auxiliary police. Two thousand, nine hundred Jews were shot."

There was a rustling in the rows of observers on the plaintiff's side. Kat looked over with the corner of her eye and saw that one of the elderly women was weeping. It cut her to the quick to think that these people had probably witnessed what this professor was itemizing. How hard it must be for them to listen to it all again.

Professor Gillen flipped through his notes and read more, "There were other reports from a Police Battalion hunting down Jews in the northern parts of Volhyn-Podolia in the fall of 1942 that occasionally referred to working with the auxiliary police."

As Professor Gillin mentioned killing after killing, Kat felt like she was going to be sick. Was her grandfather one of these men? Was he one of these auxiliary police who had been involved in the killing of Jews? It was horrible to think of all those deaths, and it was even worse to think that perhaps her own grandfather could have been responsible. She looked over to her grandfather and saw that his face was pale as stone and that he held onto the sides of his chair with a white-knuckled grip.

There was a rustling of paper to Kat's right, and then she noticed Mr. Vincent standing up.

"Your honour," he said to the judge. "I would like to ask Professor Gillin a few questions."

"The court recognizes the honourable Mr. Vincent."

"The reports you have itemized are chilling, Professor. I agree with you that these crimes of humanity must not go unpunished. However, in all of your reports, not a single one deals with the village of Orelets."

"My knowledge is based on German documents which itemize police operations in occupied territory. My testimony is not directed at the overall Ukrainian situation," replied Professor Gillin.

"In fact, all of these incidents took place more than one hundred kilometres away from where Mr. Feschuk was stationed as an auxiliary policeman. Your reports mention only occasional involvement of any auxiliary police, and you have not mentioned any incidents that could even remotely have involved my client. Why then, are you mentioning them?"

Kat sat up at this point. She had listened to the horrors one by one and had assumed that it was documentation directly related to her grandfather.

A wave of annoyance briefly passed over Professor Gillin's face, but then he regained his composure. "This information is provided to give further understanding of the role that the auxiliary police played in the massacre of Jews during World War II."

"The reports you are reading from itemize the rare involvement of auxiliary police. However, each reference you made involved those who served in police battalions, yet my client did not serve in a police battalion."

What, wondered Kat, was Mr. Vincent trying to get at? Her grandfather was clearly an auxiliary policeman.

"Mr. Feschuk performed precinct service in the towns and villages," Mr. Vincent continued. "The atrocities described by Professor Gillin were carried out by Germans."

Kat listened with interest. Now that she thought about it, on the one occasion when Professor Gillin mentioned the name of a "Ukrainian" auxiliary policeman, it had been a German name.

"On the rare occasion when auxiliary police are mentioned, they are battalion auxiliary police, not precinct auxiliary police," continued Mr. Vincent.

"A fine point, but you are correct," conceded the professor.

In Kat's mind, it was more than a fine point. It was the difference between evidence of her grandfather's guilt and innocence. She looked over at her grandfather and noticed that his knuckles were no longer white.

"And you have no documentation of atrocities carried out by any auxiliary police within one hundred kilometres of where my client was stationed?"

"That is correct."

"I have no further questions." said Mr. Vincent.

Just then, the judge himself made a comment. "It should be noted," he said, "that reports made by German officers cannot be taken at face value. They, of course, would minimize their own culpability by spreading the blame."

Mr. Vincent nodded in agreement.

Kat sat there, still trying to digest all that she had heard. Why had this expert witness been called all the way from England if he had no direct evidence against her grandfather?

The next witness was a woman with a thin bun of snow-coloured hair. Her thick wire-rimmed glasses had lenses so large that they overpowered her fragile features. She had trouble bending her knee to step into the witness stand, so Mrs. Caine jumped up from her seat and gently guided her to her chair.

Kat leaned forward, intent on hearing every word of the woman's testimony.

Mrs. Caine stood in front of the witness stand. In a gentle voice, she asked, "Could you please state your name?"

The woman leaned forward and spoke with crisp enunciation into the microphone. "My name is Mrs. Anne Pensky."

"Can you tell me what happened to you in the summer of 1941 when you were ten years old?" Mrs. Caine asked.

"I was herded into the Ozeryany ghetto with approximately 835 other Jewish men, women and children."

"Who was it that gathered you up and put you in the ghetto?" Mrs. Caine asked.

"German soldiers."

"Who guarded the ghetto?" Mrs. Caine asked.

"Ukrainian police from Ozeryany," she stated. "Some of them I knew by name."

"Can you tell me about the killings?" Mrs. Caine asked gently.

"The black uniformed German soldiers came with guns and ordered all the men and women — the adults — to ... to ... line up." Mrs. Pensky choked back tears, then took a deep breath. "There were carts following behind. Anyone who stumbled was put in a cart."

In a voice so low that it was barely audible, Mrs. Caine asked, "Could you tell the court what happened then?"

"My mother and father were part of that group," said Mrs. Pensky, gulping back tears. "They were marched to the grave-yard, where they were forced to dig their own graves, and then they were shot."

"Who was it that did the shooting?" asked Mrs. Caine.

"It was the Ukrainians," said Mrs. Pensky, in a voice clear through her tears. "They shot them."

Kat sat there stunned by what she heard. So here it was: direct testimony of Ukrainians killing Jews. Kat waited, wondering what would come next. Would the woman point her finger at her grandfather and identify him?

Just then, Kat saw Mr. Vincent stand.

"Your honour," he said. "May I ask the witness a question?"

"The court recognizes Mr. Vincent," said the judge.

Mr. Vincent smoothed down the front of his robe as he approached the woman in the witness stand. He paused for a moment, as if trying to compose himself.

"Mrs. Pensky," he said. "I am sorry that you have had to testify here today. I realize that this must be very difficult."

The woman nodded, then dabbed the corner of her eye with an embroidered handkerchief.

"This is a delicate question, but one that I must ask: where were you when the shootings took place?"

"I was in the ghetto with the other children," she replied. Kat noticed that Mrs. Pensky was staring out into the distance. It was as if she were looking into the past, seeing those scenes over and over again in her mind.

"Where exactly in the ghetto?" asked Mr. Vincent.

"We were in the school inside the ghetto. This was used as a synagogue. When the adults were led out to their deaths, we children hid there and said prayers for their souls."

"Could you see the graveyard from the school?"

Mrs. Pensky looked at the lawyer quizzically. "No, you couldn't," she said.

"Then how did you witness the killings?"

"I heard the guns fire," she said in her clear voice. "I can picture it as if I were standing right there now."

"If you didn't see the killings, how do you know that it was Ukrainians who did the killings?" he asked.

"I just know," she said emphatically. "It was the Ukrainians."

Kat's eyes had been riveted on the witness throughout this exchange. The woman was so sure, yet she hadn't seen it. Kat turned her head slightly so that she could see the men and women who had come to support the plaintiff's side. They were all nodding in agreement. It seemed that they too knew too, despite the lack of a witness.

"Mrs. Pensky, may I ask you to look at the defendant?"

Mrs. Pensky reluctantly turned her eyes in that direction. It was as if she didn't want to see Danylo.

Kat looked over at her grandfather and saw that he was staring right at Mrs. Pensky, then she saw Mrs. Pensky meet his gaze.

"Do you recognize this man?" asked Mr. Vincent.

"I know that he was one of those Ukrainian Police," said Mrs. Pensky in her clear voice.

The judge intercepted, "Please, Mrs. Pensky, answer the question."

"No, I do not recognize him."

"Mrs. Pensky, how far away is Ozeryany from Mr. Feschuk's village of Orelets?"

"Ten or twenty kilometres away," she responded.

Mr. Vincent walked over to the long wooden table on his side of the courtroom and then he reached down and picked up a black and white photograph. He walked over to the witness stand and handed the photograph to Mrs. Pensky.

"Please take a look at the photograph," Mr. Vincent said. "This is a photo of Danylo Feschuk when he was nineteen years old. Do you recognize him?"

Mrs. Pensky took the photo in her hands and stared at it. She even raised her glasses and squinted at it again before handing it back. "No," she said. "I don't recognize this man."

"I have no more questions, your honour."

Mercifully, a break was called.

"I need some fresh air," said Kat to her mother as they stood up, stretching their legs.

"Why don't you take the subway home?" suggested Orysia. She was tired herself, but she could see that this was even harder on her daughter. This was why she hadn't wanted her to come in the first place. "You could start supper for me," Orysia continued.

There was nothing that Kat wanted to do more than to get out of the courthouse. She was still trying to sort out all that she had heard. However, she had a feeling that the worst was yet to come, and she had to hear it with her own ears.

"I can't go home right now," said Kat.

Orysia looked at her watch. "You've still got ten minutes before the hearing starts back up. Why don't you at least get some fresh air?

"That's a good idea."

Not wanting to wait for the elevator, she ran down all five flights of stairs. It felt wonderful to stretch her legs.

Kat breathed in a lungful of fresh cold air as she stepped outside the main entryway, then blinked a few times to get used to the natural light. A fine dusting of snow had fallen since the morning, making everything that much brighter and cleaner looking.

She walked down the street a bit, just for the feel of the wind on her cheeks, and as she did so, she looked at the jumble of buildings around her — new skyscrapers and old churches all on the same block. She tried to imagine what this street might have looked like five decades ago in the midst of World War II.

"He did it, you know."

The voice spoke so close to Kat's ear that she gasped. She swung around and came face to face with the protester. Seeing her up close gave Kat a shock. She had known that the woman was old, but with their faces just a few inches apart, Kat realized that it wasn't just age that had etched the lines on the woman's face. Unspeakable horror, untold grief. It was all there for the world to see.

"How do you know?" asked Kat.

"They were all like that," said the woman. "They are all war criminals."

"Do you mean to tell me that you think every single Ukrainian auxiliary policeman was a war criminal?" asked Kat.

"Every one," replied the woman emphatically. "You and your family should kneel down and pray. Pray for forgiveness until your knees bleed."

Kat was taken aback by the hate in the woman's voice. Kat could think of nothing to say. She turned from the woman and walked back to the courthouse.

The next witness was a rheumy-eyed man whose sparse grey hair was combed from one side over to the other in a vain attempt to hide the fact that he was almost entirely bald. This man spoke no English, and so two translators had been called in: one for the defendant and one for the plaintiff.

Mrs. Caine stood in front of the witness box. "Can you please state your name?"

The plaintiff's translator mumbled something to the man and the other translator nodded in agreement. The man answered.

Kat hardly needed a translator. The man was speaking Ukrainian.

"My name is Pavlo Abramovich," said the man. "I was born in 1924 and raised in the village of Orelets."

"Do you know this man sitting here?" Mrs. Caine asked, pointing to Danylo.

"Yes," he replied. "I will never forget that man."

"Why is that?" asked Mrs. Caine.

"That man helped the Germans. He was a collaborator."

"Did you witness him helping the Germans?"

"Yes, I did," said the witness, nodding emphatically. "I will never forget. It was in the summer of 1941. The Germans had gone through the village and rounded up all the Jews and the Communists. Mr. Feschuk was given the job of punishing us."

"What punishment did he give you?" asked Mrs. Caine.

"He pointed his pistol at us."

"Did he threaten to shoot you?"

"Not in so many words," replied the man. "We were very frightened. We thought he was going to kill us."

"What did he do to you?" asked Mrs. Caine.

"He pointed the pistol at us, ordered some of us to get down on the ground, and then he made us do push-ups."

Kat didn't think it was very nice of her grandfather to make people do push-ups, but for the life of her, she didn't see how this constituted a war crime. She heard rustling behind her, so she turned around. One of the men from her church had his arms crossed and a sour expression of disbelief on his face. Another man shook his head and tsk-tsked under his breath.

Mr. Vincent stood up.

"Were you a Communist during World War II?" asked Mr. Vincent.

Mr. Abramovich sat up straight in his chair. "Yes," he replied. "Even in the face of the Fascist invasion, I stayed true to my political beliefs."

"Mr. Abramovich," said Mr. Vincent. "When Mr. Feschuk made you do push-ups, was that the punishment you expected?"

The witness shook his head. "I was surprised that he didn't kill us," he said.

"No more questions," said Mr. Vincent.

Mrs. Caine then called her last witness of the day. Miss Lily Solonenko was a wheelchair-bound woman with closely cropped white hair and papery thin skin. She too spoke Ukrainian and still lived in the village of Orelets. Through the translators, she explained that she was a six-year-old girl in the summer of 1941.

"What do you remember about the defendant, Danylo Feschuk?" asked Mrs. Caine.

"He was my neighbour," said Miss Solonenko. "I remember the first day he wore the armband of the auxiliary police. It scared me, but he told me that I had nothing to fear from him."

"Did you witness him harming any of the villagers?" asked Mrs. Caine.

"Not the villagers," replied Miss Solonenko, "But he was one of the guards at the prisoner of war camp."

"Can you explain," asked Mrs. Caine.

"Yes," replied Miss Solonenko. "There was a barbed wire enclosure where the Germans kept Soviet prisoners of war. The conditions were very brutal. The men were not given food or water. They were basically herded into the enclosure and left to die."

"Can you tell me what you saw regarding Mr. Feschuk?" asked Mrs. Caine.

"Yes," said Miss Solonenko. "These men were Slavs just like us. There were even two boys in there who had relatives in our village. Germans were starving them to death. It was terrible. One night I looked out from my attic window, and I saw Mr.

Feschuk standing with the German guards. I was so shocked. Even the other auxiliary police wouldn't stoop so low as to help guard the POW camp."

Mr. Vincent stood up to ask his questions. "Miss Solonenko, did anyone in the village try to feed the prisoners of war?"

"Yes," she replied. "But they weren't successful. My own mother once threw over a loaf of bread. A dozen poor starving men lunged for it at once, but instead of bread, they got a bullet in their head. The prisoners of war were not to be fed. Bread in a POW's mouth was punishable by death."

"Did any of the villagers try to release the POWs?" asked Mr. Vincent.

"How could they do that?" asked Miss Solonenko incredulously. "The Germans would have rounded up a dozen or more villagers and hanged them in retaliation."

"Would anyone be in a position to let the prisoners out?"

"There was a rumour that some had escaped to the forest, but I don't know how they would have managed it," she replied.

"No more questions," said Mr. Vincent.

And with that, the hearing was adjourned for the day. As soon as the judge left the chamber, Orysia was on her feet to talk to Mr. Vincent.

Kat and Danylo stayed sitting. Every muscle in Kat's body ached from the strain of listening so intensely and trying to make sense of it all. In her mind was an image of a barbed wire enclosure with starving men herded up like cattle. Had her grandfather actually willingly guarded such a place? She looked at him, sitting beside her. His face was grey with fatigue. Even though everyone around them was getting up, stretching their legs and gathering their belongings, Danylo sat, still as death.

"Are you okay?" asked Kat, placing her hand on her grandfather's forearm.

"My *zolota zhabka*," he said. "Through what eyes are these people viewing me? They must think I am a monster."

Kat leaned over and gave her grandfather a gentle bear hug. "You are my grandfather," she said. "And I love you."

Orysia was still talking with Mr. Vincent. His two colleagues began to gather up the books and the papers from the table and they were putting them away in wide leather briefcases. Mr. Vincent looked up and saw Danylo and Kat still sitting. He broke off his conversation with Orysia and walked over to them.

"Mr. Feschuk," he said. "I know you're tired, but could you stay for a bit longer? I need to ask you some questions."

Danylo inclined his head in a tired nod.

Orysia came over and stood beside Mr. Vincent. "Kat, why don't you take the subway home?"

Kat regarded her mother and then Mr. Vincent. She got the distinct impression that they wanted to talk about some things without her there. "Okay, Mom," she said. "That way I can start dinner."

"That would be great," said Orysia, brushing Kat's cheek lightly with a kiss.

As Kat walked to the subway stop, she marvelled at the people she passed. To them, this was just another day.

The testimony she had heard so far was devastating for a number of reasons. First, to hear what horrors so many people had lived through many decades ago. Kat had known about much of this, but it hadn't really hit home until those survivors had got up into the witness stand and given their testimony. It was also devastating for another reason. Not one of the people who had testified that day had anything specific to say against her grandfather. She was also curious about the uniforms. Her grandfather had been issued an armband only, but again and again, she heard of the black uniformed police. Were these the SS?

If the worst anyone could say against her grandfather was that he had made people do push-ups, why was he being grouped with people who had done far worse? It especially troubled her to think that her grandfather and others like him were being painted with a broad brush of guilt, even through there were no witnesses and no evidence. What was going on?

She wished her grandfather would actually talk to her about the things he'd had to live through. Maybe then she would be able to understand. It was a time in his life that he had shut the door on. Had it not been for this hearing, Kat wouldn't even know this much about it.

When she got home, she was dismayed to find a police car idling in her driveway and what looked to be the beginnings of another swastika being spray-bombed on the front of the house.

The passenger door of the police vehicle opened, and out stepped the middle-aged police officer who had been to her house before Christmas. He had a big grin on his face.

"Miss Baliuk," he said. "I am so glad that you're home. We caught your graffiti artist."

"You're kidding," said Kat.

She peered in through the back window of the car and saw a head of short dark hair and a blue winter jacket. The person turned to face Kat.

It was Michael. He looked at her with a pleading look in his eyes. She watched his lips through the cruiser window and saw them form the words, "I didn't do it."

"We caught him in the act," said the officer to Kat. "My partner had a suspicion that he'd be back today, what with the hearing and all, so we've been down this way several times."

Kat had a sick feeling in the pit of her stomach. She had just been starting to get to know Michael, and now this? What made it worse was that Michael was Mr. Vincent's son. What would this mean to her grandfather's case?

Kat grasped the officer's hand. "Thank you," she said. If only all the other matters could be solved so simply, she thought to herself.

As the officer got back into the cruiser, Kat asked, "Can I paint over his artwork, or do you still need it?"

"Go ahead and paint it. We've taken samples and photos." And with that, the cruiser backed out and pulled away.

Kat walked up the back steps and into the summer kitchen with a heavy heart. What a dreary end to a dreary week. She noticed that there were two packages sitting on the picnic table in the summer kitchen: an open box with something wrapped in newspaper nestled inside and something flat and oblong, secured with a plastic grocery bag. She opened the one in the grocery bag first, and discovered a casserole dish of chicken cacciatore. There was an envelope stuck inside the bag, so she pulled it out to read it. It was a note from her grandfather's neighbour, Mrs. Wentworth, and it read, "Dear Danylo and family, I know how you love my chicken cacciatore, so enjoy! Re-heat at 350 degrees for one hour. My prayers are with you."

Kat's eyes began to water. What a thoughtful gesture of Mrs. Wentworth.

Kat then pulled at the newspaper wrapping in the second package. Inside was a Zip-Loc bag of small crescent-shaped pastries. Kat opened the bag and pulled one out. Biting into it, she grinned with delight. They were filled with apricot preserve, just like Baba used to make. There was something wrapped in tinfoil besides the bag of cookies, and so Kat pulled back a bit of the foil to look inside. A loaf of rye bread, homemade and fresh from the oven. This package needed no note; it was from the priest's wife.

When Orysia and Danylo arrived home, they were greeted with the aroma of chicken cacciatore warming in the oven, and not a trace of graffiti on the house.

Mr. Vincent called that night and asked to speak to Orysia. She frowned with concern as she listened to what he had to say and then she handed the phone to Kat. "He would like to talk to you too," she said.

"I'm sorry about the incident with Michael at your house today," Mr. Vincent said. "But remember, innocent until proven guilty, right?"

"Right," said Kat.

"Let's put this behind us and deal with your grandfather's hearing," said Mr. Vincent.

"Absolutely," she said. "One thing at a time."

CHAPTER 26

KAT DID NOT usually sleep in on a Saturday morning, but January 12th was no usual Saturday morning. The week before, and especially the day before, had been so exhausting that she had gone to bed at nine o'clock on Friday night and didn't wake up until nearly noon when she heard a persistent tapping at her door. She looked over at Genya's bed and saw that it was neatly made. Not a trace of her older sister: had she even come home last night?

The tapping continued, and then her mother's voice called, "Kat, are you awake?"

"Come in," said Kat.

Orysia walked in, holding a mug of lemon tea.

Kat sat up in bed and gratefully took the mug of tea from her mother.

"I need your help," said Orysia.

"Sure," said Kat.

"Mr. Vincent has asked that your grandfather come to the office this afternoon. They need to go over a few things before the hearing continues on Monday, and I would like to be there with him."

"Okay," said Kat, not quite understanding how she fit into all of this.

"I have a ton of things I need done, though," said Orysia. "And your sister isn't here. We need groceries, and more rags and paint from the hardware store, and I need to drop an envelope off at the bank."

"I can do all that for you," said Kat.

"That's what I was hoping," said Orysia. "I could drive you to the mall and you could call me when you're done, and I could swing by and pick you up, even if Mr. Vincent isn't finished with your grandfather."

"Sure," she said. It would have been a lot easier had Genya stuck around, thought Kat. At least she had a driver's licence.

When she got back from doing errands, Ian was sitting on the front steps, a rolled up paper bag on his lap. When Orysia pulled the car into the driveway, Ian stood up and walked over to the driver's side of the car and opened the door for her.

"Thank you," she said. "Have a good time tonight," she said, eyes sparkling mysteriously.

Ian grinned.

Kat watched this exchange with mild curiosity, then popped the trunk and grabbed one of the grocery bags. "Can you take this in?" she asked Ian.

"Sure," he said. He took it in one arm and held his rolled up bag in the other, and walked around to the back of the house.

"What's in your bag?" Kat asked, following close behind him with more groceries.

Ian grinned. "Something to take your mind off the hearing," he said.

Kat was intrigued.

She set down her own grocery bag and grabbed Ian's and set it on the table too. She looked out the window and saw that her mother had already backed out of the driveway and was heading back to Mr. Vincent's office for the rest of the meeting.

Ian handed her the rolled up bag. Inside was something black. Kat looked up at him.

"Lisa and I decided that you need a diversion," said Ian, grinning. "So we're taking you to The Savage Garden tonight."

"*What?*" exclaimed Kat. The Savage Garden was a club where people into Goth culture hung out.

"Don't look so worried," said Ian. "It's fetish night tonight, meaning all ages are allowed in."

"I don't know...." said Kat.

"I already talked to your mother about it," said Ian. "And she thinks you should go."

This hearing really must be affecting her mind, thought Kat. Since when did her mother approve of such things?

"She said she'd drive us all there and pick us up at the stroke of midnight," said Ian.

Okay, now it sounded more like her mother. "That would be great," said Kat.

"Lisa and I will come by at 9 and we can all drive down together," said Ian.

Kat watched in amazement as he walked down the street towards his own house.

As she unpacked the groceries, she noticed that the light on the answering machine was blinking. Kat pushed "play" and listened:

"This is detective Ann Marie Foulds. Would either Iris or Walter Baliuk call when they get in?"

As soon as Orysia got home, she called the detective immediately, and Kat could see her mother's shoulders relax in relief as she listened to what the detective had to say. "Good news and bad news," she said as she hung up the phone. "The good news is that Michael Vincent is not our graffiti artist."

"Thank goodness," said Kat. Her faith was restored in humanity. Yet hadn't the police said that they had caught him in the act? "How did they clear him?"

"His fingerprints don't match the ones from the graffiti," explained Orysia. "Which leads me to the bad news. They still have no idea who did it."

Frustrating, thought Kat. But she was so happy that Michael hadn't done it.

"Why don't you give Michael a call while I start supper?" suggested Orysia.

Kat called, but Michael seemed distant. It made her feel bad that she had ever suspected him.

"Can you come over Sunday afternoon?" she asked. "I could really use some feedback on an art project I'm thinking about."

"I'll see," said Michael.

CHAPTER 27

"I DON'T KNOW how you can stand to go to the hearing," said Genya as Kat was going through her Goth clothes. "I can barely stay sane just thinking of all this stuff."

"He is our grandfather," said Kat. "And the least you could do is come to the hearing once. I know he would get strength in that."

"Kat," said Genya. "You've already lost your year. I don't want the same to happen to me."

Kat sighed. Her sister had a point. She just wished Genya hadn't decided to opt out of the family. "Why are you even here now?" asked Kat. "I mean, you hardly even sleep here any more."

"Needed a change of clothes," said Genya. She opened her chest of drawers and pulled out a sweater and a skirt, then stuffed them into her knapsack. Then she walked over to Kat's bed and looked at the items Ian had brought.

"This is neat," said Genya, holding a black short skirt up to her waist.

Kat looked at it sceptically.

Almost as if Genya knew what she was thinking, she said. "The neatest thing about this is that it's vinyl and fits like a glove." Then she put both of her hands inside the waist and pulled.

Then Genya, in her usual take-charge manner, put together an outfit for Kat from the items Ian had brought. By the time Kat struggled into the black corset top, the skintight skirt, fishnet stockings and knee-high vinyl stiletto boots, she truly did feel like she was someone else.

Genya had a huge grin on her face as she angled the door mirror so Kat could get a good look at herself. "Well," said Kat. "I sure am not me."

"Too bad you have to wear those glasses," said Genya.

"I'm blind without them," said Kat. "And you know it."

"Yeah," said Genya. "But let me do your make-up, okay?"

When they were little, Genya used to love putting make-up on Kat. She also would put make-up on her mother and even on Baba. Kat sighed with nostalgia. It would be so nice to be back in those simpler days.

Genya painted china doll lips on Kat in black eyeliner, and outlined her eyes in kohl. They didn't have white face make-up, but Genya mixed up a concoction of foundation and concealer that did a pretty good job. Kat's hair was its natural colour, but Genya gelled it wild. "Promise not to touch it," she admonished, "or you'll spoil the effect."

Kat felt giddy with anticipation as she walked on the sidewalk between Ian and Lisa on their way to The Savage Garden. They passed a small shop or two, and a garment factory. The door opened as they walked by and a haggard looking Vietnamese woman stepped outside. Under one arm was the end of a bolt of glittery cloth. She clutched it protectively as she darted past the three teens.

"This is the street where my grandparents lived when they first came to Canada," said Kat. "Baba worked in one of those garment factories too."

"It's all Vietnamese now," said Lisa. "These women can barely scrape by."

The entrance to The Savage Garden looked like a cross between a construction zone and a cave. Ian pushed on the door and Kat was greeted with a blast of retro Goth music and a swirl of cigarette smoke. She stepped in, Lisa and Ian close behind. They were enveloped in darkness and steamy warmth.

Kat could feel Ian's hand under one of her elbows, and Lisa's arm around her waist and she was grateful for their closeness because the place was packed. As her eyes adjusted to the darkness, she took in all of the outrageous outfits. Compared to some of these, she was downright conservative.

A middle aged man with red contact lenses, a black shirt with a priest's collar and a long leather skirt was standing beside a pool table, chalking a cue. Beside him was a woman in her twenties wearing skintight black leather pants and a leather bra. She was bending over the pool table, lining up her balls.

Amidst the outrageous outfits, there were a few people who must have come only to sightsee. Kat noticed that these people wore regular black clothing — black jeans, shirts, skirts — but no vinyl and nothing daring.

There were a number of small tables scattered around the room where people clustered for conversation. Each table was anchored in place with a pole that extended from floor to ceiling. The walls were mostly painted black, but some parts were metallic, and Kat could see the outline of machine sculpture through the cigarette smoke.

There were a few people dancing frenetically, but most were either talking, or just walking around, enjoying the sights. Kat looked up and saw that there were some raised platforms decorated to look like jail cells. People were dancing up there too.

"Do you want to dance?" asked Lisa, motioning her towards the centre of the floor.

"No," said Kat.

Lisa pulled Ian to the dance floor and Kat watched.

It was such a welcome change to have such extreme sensory overload. The music was so loud and the lights flashing were so intense that it blocked out all thought. She revelled in the anonymity of it all.

Chapter 28

KAT WAITED ALL day Sunday, but Michael didn't call. Once, she picked up the phone and began to dial his number, but she changed her mind halfway through and put the receiver back on the cradle.

She opened the front curtains, thinking that maybe Michael was walking down the street to her house, but all she saw was the woman with the picket sign.

She was filled with impatient energy and a million thoughts. There was really only one thing that would ever settle her down, and that was to set her mind free by creating something with her hands. It was only days after Christmas, but what Kat had the urge to create was a *pysanka* — a written egg.

It felt odd to be getting out the mason jars of dye from their dark storage area months before Easter, but the sight of them brightened her spirits. A written egg was hope. And she could never write just one egg. After all, once you got the dye out and tested it to see which colours needed replacing, and then once you found some really nice smooth and perfect chicken eggs, it seemed a shame to just make one.

On a sketchpad, Kat quickly drew the outlines of a few ideas she had swirling in her head. She wanted one or two of her eggs to be fairly traditional, but she wanted to combine the old symbols in a new way. She experimented with a motif of dots, symbolizing the Virgin's tears, and waves, symbolizing immigration, but then she scratched that out. Stylized sheaves of wheat? No. Too typical. Kat tried to think of Easter eggs she'd seen when she was younger. She remembered the first time she had seen swastikas on a Ukrainian Easter egg. She was barely seven years old. Her grandparents had taken Kat and Genya to a travelling exhibit that had come to the Ukrainian community centre and some of the eggs were from the 1800s.

"Look at that pretty egg," she had said to her grandparents, pointing to a red and white *pysanka* decorated with a broad band of yellow and black stylized crosses. The label in front of it stated that it had been made in 1882.

"That used to be pretty, but not any more," replied her grandfather.

Kat looked up, startled by the anger in his voice.

"Those crosses, the 'swastika' used to mean the wheel of life. It is ancient: thousands of years old."

"What do they mean now, Dido?" Kat had asked.

"Death," he replied huskily. "Death and hate. They shouldn't even display those eggs."

Even at that age it had startled Kat to think that something out of context could cause such pain.

She tried to reconcile this thought of Dido's reaction to the swastikas many years ago and what she had heard at the hearing. Her grandfather was repulsed at a visceral level. Yet he had worked for the Nazis. It didn't make sense.

Kat turned her attention back to her egg. She gave up on trying to sketch something altogether. "I'll just write on the egg and see where it takes me."

Kat struck a match and then lit the small stub of a candle that was nestled in a pool of hardened wax inside the lid of a peanut butter jar. She grabbed the red-handled *kistka* from the

TV tray and stuck the metal tip into the flame. She had three different *kistkas*. The red-handled one had the thickest nib and she used it to write the broad outlines of designs. It was also good for filling in broad areas of colour. The blue handled *kistka* had a narrower nib, and the white had the narrowest of all. So narrow, in fact, that it kept getting clogged with soot from the candle. Kat had bought a metal wire finer than baby hair at the Arka store to clean it out with.

When the tip of the red-handled *kistka* was blackened and warm, she dipped the head into her cake of beeswax, then blotted it on a paper towel to make sure it didn't drip. Then swiftly, without even thinking of what or where the *kistka* would take her, she began blocking out sections with broad swift lines of blackened beeswax upon the egg.

She looked down at her egg and realized that she had blocked off the traditional pattern of forty triangles. There were a number of classic base patterns to a *pysanka* and one of the most difficult to do freehand was the forty triangles. Kat had never done it before without drawing the outline lightly in pencil first. She was amazed at the steadiness of her hands. I guess it pays not to be trying too hard, she thought to herself.

She set the egg down on a dishtowel and opened up the jar of red dye. With a teaspoon, she dipped the egg in gingerly, then resealed the jar. This one would sit till tomorrow.

"I'll start one more today," she said to herself, drawn to a beautifully smooth creamy white egg that seemed more oblong than the others. Since she had so much success writing freehand before, she decided to try it again, only this time with the blue-handled *kistka*.

As she heated the tip over the candle flame, Kat thought back to the testimony she had heard. Nothing she had heard had implicated her grandfather. But she was curious about why he would have become an auxiliary police officer in the first place? What could he possibly have been thinking of?

Why hadn't he simply run away? She almost feared what he would testify.

Kat looked down at the egg she was currently working on and was startled to see that she had blocked the egg with a band down the middle and then another band perpendicular to it. It was like a motif of crosses. Behind the crosses, Kat had begun to draw a cross-hatch pattern: a fine mesh. This was a classic pattern and symbolic of a fisherman's net. Could it also be symbolic of the net that was closing in around her grandfather?

She blew out the candle, then set the egg down on the dish-towel. She opened up the mason jar of brilliant yellow, then gently plopped in the egg with a fresh teaspoon. Sealing the lid back up, she set the jar beside the one with the red dye. "I can hardly wait to see what you two eggs look like tomorrow," she said to herself.

CHAPTER 29

THE NEXT FOUR days saw more witnesses for the plaintiff. First on the stand was a retired immigration officer. Mr. Conrad Draycott had been stationed as a screening officer in Karlsruhe, Germany from 1948 to 1952. During those years, Mr. Draycott screened thousands of Eastern European displaced persons who wanted to immigrate to Canada.

Mrs. Caine began the questions. "Mr. Draycott, can you tell me how you went about deciding who could come into Canada and who was to be screened out?"

Mr. Draycott had an oblong face and a surprisingly full head of steel grey hair. While his arms and legs were long and lanky, the man also sported a substantial stomach, and in order to accommodate this, the waist of his navy blue trousers settled between his chest and navel, and his tie was tucked into his leather belt.

"Canada had an urgent need for farm labour after the war," explained Mr. Draycott.

"Were there any screening procedures in place to keep certain people out?" asked Mrs. Caine.

"With the huge backlog of refugees, it was difficult, but we did the best we could. Almost certainly some undesirables were able to sneak through. One or more of the following elements would have made a prospective immigrant unsuitable: If the person was a Communist, a member of the SS, a member of the Nazi Party, a criminal, a professional gambler, a prostitute, a black market racketeer, if the person was evasive during questioning, did not have acceptable documents, used a fictitious name, was a collaborator presently residing in previously occupied territory, a member of the Mafia or of the Italian Fascist Party, a Trotskyite or member of another revolutionary organization."

Mrs. Caine walked over to where Danylo was sitting and pointed at him. "Would you have let this man into the country had you been the one screening him?" she asked.

Mr. Draycott turned to look at Danylo and knitted his brows. "Under what grounds are you thinking, Mrs. Caine?"

"As someone who committed crimes against the local population on behalf of the Nazis," she replied.

"These people were 'collaborators' and were specifically barred from obtaining entry into Canada," he said.

"So a person who committed crimes against the local population would be barred from gaining Canadian citizenship?"

"That is correct," said Mr. Draycott.

"No more questions," said Mrs. Caine.

Mr. Vincent got to his feet.

"Mr. Draycott," he began. "Mr. Feschuk was a member of the auxiliary police force in the Ukrainian province of Volhyn from 1941 until 1943. If he told you that during his security screening, would that have barred him from entering Canada?"

"Not on those grounds. Was he a member of the SS?" asked Mr. Draycott.

"No," said Mr. Vincent.

"Did he bear the SS tattoo?"

"No," said Mr. Vincent.

"Was he a member of the Nazi Party?"

"No."

Mr. Draycott shook his head. "Simply being a local auxiliary police officer would not be considered collaboration."

"What would be considered collaboration, then?" asked Mr. Vincent.

"As I said to Mrs. Caine, if Mr. Feschuk had committed crimes against the civilian population, he would be considered a collaborator."

"How would you determine that?" asked Mr. Vincent.

"People like that were shunned by the other Displaced Persons," said Mr. Draycott. "But mostly, we would base the judgement on the personal interview."

"Thank you Mr. Draycott. I have no more questions."

The next witnesses were much the same as the first. Another immigration officer, a medical officer. Each would speak of who would and who would not have been let into Canada immediately after the war.

As Kat listened, she was troubled by the fact that month to month and year to year, there were subtle changes in who was allowed in and who wasn't. It also troubled her that Danylo's immigration papers had not been brought forward as evidence. Surely if he was being accused of misrepresenting himself, the government could settle the matter by showing the papers? But all the immigration papers from just after the war had been destroyed. One clerk testified that this wasn't malice on the part of the government, it was routine housekeeping. It left Kat to wonder at how this hearing could even be, with no surviving paperwork and no witnesses.

After the last immigration officer testified, the plaintiff rested the government's case. "To sum up," said Mrs. Caine. "We have heard testimony that Mr. Danylo Feschuk collaborated with the Nazis in Reichcommissariat Ukraine from 1941 until 1943 in his role as an auxiliary police officer. We have heard testimony about the atrocities committed by Ukrainian auxiliary police in World War II. We have also heard testimony that had

Mr. Feschuk disclosed his involvement in these crimes, he would not have been given Canadian citizenship. The fact that he gained Canadian citizenship proves that he lied to security officials during screening procedures.

"Some may try to minimize Mr. Feschuk's collaboration, saying he was forced into it. However, I want you to consider this: if a man betrays the country of his birth, what stops him from betraying his country of adoption?

"Mr. Danylo Feschuk's citizenship should be stripped and he should be deported."

Kat sat there, stunned.

Chapter 30

WHEN THE BALIUKS arrived home, Kat checked the mail, but found no hate mail. There had been a few pieces of hate mail since that first one, but now everyone knew what to do. As soon as they were opened and their contents revealed, they were dumped into a zip-lock bag and the police were notified. Several good prints had already been found.

While the hate mail was upsetting to Danylo, what upset him even more was the "fan" mail. Twice in the last week, Danylo had received letters from neo-Nazis extending their support. The writers of these "fan" letters mistakenly believed that her grandfather was a Nazi and they idolized him for it.

Kat remembered when the first such letter arrived. She had found her grandfather sitting on the sofa, a letter in hand. His face was almost purple with anger.

"What's the matter, Dido?" she had asked.

"This piece of garbage," he said, holding out the letter for her to see. "A fool is thanking me for my work in the name of Hitler. What kind of a nut would think Hitler was a good guy?"

Thankfully, these letters were few and far between, and in this particular stack, there were none. What was in this stack, however, were letters of support. Some of the letters came from fellow Ukrainian immigrants who, like Danylo, had come from a village that was right on the front, but what warmed Kat's heart the most were the letters from Canadian-born citizens who were simply appalled by a process that could strip citizenship on the basis of unproven evidence.

Kat had her own case of unproven evidence to atone for. Michael had still not returned her phone calls. She felt awful about what had happened, but she couldn't quite understand why he was so angry with her. She had not accused him of doing the graffiti, and she had not called the police. All she had done was witness his arrest. What had he expected her to do?

She picked up the phone and called one last time. This time, Michael picked up.

She was momentarily at a loss for words because she had expected to get an answering machine again. "Hi Michael, it's Kat," she said.

"Hi," he replied in a flat voice.

"Look," said Kat. "I am really sorry for what happened. I wish it didn't happen at all, but I don't know why you're so mad at me about it."

"I'm not, really," said Michael. "I'm sad about it, not mad about it."

"Can you come over, and maybe we can talk?"

"Sure," he said. "Hold on for a minute."

Kat could hear the muffled sound of a hand over the speaker of a phone.

"My dad has to drop some papers off at your house after supper tonight. He said he could drive me over at the same time."

"That would be great," said Kat. She was very relieved.

When Mr. Vincent came over, he and Kat's mother and grandfather took over the kitchen table with an assortment of files and clippings. Michael stood awkwardly in the living room, looking on.

"I'll just grab a couple of sodas and then we can go downstairs and I'll show you what I was working on," said Kat.

"Okay," said Michael.

Kat was relieved to see a faint smile on his lips.

Kat had brought a spare lawn chair into the basement so Michael would have a place to sit. Since the trial began, she had come downstairs almost every single evening to work on her eggs. She had completed seven already, and there were three more in various stages of completion.

Michael sat down on the lawn chair that faced Kat's working area. "Wow," he said. "You made all of those?"

"Yep," said Kat. She picked up the one she was most proud of: the forty triangle *pysanka* she had written freehand, and she put it in Michael's hand.

"It's still got the egg guts in it," said Michael. "Is it hard boiled?"

"No," said Kat. "You have to use raw eggs."

"Why?"

"Boiling them would ruin the finish, and the dye wouldn't take properly."

"Then how do you get the egg out once it's all done?" asked Michael.

"You don't have to," said Kat. "Traditionally, you're supposed to leave the egg guts in. They dry on their own. Also, traditionally, to take the guts out is to kill the egg. An egg is a symbol of life and hope and good wishes, so some think it turns the symbol around if you take the insides out of it."

"Hmm," said Michael. "I didn't know that." He set down the forty triangles *pysanka* and picked up another. This one had an intricate design. "This is beautiful," he said.

"I made it for you," said Kat.

Michael looked up, surprised and a bit embarrassed. "I can't take this," he said. "It is too precious."

"*Pysanky* are made to be given," said Kat. "It is like a wish or a prayer that you give to someone else."

Michael smiled. "Thank you," he said.

"So," Kat said, grinning back. "Would you like me to teach you how to make your own *pysanky*?"

His smile broke into a broad grin. "I would love it," he said.

CHAPTER 31

DANYLO'S DEFENCE BEGAN on Friday, January 18th with an opening statement by Mr. Vincent.

"The plaintiff has put forward the theory that Mr. Danylo Feschuk collaborated with the Nazis in Reichcommissariat Ukraine from 1941 until 1943 in his role as an auxiliary police officer. However, it should be noted that the plaintiff did not present a single person who witnessed atrocities committed by Mr. Feschuk. In fact, the plaintiff presented no eyewitnesses to atrocities carried out by Ukrainian auxiliary police at all.

"The court might wonder how Mr. Feschuk was targeted with this accusation in the first place. In the 1970s, a package of material was brought forward by the Soviet Secret Police — the KGB — on behalf of the Soviet government. The RCMP followed up on that information, and drew up a list of people to investigate.

"One might ask what the motivation was for the KGB to do this? Why did the list contain not a single Russian, in spite of the fact that the Soviet Union openly collaborated with Nazi Germany from 1939 until 1941? Why did the list contain not a single German citizen, in spite of the fact that only German citizens could join the Nazi party? All of the people on the list were from Eastern European countries. These were the same countries who fought Communism, but were forcibly annexed to the Soviet Union after World War II. Was the Soviet Union trying to deflect attention from their own war crimes?

"Mrs. Caine has not been able to present a single piece of evidence to personally implicate Mr. Feschuk in atrocities. She bases her case on German documents which occasionally implicate Ukrainian auxiliary police. I will bring forward an expert witness who will provide German documents that paint a different picture.

"Mrs. Caine has stated that Mr. Feschuk lied during immigration proceedings, yet she has provided no evidence to back that claim.

"In her closing statement, Mrs. Caine asks, 'if a man betrays the country of his birth, what stops him from betraying his country of adoption?'

"This is a key question. Mr. Feschuk's country of birth was Ukraine. I will show that Mr. Feschuk was a patriot.

"I call my first witness," continued Mr. Vincent after pausing. "Professor John Thompson of the University of Toronto, author of *Modern Ukraine: 1900 - 2000*."

Professor Thompson was a slim small man with tiny round glasses and greying curly hair, which he wore gelled and combed away from his face. He walked over to the witness stand and sat down, then adjusted the microphone so that it was close to his mouth.

Kat sat up to listen. She was very familiar with this man's name. Many of Professor Thompson's books graced her parents' bookshelves, but she had never read one herself.

Kat learned that when Hitler invaded Ukraine in 1941, there were many Ukrainians who welcomed the Nazis, believing they were being liberated from the Soviet Terror that had seen millions of Ukrainians go missing.

But the Nazis turned out to be as bad as the Soviets. Five million forced labourers from various countries were sent to

Germany — half of them were Ukrainian. They were known as the *Ostarbeiter* and were identified by the OST badge they were forced to wear on their clothing. The goal was to literally work these labourers to death, and they succeeded at a rate of 40,000 a month.

As Kat listened to the professor's testimony, stories that her grandmother had told her began to surface in her thoughts. Kat could never really put them in context before. A sob caught in Kat's throat. She missed her grandmother so much. But as the professor continued, Kat remembered the stories as crisply as if she were stepping into her grandmother's shoes:

A sign was posted in the village square: Limited quantity of fresh bread, post office, two o'clock, first come-first served.

Nadiya couldn't believe it. Bread? She and her mother had been surviving on handfuls of horse feed that they'd steal from the Germans' stables when they were sent in to clean them. "Mama is so sick with hunger," thought Nadiya to herself. "She'll be so proud of me if I bring home a loaf of real bread."

When Nadiya got to the post office, her heart sank. There were already more than twenty villagers lined up. Mostly, it was wretched starving old women with distended bellies, but there were a few people Nadiya's age too.

Nadiya was about to leave when a soldier came out and beckoned the half dozen young people in the crowd. "I may have some more bread in the back," he said. "Follow me."

Nadiya hesitated, but she saw that the others were eager to follow. A loaf of bread was nothing to sniff at. So she followed too. But no sooner was she inside the post office when she felt a sharp blow to her head. When she woke up, she was in a boxcar packed tight with Ukrainian boys and girls. The smell of vomit and feces was intense, but worse was the weeping and wailing of all the teens who would never see their families again.

At the munitions factory she was sent to, she was fed a bowl of gruel once a day that was mostly water with scraps of mouldy potato. She was constantly hungry and her fingers were sore and swollen from handling metal all day. At night, she slept in a small room with dozens of other women. She could hear the sound of allied bombers flying overhead. Munitions factories were prime targets. On her breast she wore the badge of shame: OST. Subhuman.

Kat could almost see her grandmother sitting beside her, telling her these stories. She had to stop thinking of it, or she would burst into tears. She tried to concentrate on what Mr. Vincent was asking the professor.

"What were Ukraine's total losses during World War II?"

"Some go as high as 14.5 million, but in my estimation, approximately 10 million Ukrainians lost their lives during World War II. Of that total, four million were civilians. This figure includes 600,000 Jewish Ukrainians."

Throughout the professor's testimony, Kat would occasionally turn in her chair slightly so that she could see the reactions on the faces of the people in the audience. She was struck by the fact that several of the people on the opposite side wore angry expressions and had their arms crossed. Kat noted in particular the girl with the hair clip. She looked like she was about to explode.

Curiously, the reaction of her grandfather's supporters were exactly the opposite. While Professor Thompson spoke of Ukrainian losses, most were perched on the edge of their chairs and nodding in agreement. Kat remembered that when the plaintiff's witnesses were testifying, the reactions had been reversed.

This appalled Kat. Why were both sides not equally concerned with all the deaths? Was one human not equal to another? Kat's heart ached for all of the people who had been destroyed so long ago by two madmen. Whether Jews or Gypsies, Ukrainians or Poles, Russians or Germans, each of these people had been killed because of their race. Kat had assumed that the world had matured since then, but when she looked at the reactions of the people in the courtroom, she realized how little progress had actually been made.

At the first break, Kat didn't go down to the cafeteria for coffee with the others. Instead, she took the subway home. Professor Thompson had a stack of papers six inches high, and Kat had a feeling he'd be testifying all day. She didn't need a history lesson right now. What she needed was time to think. Thank goodness tomorrow was Saturday.

CHAPTER 32

KAT WAS SUFFERING from information overload. Her head was still swimming with all the facts and figures from the historian. She had wanted to get home and clear her head, but as soon as her house came into view, she realized that would be impossible. While they were gone, the house had again been attacked by the crazed swastika artist. On top of that, there was so much mail that it wouldn't even fit in the mailbox. Instead, the letter carrier had left the thick elastic-fastened bundle leaning against their front door. Too much information, Kat's mind screamed at her. She grabbed the mail bundle and walked around to the back door. On the summer kitchen table was more food — a casserole dish of cabbage rolls and perogies from the church women, a lemon cake from a neighbour, spring rolls from the Nguyens. Between the letter carrier and all these people dropping by and the police on top of it, Kat wondered how the graffiti artist ever found time to do his work.

She unlocked the door between the summer kitchen and the kitchen and carried the food and the mail inside. The first thing she wanted to do was to report the graffiti, so she walked to the phone. It was already blinking the number three. She pushed the "play" button on the answering machine. The first message was for her mother. It was from one of the women at the church, calling to let her know that a petition to the Minister of Justice was being circulated for signatures.

The second message was from her father in Oregon. It was short and sweet. "Dearest Orysia, I love you. I am thinking of you and the girls and your father."

The message comforted Kat. She missed her father terribly, and she knew her mother did too.

The third beep sounded, and a gruff voice said, "You're all a bunch of Nazi-pig-murderers."

The words hit Kat like a slap across the face. How did this nut get their unlisted number? She was about to hit delete, but then she remembered that by doing so, she would destroy evidence. She called the police instead.

CHAPTER 33

TESTIMONY FOR DANYLO'S defence resumed on Monday. Wasyl Kozenchuk was a professor from the university of Sorbonne in Paris, France and he was the first witness to be called.

"Professor Kozenchuk, can you tell me your background?" asked Mr. Vincent.

Danylo noticed that Professor Kozenchuk was an exquisitely dressed man with manicured fingernails and carefully combed brown hair that had not even a hint of grey. He must be close to my age, estimated Danylo, but he looked much more fit and athletic.

"I was born in Soviet Ukraine in 1924, but escaped to France in 1938 with my parents. Even as a boy, my gift for language was noticed, and I received a scholarship to the University of Sorbonne, where I studied languages and political history. I am now a full professor of history. I am fluent in German, Russian, Ukrainian, Polish, French and English."

"Professor Kozenchuk, what is your current research?"

"I have spent the last decade poring through government documents from the Third Reich."

"What is your key area of study?" asked Mr. Vincent.

"I am a French citizen, but my heritage is Ukrainian. I am

intensely interested in the Ukrainian question and the Third Reich."

"Thank you," said Mr. Vincent. "As you know, the reason we are here today is because Mr. Danylo Feschuk is accused of being a collaborator with the Nazis between 1941 and 1943 in his role as a Ukrainian auxiliary police officer in Orelets, a village in the region of Volhyn, Ukraine."

"It must be pointed out," replied the professor, "that the Volhyn region of Ukraine was a problem area for the Germans. In World War II, this area was still heavily forested and swampy. For weeks and even months, German control of this area was limited to the main roads. Resistance activity, from both the Ukrainian patriots and the Red partisans, was heavy. The locals knew the forests and the swamps, but the Germans didn't."

"Can you explain what this has to do with Mr. Feschuk and his role as an auxiliary police officer?"

Professor Kozenchuk flipped through a sheaf of notes that he had brought with him to the witness stand. "Mr. Feschuk joined the auxiliary police in August of 1941, correct?"

"That is correct, Professor."

"That was two months after Stefan Bandera and the OUN — the Organization of Ukrainian Nationalists — had declared Ukrainian independence from Germany, only to be arrested by the Nazis and thrown into a concentration camp. The OUN members who were not arrested went underground and into the forests of Volhyn and Polessia, where they continued their resistance against the Nazis."

"How did they set out to accomplish this?" asked Mr. Vincent.

"By sabotage and infiltration. They took jobs with the Germans in administration, as interpreters, mayors and so on, in order to monitor the actions of the Germans and to plan their next move."

"Can you explain how Danylo Feschuk fits into this?" asked Mr. Vincent.

"Another area of infiltration was the auxiliary police. Bandera's resistance movement needed weapons. The only way to get weapons was from the police and from the militia. They hid their true purpose and stockpiled weapons for more than a year — until February of 1943. At that time, three thousand Ukrainian auxiliary police in Volhyn simultaneously took to the forests. They killed their Nazi superiors and brought with them their stockpiles of weapons."

Danylo remembered what it was like to actually live through that time. Danylo and his fellow auxiliary police were to congregate at sunrise each morning for their orders from the Chief of Police, a German named Oskar Behr. In addition to the Ukrainian auxiliary police, there were three German police, and Danylo had to step carefully in order to make sure these Germans didn't suspect what he was up to. As far as the Ukrainian auxiliary police were concerned, all but one of them were secretly working with the resistance — the Organization of Ukrainian Nationalists.

It was a dangerous game. Once a week, the orders from the German-controlled headquarters in Rivne would arrive. How many slave labourers were required; how many girls for the German brothels; how many blonde and blue-eyed Ukrainian girls to be impregnated by Aryan soldiers, then discarded once the babies were born.

The auxiliary police outnumbered the Germans, but they were issued sometimes a pistol with no more than two bullets, sometimes no weapon at all. In addition to that, every rebellion was treated brutally. For the sake of the villagers, as much as for Danylo himself, it was imperative that the Germans didn't catch on to their game.

When the first orders for workers to Germany came in, some of the villagers willingly signed up. How bad could it be, they thought? Germans are civilized. But those first workers sent word back home. The villagers soon realized that to be shipped as an *Ostarbeiter* to Germany was nothing short of becoming a slave.

Danylo remembered all too well when the next orders — *oblava* — came in. On his rounds of the village that day, Danylo whispered to all he met, "*Oblava* — go underground until sunset."

When the Germans swept through the village to make their quota, they were sorely disappointed. The only people they managed to catch were an old chicken thief and a wife beater.

Danylo's attention was drawn back to the witness's testimony.

"Professor Kozenchuk," said Mr. Vincent. "The court heard expert testimony yesterday from Professor Chris Gillin regarding killings allegedly done by auxiliary police in Volhyn. From the documents you have studied, would you be able to shed more light on this question?"

"I certainly can," replied Professor Kozenchuk. "There is evidence that some Ukrainian auxiliary police were involved in killings. Thugs and common criminals were often glad to take these jobs. These auxiliary police killed not only Jews, but OUN members."

"So you are agreeing with Professor Gillin that some auxiliary police were involved in the killing of civilians?"

"I am. But certainly not all, or even most. The documents point to the fact that these jobs were infiltrated heavily by the OUN, and it is not credible that members of the OUN would commit murder on behalf of their German enslavers."

That was the understatement of the year, thought Danylo. In fact, it was difficult to restrain the OUN infiltrators from killing the Nazis too soon. Everything had to be orchestrated precisely, or the *Einsatzgruppen* — the elite Nazi killing units — would arrive and butcher the whole of Orelets.

"If the Ukrainians were so unreliable, why did the Germans continue to use them at all?" asked Mr. Vincent.

"By sheer necessity. They didn't have enough manpower," said the Professor. "But the documents reveal that the Germans didn't trust Ukrainians with important jobs. For example, let me read you this report from the Chief of the Security Police and the SD. It is from Berlin, and is dated December 8, 1941."

After he finished reading the report, the professor said, "This document shows clearly that even as early as 1941, the Germans were quite aware that Ukrainians could not be trusted to support them. It is not reasonable that the Germans would trust all auxiliary police with such an important role as mass killing. There was the risk that the Ukrainians would turn on the Germans and kill them instead."

"Professor Kozenchuk, another Soviet accusation is that the OUN was an anti-Semitic organization. Do any of the documents you've examined illuminate that issue?"

"In fact," replied the professor, "the Nazis were alarmed by what they saw as Jewish influence in the OUN. For example, in this report from Berlin, dated March 30, 1942, the Chief of the Security Police and the Security Service "Report on events in the USSR no. 187" states: "Today, it has been clearly established that the Bandera movement provided forged passports not only for its own members, but also for Jews.""

"Thank you, Professor Kozenchuk," said Mr. Vincent. "I have no more questions."

The judge looked up from his notes and regarded the plaintiff's lawyer, Mrs. Caine, who was still sitting. "Do you have any questions for the professor?" asked the judge.

Mrs. Caine stood up from her chair and walked over to the witness. "Professor Kozenchuk, in all of your testimony, you have not once produced a document vindicating Mr. Feschuk from atrocities. Do you have any specific proof that Mr. Danylo Feschuk was not involved in crimes against civilians?"

"No, I do not," said the professor.

"No more questions," said Mrs. Caine.

The professor wearily stepped down from the witness stand. It had been a gruelling day for him and everyone else.

Kat stood up from her seat and stretched. As she turned and joined the others who were milling out of the courtroom and into the hallway, she noticed in the back row a head that had to be Ian's. His hair was stark platinum white. He was wearing one of his father's suits and his face was scrubbed clean of make-up. He caught her eye and smiled. As she passed his spot, he stepped in beside her and walked out of the courtroom at her side.

"Hey there," he said. "I just caught the tail end of that testimony, but it sounded like pretty powerful stuff."

"It was," said Kat. Then she looked at him quizzically. "Why aren't you in school?"

"I skipped out of my last period, hoping to catch you here."

"Why?"

"Thursday night is the winter concert," he said. "I haven't talked to you forever, and I was hoping that you hadn't forgotten."

Kat had forgotten. With all that had been going on with her grandfather, the school concert had been the last thing on her mind.

"You'll still be able to help with the backdrop, won't you?" asked Ian with a pleading look in his eyes. "Lisa can't do it on her own. We tried."

Kat considered for a moment. It would actually be nice to be doing something entirely different for a change. She hadn't been back to the school since before the hearing started. "Sure," she said. "But Lisa and I need to do a dry run before the concert."

"Can you meet us at school on Thursday right after you leave the hearing?" asked Ian.

"I'll try," said Kat.

CHAPTER 34

WHEN THE FIRST witness was announced on Tuesday morning, there was a ripple of whispers in the courtroom. Doctor Samuel Sterzer walked over to the witness stand with methodical determination.

Orysia hadn't told Danylo that Dr. Sterzer had agreed to testify at his hearing. He hadn't seen him for more than four decades, but Danylo thought that if he had encountered him on the street, he would have recognized him immediately.

Dr. Sterzer was very short and slim, and his leathery skin was tanned but surprisingly unwrinkled. He wore no jewellery — not even a wedding ring. And his blue suit was crisp and conservative. Once he sat down in the witness stand, he looked around until his eyes met Danylo's, and then he nodded slightly in acknowledgement.

"Doctor Sterzer," began Mr. Vincent. "Can you tell me your background?"

"I am a medical doctor with a family practice in Tel-Aviv, Israel."

"Can you tell me your relationship to the defendant, Mr. Danylo Feschuk?"

"Certainly," replied Dr. Sterzer. "We were both in the UPA

— Ukrainian Insurgent Army — from 1943 to 1945."

"Can you tell me what you know about the defendant, Mr. Danylo Feschuk?" asked Mr. Vincent.

Dr. Sterzer regarded the lawyer for a moment and then he looked over at Danylo. "He was one of the many UPA soldiers in the Volhyn region. I met him when he brought me a patient. A girl who had been tortured by the Gestapo. He carried her in his arms for more than a mile to get to my underground hospital. I will never forget his face."

"Dr. Sterzer, was Danylo Feschuk a Nazi collaborator?"

"No, he was not," replied the doctor.

"No more questions."

Mrs. Caine got up from her chair and approached the witness stand. "Did you know Mr. Feschuk between 1941 and 1943?"

"I met him in 1943."

"So you have no way of knowing what sort of man he was before he joined the UPA?"

"Madame," said the doctor. "The UPA was a disciplined fighting unit and they were people of the highest principals. Even seemingly minor infractions like swearing or drinking were not allowed. To hurt a villager was punishable by death. If Mr. Feschuk had been a collaborator, the UPA would have sentenced him to death."

Dr. Sterzer's answer caused a ripple of whispers in the courtroom.

"Order," admonished the judge. "If you can't hold your tongue, you will have to step outside."

The whispers ceased.

"I have no further questions," said Mrs. Caine.

Kat was surprised by Doctor Sterzer's testimony. This was a whole side of World War II that she had never had an inkling about. As he spoke, the image of a whole army hidden in the woods formed in her mind. But it also raised a question for her. How did her grandfather transform himself from an auxiliary

policeman to an UPA soldier? She hoped some of the other witnesses would shed light on this question.

Chapter 35

"This first *pysanka* is going to be awesome," said Kat, blotting the black mottled thing she had pulled out of the mason jar of dye with a paper towel.

Michael grimaced. "Somehow, I find that hard to believe."

This Tuesday night was the fourth time that he had come by after supper in the past week. Since Kat had first shown him her *pysanky*, he became determined to perfect the process for himself.

What had confused him the most was the concept of doing everything backwards. The melted beeswax went on like black ink, but it was used only as a temporary seal for the colour underneath it.

Each day before he left, Kat submerged his egg into a different mason jar of dye, starting with the lightest first: yellow, then red, then black. By the time she fished it out of the last jar and blotted it dry, it was totally black and mottled with bumps and ridges.

Michael's eyebrows frowned in confusion. "Okay," he said. "I know that all the colours are underneath the wax, but how do you get the wax off?"

"Very carefully," said Kat with a smile.

She lit the small stub of the candle on her table, then waited for the flame to burn clean and long. "Now watch."

Holding the blackened egg between her thumb and forefinger, she held it close beside the flame. Within seconds, the beeswax heated up and began to liquefy and drip. With a quick motion, Kat grabbed a facial tissue and blotted away about an inch square of melted wax. A tiny bit of Michael's colourful pattern was peeping through. Kat held the egg at a slightly different angle and again held it close to the flame, then blotted away the melted wax. More pattern was revealed, and the tedious process continued.

"Why don't you just put the whole thing in the microwave?" asked Michael.

"It would explode," said Kat.

"Oh."

Kat didn't want to confuse him by telling him that it was actually possible to microwave the beeswax off *pysanky*, but first, the raw egg had to be removed from inside. And it had to be removed after the succession of wax and dye had been applied. It was incredibly tricky to do it without breaking the egg and without disturbing the design. One time, when Kat had accompanied her grandmother to the chemotherapy room, she had joked about the big-barrelled syringe the nurse used to inject the anti-cancer concoction they had nick-named the "red devil" because of its vile side-effects. "Wouldn't that be a great syringe for *pysanky*?" her grandmother had remarked.

After a few minutes, Kat had removed almost all of the wax. There were a few places where it stuck, so she scraped the remaining bits away with her fingernail, and then she held the finished work up with a grin. "See?" she said. "I told you it would be awesome."

Michael's egg pattern was one that Kat had sketched out for him as a good one to start with. It consisted of two stylized eight pointed stars: one on the front and one the back. The points were each so elongated that they connected up with their mirror image on the other side of the egg. The result was stunning, although there were a couple of fingerprint smudges and one or two places where the wax had loosened and dye had bled through in the wrong place.

"Why did that happen?" asked Michael, pointing at the imperfections.

"You were holding the egg too tightly," explained Kat. "Next time, don't try so hard."

Michael nodded in understanding.

CHAPTER 36

THE TESTIMONY ON Wednesday consisted of a succession of villagers. Kat secretly agreed with her father's opinion. It would have been just as effective and much cheaper if one or two of them had testified. They all said the same thing: that Danylo had walked a tightrope in his role as an auxiliary police officer. He had to make the Germans think he was obeying them, while all the time he was working against them. None had witnessed brutality on his part.

One witness from New Jersey had a different story to tell. Kat watched as the white haired man with piercing blue eyes entered the witness stand.

"What is your name?" asked Mr. Vincent.

"Sergei Kovalenko," he said.

"Can you tell me about yourself?" asked Mr. Vincent.

"I am a retired insurance salesman," said the man. "I was born in Russia. I came to the United States from a Displaced Persons camp after the war."

"How do you know Mr. Feschuk?" asked Mr. Vincent.

"I will never forget that man," said Mr. Kovalenko, nodding in Danylo's direction. "I was a prisoner of war, and he helped me escape." Sergei then told the courtroom of that fateful time.

Within the barbed wire enclosure, the odour was overwhelming. Some of the prisoners had died, but the guards didn't remove the bodies right away. The stench of the corpses competed with the smell of dried vomit and feces. The prisoners were not fed, and they were not given water and so it was a wonder they were able to create such a mess, but the mess was there for all to see. And smell.

Sergei had tried to stay away from the other prisoners of war. Although he had no hope of surviving beyond a couple of days, he felt a moral obligation to try to stay as healthy as he could for as long as he could.

Within the barbed wire enclosure, there were perhaps 500 men. Each day, more were brought in, but each day many died, so the number was constant. Sergei was already in his second day, so he knew his time was near. He would sit as still as he could to conserve his energy, and he would watch the guards.

One day, a Ukrainian auxiliary policeman brushed past him, just inches from his face. "Watch the gate. Escape," the man said, then continued walking.

Escape? Could he even hope for that? And what was he to watch the gate for? Something different, he presumed. He gestured to a couple of others who were healthy like him and told them what the policeman said. So there were about five of them, surreptitiously keeping their eyes on the gate, not knowing what they were supposed to see.

It happened the next day. A beautiful, young and healthy girl walked past with a basket of eggs at the exact same time the corpses were being removed. The one guard left at the gate was momentarily startled when the girl tripped and fell.

Sergei and his friends were ready. They slipped out.

Sergei and the others went to the forest, and they found many others like themselves. Some of the villagers came out to find them and brought food. Others brought weapons.

Sergei never saw the policeman again until one memorable day in February of 1943, when thousands of Ukrainian policemen escaped to the woods.

"Mr. Kovalenko," Mr. Vincent asked. "What was the approximate date of your escape from the POW camp?"

"It was in 1941," replied Sergei. "I do not know the exact date, but it was in the fall."

"So as early as 1941, you witnessed Mr. Feschuk performing anti-Nazi activity."

"That is correct."

"What would have happened if Mr. Feschuk had been caught helping you to escape?"

Sergei shook his head in dismay. "I don't even want to think about it," he replied. "He would have been killed, and many other villagers would have been killed too."

"Thank you, Mr. Kovelenko," said Mr. Vincent. "No further questions."

Mrs. Caine stood up. "Mr. Kovelenko, how did you become a prisoner of war?"

"My whole unit surrendered to the Germans."

"You refused to fight the Nazis?" asked Mrs. Caine.

Mr. Kovelenko sat up straight in his chair and regarded Mrs. Caine sternly. "I fought the Nazis once I was in the UPA. In the Red Army, we were issued one rifle for every two soldiers. The Germans arrived in tanks. What did you expect us to do?"

"I would have expected you to die with honour," said Mrs. Caine. "No more questions."

It was only 2:45.

The judge looked from the plaintiff to the defence. "We have one more witness," he said. "And that is Danylo Feschuk."

Then the judge removed his glasses and regarded Danylo.

"Would you like to testify today, or would you like to wait until tomorrow?"

Danylo leaned towards a microphone to answer, but before he did, Mr. Vincent stood up.

"We ask that the hearing be adjourned for the day. Mr. Feschuk is tired."

"Fine," said the judge, banging his gavel. "The court will resume tomorrow at 9 am."

CHAPTER 37

BY THE TIME Kat arrived at Cawthra, Lisa had taken the parachute out of the knapsack and it was draped out on the stage floor. It was amazingly huge: it stretched all the way from one side of the stage to the other.

Lisa and Kat tried to hang it with the three huge scallops like they had before, but they couldn't get the knack anymore. It kept on looking lopsided. They experimented with different ways to hang it, and Ian stood at the back of the auditorium and watched. "That's perfect," he called out on their sixth attempt.

The two girls stepped back to view their work. It was angled in such a way that the khaki satiny material formed into one huge loopy triangle, with the small end at the top, widening to the full expanse of the stage at floor level. The velvet maroon curtains contrasted nicely in texture and colour as a backdrop to the set. It was an elegant and stark setting for Ian, with his white hair and long black coat with the red satin lining.

Ian walked down the centre aisle towards the stage as Lisa climbed up a ladder to unfasten the top of the parachute. A moment later, it was in billows on the floor. Ian bent down to wind it into a compact ball. He unzipped the knapsack carrying case and drew out a bundle of chamois. Inside was the ornate Victorian knife that he had bought at the surplus store.

"Why are you still carrying that around?" asked Kat, a note of concern in her voice.

"No reason," said Ian. "I just like the look of it." He ran his finger over the polished blade with admiration.

Kat was not convinced. "You don't take a knife to school just because you like the look of it," she said.

"I do."

"Even a pen knife on a key chain is forbidden," said Kat angrily. "Do you want to get kicked out of Cawthra? I can't believe you could be so dumb."

Ian looked up at her with an annoyed expression on his face. "You are such an incredible priss sometimes," he said. He had finished bundling the parachute by this time and shoved it into the knapsack. He wrapped the knife in the piece of chamois and placed it inside the front of his leather jacket.

They walked out of the auditorium and into the school hallway together.

"I'm calling my mom to pick me up," said Kat, walking towards the pay phone at the front of the school. "Do you guys want a ride home?"

Ian looked at her with a scowl. "I'll catch the bus," he said, turning his back on them both and walking out the front door of the school.

Lisa looked from Ian's back to Kat and rolled her eyes. "I'll take a ride if the offer's open."

Kat called home and was surprised when Genya answered. "Mom's lying down," she said. "But I'll come and get you."

"Don't be too upset with Ian," said Lisa. "He's always in a bad mood before a concert."

Kat just shrugged. Ian had been so patient with all of her strange moods of late. The least she could do was be patient when he had something on his mind. As they walked towards

Lisa's locker, Kat updated Lisa on the latest developments of her grandfather's case.

Ian was still angry by the time he had reached the bus stop. Kat was a nice kid, but she was so conservative that sometimes it made him want to scream. Why was she always looking at him with such disapproval? What was the big deal about carrying a knife, anyway? Couldn't she see that it was an awesome looking knife?

He was the only person waiting by the bus stop, and he paced back and forth to keep himself warm in the January air, hoping that he hadn't just missed a bus. He didn't still want to be standing there when Kat's ride arrived. The parachute knapsack was strapped to his back, and he carried the other one filled with his books. He didn't even know why he had brought his books home. He wasn't about to do any homework on concert night. However, if he walked back to his locker to get rid of the stuff, he would exit at the exact same time as Kat and Lisa. And he was mad at Kat.

He looked up the street and noticed that a couple of jocks from another high school were walking towards him. Ian hated jocks. He used to be one himself, and he knew that they looked upon people like him with utter disdain. He looked down the street to see if the bus was coming yet, but none was in sight. He looked back and noticed that the jocks — there were three of them — were coming straight towards him.

Where was that stupid bus?

Ian surveyed the three when they were just a dozen feet away from him. The tallest was the jerk Kat seemed to know. Dylan and he had been on the same all-star hockey team eons ago. The other two he didn't know.

"Hey Ian, is that you?" said Dylan as he came up and stood beside the bus stop.

Ian looked at his team mate of long ago and scowled a nod.

Dylan was a full head taller than he was and probably weighed at least fifty pounds more.

His two friends weren't much smaller.

One of Dylan's friends pushed Ian's shoulder with rough jocularity and asked, "Are you a fag, or what?"

Ian rolled his eyes. Puhlease, he thought. What was this guy's problem?

"Hey," said the jock angrily. "I asked you a question." He poked Ian roughly. "You look like a fag to me."

"What I am is no business of yours," replied Ian with cold anger.

"So you think," he taunted.

Ian was doing a slow burn by this time. He looked down the street and saw that there was still no bus in sight. He stepped away from the three other teens and began walking down the street. Perhaps he would hitch a ride home.

"Hey, my friend was talking to you," said Dylan.

Ian continued walking. He could hear three sets of Nikes close behind him, but he didn't want to turn around. Suddenly, he felt a punch on his arm.

Ian reached into his jacket and unwrapped the ornate Victorian knife. He felt someone pulling on his knapsack. He swung around, knife in hand. "Leave me alone!" he shouted.

Dylan saw the knife and in a flash, he had grabbed Ian's wrist and squeezed it. The pressure made Ian drop the knife with a clatter onto the sidewalk.

One of Dylan's friends picked it up. "We'll show you, you fag."

Dylan grabbed a huge handful of Ian's hair and pulled with all his might. Ian's legs buckled, and before he knew it, he was kneeling on the ground. The teen with the knife fell upon him. Ian felt a sharp pain on his scalp, and then a warm gush. Through a veil of blood, Ian could see that the teen with the knife was grinning and holding a handful of white hair.

The teen threw it down on the sidewalk, then wiped the remnants of blood from his hand onto Ian's jacket.

"Ew," he said. "I hope I don't get AIDS now."

Next, Dylan grabbed the knapsack that had fallen from Ian's hands and ripped it open, scattering school books all over the sidewalk. Someone cut the straps of the other knapsack from his back and opened it up.

"What do we have here?" one of them asked.

Ian's eyes were closed in pain, but he could hear the sickening sound of ripping fabric. He felt the dull thud of someone kicking him in the ribs.

"GET OFF HIM!"

Ian heard the shrill scream as blackness enveloped him.

With strength they didn't know they had, Kat and Lisa punched and bit the three large teens who were attacking Ian. Dylan and his friends looked up at complete shock and amazement when they saw who Ian's champions were.

They dropped the knife and scattered.

Kat was utterly shocked that Dylan would be involved in such an incident of violence. What had gotten in to him?

Ian lay, still as death, on the sidewalk. The blood from his scalp wound had spilled onto the sidewalk and was beginning to form a small pool. Long strips of cut parachute fluttered in the wind. Lisa gathered it up as best she could while Kat took a strip of it and stanched the wound on Ian's head. She was thankful to see that the thugs had not yet torn out his nose ring. Small comfort.

The knife lay on the ground, smudges of Ian's blood and a wisp of hair still visible on the blade. A clump of white hair was stuck to the sidewalk, looking like a stomped mouse. The sight made Kat want to vomit.

Lisa followed Kat's gaze. "We can't just leave that," she said. She rooted through her knapsack for her binder and then tore out a sheet of paper. Gingerly, she wrapped the knife up into it and then placed it in her own knapsack. Then she pulled the hank of hair from the sidewalk and wrapped it in a separate sheet of paper. Next she gathered up Ian's scattered school books and put them back into his other knapsack.

"When is your sister getting here?" asked Lisa. "Do you want to call her on my cell phone?"

"She'll be here any minute," said Kat, still holding the bit of fabric to Ian's wound and fighting back tears.

Genya had come upon the scene moments later, although to Lisa and Kat it had seemed like hours. As usual, Genya's calm efficiency was an asset. She had assessed the situation before even stopping the car. She pulled up right at the bus stop and set her emergency lights on flash then scrambled out of the car.

"We've got to take him to the hospital," cried Kat to her sister.

"Not so fast," said Genya. "We don't want to move him in case he has a neck injury. We've got to call an ambulance."

Lisa flipped open her cell phone and called 911. When the ambulance came, Lisa scrambled in beside Ian's stretcher, leaving Ian's two knapsacks behind. Kat picked them up and put them in the trunk of the car, and then she and her sister followed behind the ambulance.

Thankfully, Ian's injuries were superficial. He needed twelve stitches to his scalp, and his ribs were terribly bruised, but that was all. Kat phoned home to let them know why she and Genya would be late, and then she called Ian's house.

His mother answered the phone. Once Kat explained the situation, she could hear the clatter of a phone being dropped, and then she could hear the slam of a door.

Kat and Genya and Lisa were still waiting anxiously for Ian's stitching to be finished when his mother burst through the doors of Emergency fifteen minutes later. Mrs. Smith's expensively tailored jacket was buttoned awry and streaks of mascara stained her face. Her facade of polished perfection was gone. As her eyes darted urgently from Genya to Lisa and Kat, she asked, "Where is he?"

Kat pointed to the door of the room where Ian was being treated. Mrs. Smith didn't even knock. She pushed the door and rushed in.

As they waited, Genya looked at the two younger girls. "Did you recognize any of the guys who attacked Ian?"

Kat looked at Lisa, then back at her sister. "One of them was vaguely familiar. I think he's on some high school football team," she said evasively.

"By the looks of them, all of them were," said Lisa. "But they weren't from Cawthra, and they weren't from St. Paul's."

Kat nodded in agreement.

About a minute after that, Ian's father showed up. Kat noted that he had a look of angry determination on his face. Before doing anything else, Mr. Smith approached the reception desk and identified himself. The nurse apprised him of his son's condition and his shoulders immediately relaxed in relief. Instead of bursting into the treatment room as his wife had done, he sat down with the girls and waited.

"Tell me what happened," he said to them.

This was the first time Kat had seen Mr. Smith up close. She was struck by the physical similarity between him and Ian. Had Mr. Smith dyed his hair platinum, he would have looked identical to the Ian who showed up at the courtroom yesterday. They were both tall and lean with blond, almost feminine good looks. Mr. Smith had Ian's long tapered fingers, except these had only one adornment: a plain gold wedding band.

Kat told Mr. Smith about the scene they had happened upon. She didn't mention that they had found Ian's knife on the ground, nor did Lisa. They also didn't tell him that any of the kids looked familiar to them.

As they talked, the door to the treatment room opened and two figures emerged: Mrs. Smith, with her arm looped protectively around Ian's waist. In any other context, the image would have been absurd. Ian was more than a head taller than his mother, yet it was she who was supporting him. He had all of the energy of a rag doll and he leaned heavily on his mother, who no longer looked fragile or frantic.

One side of Ian's head had been shaven and the twelve black stitches were clearly visible. There were still traces of blood on his face and his iridescent shirt was splattered red. His leather pants were torn at the knees and his hands were scraped.

Ian's father jumped up from the chair and strode over to his son. "Are you okay?" he asked.

"I'm fine," said Ian, not looking fine at all. "I'm just bruised."

"We've got to press charges," said his father. "Did you recognize any of the kids who did this to you?"

Ian looked at his father with angry frustration. Did his father really think that pressing charges would make this better?

"They must have been from out of town," lied Ian. "None of them looked remotely familiar."

Genya opened her mouth to say something, but Kat gave her sister a meaningful look. Genya remained silent.

"Let's get home so I can get cleaned up. I don't want to be late for the concert."

Ian's mother looked up at him in amazement. "You can't perform in your condition."

"Just watch me," said Ian.

He flashed a weak smile at Lisa, Kat and Genya then said, "Thanks guys. See you at the school, okay?"

Then he walked with slow determination out of the hospital, still supported by his mother.

CHAPTER 38

DANYLO WAS PACING with agitation by the time Kat and Genya came home from the hospital. "How is Ian?" he asked urgently as soon as Kat stepped through the door.

"Fine," replied Kat. "No broken bones, just stitches and bruises."

Danylo sighed with relief. "It is too bad about his concert, though," said Danylo. "Has he cancelled?"

"Believe it or not, he said he was still going to play tonight."

A smile of admiration formed on Danylo's lips. "Then we'll have to hurry up and have supper so we can get over to the school," he said.

Orysia and Danylo both decided to go to the concert with Kat. Genya, as usual, went over to a friend's house. When they got to Cawthra, it was still early so there were only a few cars in the parking lot. Kat recognized Ian's father's Mercedes and sighed with relief. She was afraid that he might have changed his mind and not come. She also saw Lisa getting out of her parents' SUV. Lisa was dressed in her usual black, but instead of a short leather skirt and ripped stockings, she was wearing black jeans and a black leather jacket. She wore a silver spiked leather dog collar around her neck and her nails were painted black. Surprisingly, she wasn't wearing her usual ghastly makeup. Kat figured it was a concession to her parents being with her. Kat called out to Lisa to get her attention, and Lisa and her parents walked over to the Baliuk car.

Lisa's father reached out his hand and clasped Danylo's firmly. "How was the testimony today?" he asked.

"Good," replied Danylo.

"It was better than that," said Orysia. "Mr. Vincent has presented my father's case very thoroughly."

"I am glad to her it," said Dr. Nguyen, then he turned to Danylo. "Lisa tells me that you will be on the witness stand tomorrow."

"Yes," replied Danylo.

"I shall do my best to attend," said Dr. Nguyen. "Every bit of moral support helps."

Danylo bowed his head in gratitude. "Thank you," he said.

And then he and the Nguyens and Orysia ambled towards the school together, leaving Kat and Lisa by the car.

"Did you remember Ian's knapsack?" asked Lisa.

"I did," said Kat. Then she opened the trunk of the car and grabbed out the knapsack containing the mutilated parachute. "I don't think he'll want it now, though." Not that she wanted it in the car. It gave her the creeps.

"I've got an idea," said Lisa. "Bring it with you."

When they got into the auditorium, Lisa made a beeline over to the principal. Kat stood within hearing range, but kept her distance so as not to look like she was butting in.

"... and if he goes on first, he can get home and rest," Lisa was explaining.

Dr. Bradley nodded in sympathy. "Yes," she said. "It will be a bit disruptive for the others involved, but this is an unusual circumstance. I'm sure no one will complain about these last minute changes."

Lisa smiled grimly, then thanked Dr. Bradley, who quickly walked off, no doubt to inform the other students. "Come on," she said to Kat, motioning for her to follow.

Kat looked over her shoulder and noticed that the families were sitting together: Danylo, Orysia, Lisa's parents and Ian's parents. Kat almost laughed out loud. What an unlikely group. What would they ever talk about?

She followed Lisa onto the stage and then watched as Lisa unzipped the knapsack and unfurled the ripped parachute. "Here, take the end," Lisa directed.

Kat took the one end, and just as they had practised many times, she draped it across the curtains and fastened it. Once it was hung, they both stepped back. It looked terrible. Ribbons of hacked khaki coloured material dangled limply from the deep crimson backdrop. It was worse than no set at all. Kat walked back to pull down her end, but Lisa held her arm. "Just a minute," she said. "Let me think."

Kat shrugged her shoulders. She was too emotionally drained to think anything more about it, but if Lisa had a better idea, that was fine by her.

"Let's turn it upside down," said Lisa.

Kat was about to disagree, but then she understood what Lisa was doing. The parachute had been cut in strips, and by hanging how it was now with the narrow end at the top, it looked forlorn and straggled. Lisa pulled a ladder to one end of the stage and Kat dragged one over to the other end. They each held a bottom corner up high to see what would happen. Instantly, instead of looking forlorn and bedraggled, the strips looked intentional. The backdrop was suddenly transformed with fluttering jagged stripes. The hacked khaki strips of parachute stood out brave and proud.

Kat grinned at Lisa from her perch on the ladder and gave her the thumbs up sign.

There were seats in the orchestra pit for both Kat and Lisa to sit in while Ian played the piano. From that vantage point, they had a skewed, though close view of the stage. When the lights darkened after his piece, it would take moments for them to jump up and pull down the parachute.

Kat watched as parents and students streamed into the auditorium and found places to sit. She noticed Michael and his family come in, so she waved frantically to get his attention. Before sitting down in his own seat, he walked down the aisle and kneeled down in front of the pit.

"I'm coming to the hearing tomorrow," he said. "Dad agreed to let me miss school."

Kat was touched. "Thank you," she said. "I know my grandfather will appreciate it."

"Talk to you later," said Michael, scampering to his seat before the lights dimmed.

As she watched Michael walk back to his own seat, Kat noticed three familiar burly figures slouch in and sit in the back row. Kat nudged Lisa. "I noticed," said Lisa. It was the three jocks who had beaten Ian.

"I wonder what they're doing here?" whispered Kat.

"Getting a little culture, I guess," replied Lisa with sarcasm.

Beth and Callie also came in together, sitting in front of the three burly teens. Kat noticed that they turned and giggled flirtatiously. It seemed ages ago that these two had been friends of hers. Kat hadn't realized until this moment how distant she felt towards them.

The lights dimmed. Dr. Bradley stepped up onto the stage and announced the changes in the program.

Lisa switched on the spotlights she had arranged for Ian's entrance. The whole stage was plunged into darkness except for the piano in the pit. The ribbons of torn parachute cast an eerie shadow behind the pit and did seem fitting. The auditorium was silent with expectation. Suddenly, a figure burst through the curtains. A collective gasp rose throughout the auditorium. Ian had completely shaven his head, and the black stitches looked like a slash across his scalp. Instead of wearing the long black coat as he had planned, Ian had on his torn and bloodstained shirt and pants from the beating. The most astonishing thing about Ian's appearance was his expression. Ian was the gentlest person Kat knew, but right now his face flashed an angry scowl that was frightening in its intensity. Ian surveyed the audience and his eyes seemed to lock on the three sitting in the back row. Kat followed his gaze and noted with satisfaction that they seemed to squirm.

Ian strode over to the piano and sat down on the bench. As his fingers made contact with the ivory keys, all the anger drained out of his face and was replaced with a look of total concentration.

As the familiar ballade began to unfold, Kat tried to fill her mind with nothing but the music. She searched the faces in the audience and found her grandfather. As the music began, she saw her grandfather's eyes meet her own, and then he looked above her, to Ian. Perhaps he could lose himself in the music and forget about his burden just for a moment?

Danylo looked down at Kataryna's friend on the stage and sighed deeply as he felt the music wash over him. How was it that such beautiful music could come from such an unlikely source? When Kat had phoned Danylo to tell him of Ian's accident, he was horrified, but not really surprised. People tended to hate what they didn't understand. What did surprise him was the strength of this thin pale boy. Not only in the fact that he was able to come out in public like this after such a brutal beating, but that he had the strength and the gift to produce this intricate music.

The ballade began with a pounding intensity that brought to Danylo's mind a vision of violence. He wondered if it had the same effect on Ian? Was he beating the piano just as he had been beaten by those boys? The experience was so sharp that Danylo found himself gripping onto the armrests of his seat. A sob caught in Danylo's throat as he noticed a slight reflection of wetness on Ian's cheek. The boy was weeping.

It brought back the memory of that other pale thin boy, decades earlier. Seeing him again in the courtroom made it seem as if it were just yesterday.

The Nazis had built a huge barbed wire enclosure at the outskirts of Orelets. As Red Army soldiers were captured or surrendered, they were thrown into the open air prison to die of exposure, starvation or thirst. Villagers were tormented by the sight of so many starving prisoners of war — some of whom were neighbours or relatives. One boy could have been no more than 14. His pale thin face showed the first wisps of a beard and his eyes were often filled with tears. It cut Danylo to the core to see this young boy and the others waiting to die.

The Nazi guards had a game. They would pretend not to see when a village woman tossed food over the barbed wire, but then as the starving POWs fought each other for a morsel, the soldiers would shoot into the huddled mass of humanity, killing whomever succeeded in getting a bite. And because the POWs were considered not quite human by their Aryan taskmasters, this activity was considered no more immoral than shooting fish in a barrel. It was unbearable for Danylo to watch this happen without being able to do anything about it. He sent word to his sister in the forest, and they devised a plan.

The next time the guards checked the enclosure for corpses and only one man guarded the open gate, Kataryna made her appearance. Dressed in an open-necked blouse and a tightly cinched skirt, she walked past the entrance, carrying a basket of eggs. Just as the lone guard at the entrance noticed her pass, she caught his eye and smiled. But then her foot caught on a loose stone and she stumbled, eggs scattering around her. As the guard ran to help her back to her feet, some of the POWs were able to escape.

Once they had passed the gate and were heading towards the woods, Danylo walked over to his sister and grasped her elbow. They walked away together as the guard went back to the gate and locked it, never realizing what had just happened.

When they got back to their own cottage, Danylo almost vomited with relief. Had they been caught, both he and Kataryna would have been executed, but that's not what had worried him. It was the "collective responsibility" that was most on his mind. They rounded up villagers for each instance of defiance. He remembered the first time, when a Nazi officer had been killed. That resulted in one dozen villagers being chosen at random, marched into the centre of town, and executed in full view of their neighbours. The bodies were left swinging from ropes in the village square until they rotted and fell down.

How would the Nazis retaliate if they discovered POWs had been set free? But if he and Kataryna hadn't taken the risk, that 14-year-old's eyes would have haunted him forever.

Danylo was brought out of his memory when the music changed. It mellowed and became quiet, almost gentle. Danylo's knuckles relaxed and he was lulled momentarily into thinking the music would be simply pleasurable from now on. It almost sounded like a traditional ballad for a minute or so.

Then it built again. Danylo watched Ian's face and noticed that the boy was no longer weeping. There was a distanced coldness to the face. The hands moved across the keyboard more slowly now, and Danylo waited for the ballade to end. Unexpectedly, the momentum changed. Instead of winding down, it began to build back up with a slow but increasing fierceness. Tears sprung to Danylo's eyes as he remembered what happened just weeks after the POW camps had been established — black uniformed SS swooping down into their village.

Their first target was the Jews, but they came so swiftly that the villagers didn't grasp what was happening. A notice had been put up, requesting that the Jews pack one piece of luggage each and dress in their travel clothing. They were to congregate in the village square at 9 am sharp. The notice stated that they were to be evacuated beyond the war zone for their safety. Some of the Jews were fearful. Rumours of mass killings had drifted into even this remote village, but they were discounted. Germans were civilized, after all. Most packed their bags and congregated as they had been requested to do.

But hours after the boxcars of Jews had left, a strange rumbling could be heard in the distance. It wasn't thunder. Days later, there were fearful whisperings throughout the village. The Jews had been taken only miles away and forced to dig their own graves. And then they were shot.

The terror didn't stop there. Many Jews were found hidden with the other villagers. For each Jew found, a Ukrainian family was shot.

Then the Nazis began the *Oblava* — rounding up Ukrainian young people from schools, churches, the streets, and loading them into cattle cars for slave labour in Nazi Germany.

Sometimes the auxiliary police would get advance warning of these raids, and when that happened, Danylo could sometimes warn his neighbours to hide their young. But more often than not, the raids were a complete surprise.

Danylo got angrier and angrier as his memories flooded in. The music fit his mood perfectly.

The distanced coldness on Ian's face was replaced by a look of raw anger. He pounded the keys like a punch to the face. Danylo gripped the armrests again, holding on for dear life. Suddenly, the music changed again. The anger diminished and the complexity increased. Ian's shoulders relaxed and he leaned back a bit from the keyboard, playing the notes with a sheer cold showiness. Danylo noticed that the anger was gone from Ian's face. In fact, all emotion was gone.

The music built up again with the same power and intensity, and then, suddenly, it segued into utter abject sorrow. Ian's mask of indifference melted in an instant and was replaced with a look of despair. Watching him, Danylo was also filled with despair.

Danylo gripped the two rings that hung from chain around his neck and remembered when he first began to wear them.

The Nazis continued with the hated policy of communal farming that had been initiated by the Soviets. And as the months passed, their food requisitions became ever more impossible to meet. The resistance fighters who were hiding in the forest depended on the villagers to hide food for them. They also depended on them to steal medical supplies and weapons. Very young girls and old women were the best couriers. They could hide a pistol in the fold of a skirt, or vial of morphine in their head scarf, and the Nazis, who were disdainful of Slavs, took a long time to catch on to what they were up to.

Danylo had managed to steal three pistols from the police station and he had hidden them under the manure pile. His mother was an expert courier, but she was caught on her way to the forest with the third pistol hidden at the bottom of a basket. For her transgression, the Nazis not only sentenced her to death, but they made her choose six other village women to join her. If she didn't choose, she knew that the Nazis would, so with a shaking hand, she pointed out the six eldest women in the village. After they were shot, Danylo was ordered to dig the grave. Before he buried his own mother, he gently tugged her wedding ring past her knuckle, and then he removed his father's ring from a strap around his mother's neck.

So much grief. Too much for one soul to bear.

Then the ballade ended.

Ian sat with his head down, his hands stretched over the keyboard as if he were calming it, comforting it.

The audience sat in stunned silence. Danylo sat in his chair feeling limp. How could mere music have such a powerful effect?

The auditorium was so still that it could have been empty.

Danylo pushed himself up to a standing position and with slow determination, began to clap his hands. For moments on end, the only sound in the whole room was of Danylo's two hands slapping together. Then another pair joined in. And another. Danylo noticed through the corner of his eye that Lisa's parents had stood up beside him. He turned to face Mrs. Nguyen and he nodded in acknowledgement. Danylo looked down and saw that Ian's mother's face was wet with tears, but she was grinning. She stood up, and so did Mr. Smith. And they continued clapping. Pockets of people throughout the audience stood too. By this time, the clapping had changed from a small peppering to a rhythmic intensity. Almost a chant. Within moments, the whole audience was on its feet, clapping and chanting, "More! More! More!"

Danylo looked up to Ian on the stage. The boy was standing in stunned silence beside his piano. It was as if he were trying to figure out what all of this clapping was for. Ian had been so wrapped up in the music that he had forgotten about the audience. He was just now coming back to earth and it dawned on him that these people were clapping for him. That they actually approved of him. What a strange world it was.

Ian bowed to the audience in thanks, and then held up one hand, asking for silence. "Thank you," he said. He walked towards the piano bench, and the people in the audience began to sink back into their seats, expecting him to play an encore. He hesitated for a moment in front of the bench, then shook his head slightly. He looked back up at the audience and said in a loud clear voice, "Thank you. Please enjoy the rest of the concert."

Then he turned and disappeared behind the curtains.

Lisa turned off the spotlight and the stage was plunged into darkness. The audience was murmuring their surprise and they were totally unaware of Lisa and Kat who had scrambled onto the stage to pull down the ribbons of cloth. In a flash it was down, and the two girls darted through the curtains close on the heels of Ian.

Kat could see the light go back on the other side of the curtain, and Dr. Bradley was back on the stage introducing the next performance. She quickly followed Lisa and Ian as they walked away from the back of the stage and out a door that led to a school corridor.

"That was fantastic," said Lisa.

Ian looked at her with an expression of incomprehension. Kat understood. When she was in the midst of sculpting, she was totally in another world. The school could burn down and she wouldn't know it. He looked utterly exhausted. The best thing for him would be to get home and go to bed, but his parents were still in the auditorium.

The three friends walked down the corridor that lead to the front of the school and they stepped outside into the winter air. The cold seemed to revive Ian somewhat. He breathed in, and then stretched out his arms as if to embrace the world.

"It feels so good to get that over with," he said. "I had no idea whether I would be able to go through with it or not."

"I'm amazed that you did," said Lisa. "You must be tired."

"And sore," said Kat.

"I am," said Ian. "And I couldn't have done it without your help." With that, he gave both girls a bear hug.

Just then, the front door of the school opened and Dylan and his friends walked out.

"That was quite the performance," said Dylan with a smirk. "Didn't think you'd be up to it."

"Why don't you just get out of here?" said Kat angrily. "Don't you think you've done enough damage?" Kat had trouble reconciling this new Dylan with the one she used to know. What was his problem, anyway?

Dylan regarded Kat with an offended look on his face and addressed Ian, "I see you've got your bodyguards with you."

At that, Dylan's friends chuckled. "Two girls and a fag. I'm scared," Dylan said in a taunting voice.

Ian stepped away from Kat and Lisa, then walked over to where Dylan stood. "You wouldn't be so brave without your own body guards," he said, pointing at Dylan's husky friends.

"I'll fight you anytime, anywhere. Just name the place," said Dylan, anger flashing in his eyes. His fist was midway in the air when the door of the school opened again.

Dr. Bradley stepped out of the front doors of the school. She was accompanied by an artsy-looking man wearing a camel hair sports jacket over a T-shirt and jeans. She looked from Ian to Dylan and surmised what was going on. "I take it you three are leaving the concert?" she said to Dylan and his friends. "Students from other schools are not allowed to loiter at Cawthra. If you're not off school property in one minute, I'll call the police."

"Come on guys, this place is boring," said Dylan. The three slouched away into the night.

"Were those the boys who beat you up today, Ian?" asked Dr. Bradley.

"I didn't get a good look at them," said Ian evasively. Kat and Lisa remained silent.

During this exchange, the man quietly waited a few steps behind Dr. Bradley. When it was clear that nothing more was to be said on the subject, he stepped forward and reached out his hand to Ian.

"My name is Hal Stevens," he said. "I would like you to give me a call."

Ian looked at the card. It said, "talent agent". He frowned in confusion and stuffed it in his back pocket.

Chapter 39

When Kat woke up the next morning, she was surprised to see Genya up and dressed. "You're not wearing a uniform to school today?" Kat asked.

"I'm going to the hearing," replied Genya. "Dido's testifying today, isn't he?"

It was as if they were almost a family again, thought Kat as the four of them walked into the hearing room. If only her father were here. She surveyed the audience and noticed that there were more people than usual sitting on the plaintiff's side. On Danylo's side, Kat was delighted to see several familiar faces. In addition to Michael, both Ian and Lisa were there, as well as Lisa's father and grandmother. Danylo's friends from the Ukrainian community were also out in full force. In fact, there were so many people that some of them ended up sitting in the last row on the plaintiff's side. Genya sat between Kat and Orysia in the front row of the defendant's side.

When Danylo took the stand, he wore a brilliantly white starched shirt under his grey suit. Kat had expected his face to be pale and his hands to tremble, but she was wrong. Her grandfather looked full of anticipation. As if he were finally being given the opportunity to set the record straight. For his sake as much as hers, she hoped that was possible. She glanced over at Genya, and noticed her sceptic's demeanour: arms crossed and brow furrowed.

Kat looked back at her grandfather on the stand. He nodded courteously towards the people who had come to support him.

Step by step, Mr. Vincent took Danylo through the fateful years between 1939 and 1945. She listened in awe as he described how his position with the auxiliary police had been planned from the beginning by the organizers of the resistance. He hadn't gone from policeman to fighter: he had been a patriot all along. As Danylo spoke, Kat watched Genya's demeanour from the corner of her glasses. Slowly the arms uncrossed and the brows unfurled. Almost imperceptibly, Genya began to sit a bit straighter in her seat. It was as if she were no longer ashamed of her grandfather. Could she even be a little bit proud? wondered Kat.

"Mr. Feschuk," said Mr. Vincent. "Why did you and your fellow auxiliary police wait until the winter of 1942-43 to defy the Nazis?"

"How do you rebel with no strength?" asked Danylo. "We had no government, no weapons, no organization."

As soon as the Nazis arrived, Kataryna and the others had fled to the forest. She knew she was safer there than in the village because the Germans lost their way each time they came there. But Kataryna and her friends could not fight the Nazis yet, they could only hide. They had no weapons. They had no military training. While Kataryna and her friends prepared the forests with bunkers and hideouts, other resistance fighters stayed in Orelets and let the Germans think they were on their side. How else to steal weapons and information?

"Mr. Feschuk," said Mr. Vincent. "On a single day in February, 1943, three thousand Ukrainian auxiliary police suddenly turned on their German superiors and killed them, and then all three thousand fled to the woods. Why was that particular time chosen for a mass revolt?"

"The leaders of the Ukrainian underground initially wanted us all to wait just a little bit longer. Our undercover members were a key source of information on German movements. However, when the villagers in Volhyn refused to provide any more slave labourers for the Ostarbeiter program, the Germans initiated even more brutal reprisals."

"What would they do?" asked Mr. Vincent.

"By the fall of 1942, the Germans were burning down whole villages."

"How many times did this happen?" asked Mr. Vincent.

"In all of Ukraine, the Germans exterminated every single person in 459 villages. They burned down 28,000 villages. We knew that if we rebelled in an uncoordinated way, the Germans would accelerate their rampage," explained Danylo. "So we had to wait until the time was exactly right."

"And when did that happen?"

"When we had stolen enough weapons, and when most of the population had prepared refuge in the forests and in underground bunkers. Had they not been able to hide when we rebelled, the *Enzattzgruppen* would have come in and murdered them all."

In his mind's eye, Danylo relived that fateful day.

Danylo's nostrils flared at the distant smell of fire. He stepped out of the police station and scanned the horizon. Smoke was billowing from three distinct spots. Had the Nazis locked yet more villagers into churches and then set them on fire? How many times could they do this and still get away with it? Who would be left in Ukraine by the time they were done?

Just then, Myroslaw appeared beside him. "The time has come," he whispered.

Danylo had been waiting for this moment. He and Myroslaw quickly told the others and then they retrieved a small stash of rifles. Most of the weapons that they had stolen were already in the forest, but they had kept one automatic rifle each hidden in the latrine.

It was early in the morning, and so the black uniformed SS officer was still sitting in the kitchen sipping a second cup of tea. Myroslaw, Danylo and the others burst through, and without warning, shot him dead.

Petro Manchuk, the traitor, had not been with the officer, and he had not reported for duty yet that day. Danylo saw Myroslaw leave the police building, rifle in hand, walk towards Manchuk's house. Moments later, Danylo heard gunshot, and then he saw Myroslaw walk briskly back up the street.

"It is done," he said. "Now we must get the rest of the villagers into the woods before the killing units arrive."

Kat listened to this testimony in wonder. She could almost smell the fire from the villages.

Mr. Vincent paced back and forth in front of Danylo. "You mention that there were some auxiliary police who did collaborate with the Nazis, and that some of these men hurt civilians."

"That is correct," replied Danylo.

"Did any of these men join the Ukrainian Insurgent Army, the UPA?"

"Some tried," replied Danylo.

A ripple of murmurs filled the courtroom. Danylo's mind flashed to the past.

A clearing in the heart of the forest. A firing squad standing at attention. In front of them, stands Commander Krymka. One soldier, hands tied, is brought forward.

"You have been sentenced to death for crimes against civilians," states the commander.

The man is offered a blindfold, but he refuses. He faces the firing squad, and is executed.

"Mr. Feschuk," said Mr. Vincent. "Was the UPA only for Ukrainians?"

"Most UPA members were Ukrainians," answered Danylo. "But there were Hungarians, Jews, Poles, and Russians. There were also Germans. The one thing we had in common was a love of freedom. Freedom is more precious than gold."

"One more question," said Mr. Vincent. "Did immigration authorities ever ask what you did during the war?"

"No, they did not," replied Danylo.

"Thank you," said Mr. Vincent. "No more questions."

Mrs. Caine stood up. "Mr. Feschuk," she said. "Were you forced to become an auxiliary police officer?"

Danylo looked confused.

"Let me rephrase my question," she continued. "If you hadn't become an auxiliary police officer, would you have been sent to Germany as an *Ostarbeiter*?"

"I may have been," said Danylo. "Or I may have been shot, or hanged, or burned to death like other Ukrainians. Or I may have been put in a concentration camp like other Ukrainian patriots."

"So basically, you collaborated with the Nazis to avoid harsh treatment."

"Madame," said Danylo. "I did not collaborate, I infiltrated."

"And by doing so, you survived."

"Had I been caught as an infiltrator by either the Nazis or the Communists, Madame, I would have been executed."

She regarded him sceptically, but abandoned the line of questioning. Mrs. Caine paced in front of Danylo for a moment or two, as if trying to think of a diplomatic way to phrase her next question. "Mr. Feschuk," she said. "Did the UPA turn away some Jews who had escaped the Nazis and fled into the woods?"

"You are correct, Madame," replied Danylo. "There was much distrust between Jews and Ukrainians when the Germans first arrived. Ukrainians associated Jews with the Communists, and Jews associated Ukrainians with the Nazis. We were both wrong."

There was a ripple of outraged whispering from both sides of the audience. "Order!" said the judge. The silence was immediate.

"No more questions," said Mrs. Caine.

Kat sat back. That was it? No more questions? It was clear to Kat that her grandfather had not collaborated with the Nazis.

Mrs. Caine gave her final summary. "It is clear that Danylo Feschuk collaborated with the Nazis in his role as an auxiliary police officer in Orelets between 1941 and 1943," she began. "It is also probable that Mr. Feschuk did not mention to immigration authorities that he had collaborated with the Nazis. Had he done so, he would not have been allowed to become a Canadian citizen. Therefore, he obtained his citizenship by fraud. It is my recommendation to this court that Mr. Feschuk's citizenship should be revoked, and that he should be deported from this country."

Kat sat there, stunned at Mrs. Caine's view of the situation. There was a ripple of murmurs in the audience, some approving what she said, and others not.

The judge banged his gavel. "Order," he said. Then he regarded Mr. Vincent. "The summary for the defence."

Mr. Vincent stood up. "This court has listened to countless experts and countless witnesses, and yet not a single piece of evidence has been brought forward to show that Mr. Feschuk collaborated with the Nazis."

Kat glanced over at Genya and noticed that her sister was listening intently.

"Additionally, there has been no evidence brought forward to show that Mr. Feschuk lied to immigration officials. Indeed, why would he lie? Being an auxiliary policeman in Ukraine was not a prohibited category.

"Given the fact that there is no evidence of criminality, and given the fact that there is no evidence that the defendant lied during immigration proceedings, I have to wonder why this case was brought forward in the first place?"

Mr. Vincent's final statement stuck in Kat's mind: "Imagine yourself as a teenager in a Canada with no government, no army, no weapons," said Mr. Vincent. "Now imagine that the Russian army and navy and air force attacks on one front, and the American army and navy and air force attacks on another. What would you do? Would you do what Danylo did when he was a teen? Would you fight for your country as he did?

"Mrs. Caine asked a question earlier on. She asked, 'if a man betrays the country of his birth, what stops him from betraying his country of adoption?' The reverse is true too: if a man fights for his country of birth, he is the kind of man who will fight for his country of adoption. Mr. Feschuk has earned the right to call himself a Canadian."

Kat looked over to Genya. Their eyes met. Kat saw that her older sister's eyes were wet with tears.

Then the hearing was over. Kat breathed a sigh of relief; her grandfather was clearly innocent.

"I will review the evidence before me," said the judge. "I hope to have a decision soon. The court is adjourned."

As people filed out silently, two people stayed behind from across the aisle: the protester, and the girl with the hair clip. They waited until most of Danylo's supporters had left and then they walked up to Danylo and his family.

The protester looked troubled and agitated. She held out her hand to Danylo, and he grasped it gently.

"I survived the Holocaust," the woman said. "And what I remember is being led away at gun point by the Nazis, while the Ukrainians looked on. They did nothing to save us."

Danylo understood how her memories could be shaped that way.

"What I realize now is that the Ukrainians were as helpless as the Jews." Tears welled up in the woman's eyes. "My name is Sarah Goldman," she said. "And this is my granddaughter Carol."

The teen stepped forward and shook Danylo's hand and then she looked at Kat and smiled.

Throughout this exchange, Danylo's supporters had listened in silence. Dr. Nguyen stepped beside Danylo and placed a hand on his shoulder. Ian and Lisa were close behind.

"Mr. Feschuk," said Dr. Nguyen. "I would like to invite you to a get-together at our house tonight."

Danylo turned to Dr. Nguyen in gratitude.

"Yes," said Lisa, stepping forward. "A potluck. All these people here," she motioned with her hands to show Danylo's friends and supporters, Mrs. Goldman and her daughter, "are invited too."

CHAPTER 40

THE PHONE RANG.

Kat had just changed from her court clothing into jeans and a sweater. When no one else answered, she flew down the stairs and grabbed the phone. It was for her mother.

Orysia listened with surprise, and then put the phone back on its cradle. "They think they've found the graffiti artist again," her mother said.

Kat frowned sceptically. "Let's hope they have some evidence this time."

"Actually," said Orysia. "They think it was Dylan Tomblin, that boy you used to go to camp with."

"Dylan?" exclaimed Kat. "Why would he do such a thing?"

"I don't know," said Orysia, "but Dr. Bradley called the police last night after the concert because she was concerned about vandalism. When they got there, they caught this boy on school property with a spray can in his pocket."

"And from that, they think he's our graffiti artist?"

"No," said her mother. "They ran his fingerprints through the system, and it matched."

When Danylo stepped through the threshold at the Nguyens'

house, he was enveloped in hugs, handshakes, and the steamy scent of lemon grass simmering in broth. He felt as if he were in a dream state as he looked around him and saw so many familiar faces, all regarding him with happy smiles. His friends from the church and the Ukrainian community were there, and his neighbour, Mrs. Wentworth, as were the Vincents, Ian and his family, and even Karen — Genya's friend.

Danylo could feel tears of gratitude fill his throat. This hearing had been so hard on him, yet these people had not pre-judged. They listened to the testimony and drew their own conclusions. It gave him a sense of relief to know that Canada worked differently than the regimes he had fled.

Lisa's parents had set up a table along one wall of the kitchen. She handed Danylo the first plate, and grabbed him by the hand and led him to the head of the line. There were fragrant casserole dishes, and bowls and platters of food. Many of the dishes were entirely new to him, but they all smelled wonderful. He spooned a bit of each onto his plate and savoured the moment.

The weekend passed and there was no word from the judge. In spite of the fact that she had pretty well lost the year, Kat went to school on Monday. She craved a routine: something to take her mind off of her grandfather's trial.

She walked into art class with a sense of déjà vu. It was as if time had stood still. All the same people she had not seen or even thought about in the last few weeks were all there, and they were all chattering away about the usual things: music, clothes, who had the hots for whom. There was not even a rip-ple of attention or interest at her sudden return.

Well, that wasn't entirely so: Beth turned in her chair and regarded Kat appraisingly.

"You've got a lot of catching up to do," she said.

"I know," said Kat. "But I've been doing some projects at home too."

"Did your grandfather get his papers filled out?" she asked.

"Sort of," replied Kat. "We're still waiting to hear from the judge."

Just then, Michael walked in, and he slipped into the desk beside Kat. He gave her a grin.

"Your father was awesome on Friday," said Kat.

"Your grandfather wasn't so bad either," replied Michael.

At lunch, Kat noticed that there had been changes. Callie and Beth sat together at the table with the other grade ten arts students, but Michael wasn't there. Kat stood at the cafeteria entrance with her laden tray and scanned the room. It didn't take her long to spot Ian's shaved head. As if his unusual scalp wasn't enough, he was standing, flailing his arms so she'd notice. As she walked closer, she noticed that not only was Lisa sitting with him, but so was Michael.

Kat set down her tray and regarded these three true friends of hers. Who would have thought that this unlikely trio would have stuck with her through thick and thin?

Lisa swallowed a spoonful of chocolate pudding and then looked up at Kat with an excited grin. "Ian has news," she said.

Kat set her tray down beside Michael and across from Lisa and Ian. "What?" she asked. She looked over at Ian and saw that he looked like he was about to burst.

"Remember that guy who came out of the concert with Dr. Bradley?" he asked Kat, his eyes shining with excitement.

The concert seemed like a million years away. Kat thought about it. "Oh yeah," she said. "The agent."

"That's right," grinned Ian. "I tried out for a TV commercial yesterday."

"You're kidding," said Kat, her eyes glowing with pleasure. "Did you play the piano for him?"

Ian's grin diminished almost imperceptibly. "No," he said. "He was interested in my look, not my music."

"Oh," said Kat.

Lisa, who could barely contain her excitement throughout this exchange, bumped her shoulder against Ian's affectionately and said, "Come on, Ian, just tell her what happened."

Kat looked at Ian questioningly.

"I got cast in a TV commercial for an Internet banking company," said Ian.

"That's a riot," said Kat. "I would have never pegged you as a banker type."

Ian smiled. "You're always underestimating me."

CHAPTER 41

A WEEK WENT by. Then another. And another. Time stood still at the Baliuk residence. Every time the phone rang, Orysia jumped to answer it. Kat would watch her mother's face, her heart pumping in anticipation, but soon she would realize that the caller was yet another neighbour or well-wisher or friend.

Kat's father was still posted in Oregon, and her grandfather was still in Genya's bedroom. There was only one thing that didn't stand still in the Baliuk household, and that was Genya. Once the hearing was over, she plunged herself into her school-work as if nothing else mattered.

There was a voice mail message when Kat got home from school on the first Tuesday in early March.

"This is Mr. Vincent," the message said. "Iris, please call when you get home."

Orysia was at the old house with Danylo, packing up the last of the rooms. Kat ran all the way there. "Call Mr. Vincent," she said breathlessly. "I think the judge has made his decision."

Danylo's phone had already been disconnected, so they had to walk all the way back home before returning the call. Danylo slumped on the sofa in exhaustion, and Kat sat beside him and held his hand while her mother called the lawyer.

Orysia put the phone down. "We're to be at court tomorrow at 9," she said.

With such short notice, there were not many observers. Mrs. Caine was there, as was Mr. Vincent, but aside from Danylo, Orysia and Kat, the only other people present were a couple of reporters.

The judge regarded the almost empty room, then sat down in his usual place high up on the platform. He cleared his throat, then began to read from a paper in front of him.

Kat tried to listen as the judge summarized the details of her grandfather's hearing. He pointed out that this was not a criminal trial, but a deportation hearing. "I am not here to judge whether Mr. Feschuk is a war criminal," he said. "My job today is to determine whether, on the balance of probabilities, Mr. Danylo Feschuk lied to immigration authorities when he came to Canada."

Why then, Kat wondered, had all of those witnesses been called?

"There were a number of banned immigrant categories at the time Mr. Feschuk came to Canada," said the judge. "Let us go over them and see how Mr. Feschuk fits. Was he a Communist? No. Was he a member of the SS? No. In fact, he couldn't have been a member of the SS because he was not Aryan. Was he a member of the Nazi Party? Again, he wasn't eligible. Only German citizens were allowed to join the Nazi Party. Was he a criminal? No. A professional gambler, a prostitute, a black market racketeer? No, Mr. Feschuk was none of these things."

The judge flipped over his page and considered what he had written on the next page. "Mr. Feschuk did not use a fictitious name, he wasn't a member of the Mafia, nor of the Italian Fascist Party and he wasn't a Trotskyite."

The judge then looked over his glasses at Danylo. "However, the next category is more problematical. Was he a member of a revolutionary organization?"

Danylo regarded the judge unflinchingly, waiting for his answer. "No," said the judge. "There is nothing revolutionary about defending your country."

Danylo breathed a sigh of relief.

"However," continued the judge. "On the balance of probabilities, I find that Danylo Feschuk lied during his immigration screening."

Kat raised her hand to her mouth, stunned.

"I believe that if Mr. Feschuk had told immigration authorities that he was an auxiliary policeman, they would have questioned him very carefully about this, even though this would not have been a reason to deny him entry."

Kat stared at the judge in confusion.

"The fact that he claims not to remember much about the interview implies to me that he wasn't subjected to such questioning, and therefore must have lied about what really happened," continued the judge. "I find, on the balance of probabilities, that Mr. Feschuk obtained Canadian citizenship by false representation or by knowingly concealing material circumstances."

Kat felt a slow flush of anger envelop her. She wanted nothing more than to go over and shake the judge. Did he really think that his judgement was justice? She looked over at her grandfather, who was sitting between Kat and her mother. Danylo's face was pasty white in shock. She saw that her mother had grabbed one of Danylo's hands in a white knuckled grip, and Kat reached out and clasped the other.

The judge set down his papers and took off his glasses. He looked over at Danylo and his family and seemed to understand the emotional turmoil they were in. Gently, he said, "The Minister of Citizenship may wish to consider the following points: there is no evidence that Mr. Feschuk lied during immigration proceedings. There is no evidence that Mr. Feschuk was a Nazi; there is no evidence that Mr. Feschuk committed any crimes in his position as an auxiliary police officer. There is evidence that Mr. Feschuk used his position with the auxiliary police to work against the Nazis. While the Minister may consider these points, it is not in the scope of this court to do so."

With that, the judge stood up and walked out of the chambers.

Danylo, Kat and Orysia did not move. Instead, they sat, hands locked in each other's. One of the reporters flipped his steno pad shut and walked out of the room, but the other one approached the family. He was a young man with wire-rimmed glasses and an earnest expression.

"Mr. Feschuk," the reporter said, pen poised over steno pad. "What will you do now?"

Danylo looked into the reporter's face, but did not reply. After a few moments of uncomfortable silence, the reporter left.

The only people in the courtroom now were Mrs. Caine, Mr. Vincent, Danylo, Orysia and Kat. Mrs. Caine stuffed some sheets of paper into her briefcase and then clicked it shut. She smiled triumphantly at Danylo as she walked past him to the exit.

"He had nothing to lie about," Orysia said to Mr. Vincent.

"I know," he replied.

"What do we do now?" she asked.

"There is no appeal to a deportation and denaturalization hearing," said Mr. Vincent in a strained voice. "I don't know what to say."

CHAPTER 42

THAT NIGHT, KAT tossed and turned. She kept on dreaming about what was going to happen to her grandfather. Were the RCMP going to show up at their door and handcuff Dido? Where would they take him? If they deported him back to Ukraine, where would he live? Kat knew that no family had survived in Orelets.

Kat still hadn't slept a wink when she heard the squeak of the front door opening and the thunk of a newspaper being dropped in. She shivered slightly as she got out of bed so she grabbed a sweatshirt and pulled it over her nightgown for warmth and then padded down the stairs. It was still dark out, but already, both the *Globe & Mail* and the *Toronto Star* were sitting between the doors. She grabbed them both and sat down on the living room sofa. A headline on the bottom of the front page of the *Globe* caught her eye, "Ex-Nazi set for deportation."

The judge had found that her grandfather was not a Nazi, but they weren't going to let that fact get in the way of a good headline, she thought cynically. Kat didn't even have the heart to read the article. The newspaper slid from her lap and landed on the floor.

The front page of the *Star* was even more sensational, "Ex-Nazi lied to live here." Kat felt her face redden in anger. Where did this "ex-Nazi" stuff come from? As she scanned the article, anger turned to a feeling of hopelessness. There was no mention of the fact that her grandfather had worked with the Ukrainian resistance. The implication was that her grandfather had joined the auxiliary police in order to avoid farm labour in Germany. And to kill Jews. Kat threw the paper down onto the floor. How could this sort of thing happen in a country like Canada?

She walked across the living room, into the kitchen, and opened the basement door. She was so angry and distressed that only one thing could settle her, and that was her art. She didn't even bother turning on the light, but instead, relied on the glimmers of sunrise that were peeking through the basement windows. On her TV tray sat several of the *pysanky* she had worked on so carefully during the hearing. They had brought her comfort and hope each evening as she had a chance to sit by herself and understand what each witness had been trying to convey. What was the point, anyway, she thought now. Who had been listening? The judge had heard all the same points that she had, yet he had managed to come to a completely different conclusion.

Kat picked up her favourite egg. It was the one, that for her, embodied life and hope. It was the first one she had made during her grandfather's hearing: the one with forty triangles. Legend had it that far away, a monster was chained to a cliff. Once a year, the monster's servants would travel the world and count how many new *pysanky* had been made. Each year that there were fewer than the year before, the chains were loosened, and there was more evil let loose in the world. Making *pysanky* was Kat's pleasant chore to keep evil at bay.

But after reading those newspaper accounts of her grandfather, all Kat could think of was that evil had been let loose. She reached into her shoe box of dyes and implements, and pulled out the huge chemo syringe that reminded her of Baba, but in an ugly, deathly way. She took a deep breath and plunged it into the fortieth triangle at the bottom of the egg. With cold precision, Kat drew out the yolk and the white of her favourite egg. By doing so, she killed it, but she also saved it from bursting from rot in years to come.

When she was finished, she held up the empty shell about 6 inches from her face. It was beautiful, but empty: no longer a symbol of hope and love. Just an empty shell. With anger born of despair, she took that beautiful egg and smashed it on the TV tray. And then she walked back upstairs.

She stood in the living room and stared out the window, watching the sun slowly rise. One sob escaped her throat, then another, and another.

From behind the closed door of his bedroom, Danylo could hear his *zolota zhabka* weeping. It broke his heart to hear it. What did she think of him now that the judge had ruled against him, he wondered. Did she still love him? And did she understand the truth? He could only hope.

He took his terry cloth robe down from the hook on the back of the door and put it on over his pyjamas. He opened the door and looked out. There she was, his golden frog, his *zolota zhabka*, with a broken heart. It was his fault. Perhaps he should have packed his bags and left when the deportation order had first come. Perhaps then, she would have been saved this sorrow?

He stepped out of the bedroom and approached Kat. She looked up and quickly wiped her tears. When he sat down beside her, she showed him the ugly words from the newspapers. Tears began to form in his eyes too. It was bad enough that they were stripping his citizenship, but to call him a Nazi — that was too much. Perhaps he should leave this country. He had obviously overestimated the Canadian sense of justice.

The two sat together on the sofa without exchanging words. Moments and minutes and hours passed. The sun rose.

Genya came down the stairs and walked into the living room, rubbing the sleep out of her eyes. "What's the matter?" she asked, glancing from her sister to her grandfather.

Kat looked up. "Read this," she said, gathering up the

papers at her feet and handing them to her sister. She watched Genya's expression change from bored sleepiness, to incomprehension, to anger.

"This is crap," said Genya. Danylo looked up and met his older granddaughter's eyes. He felt a glimmer of gratitude. Of all people, he felt that Genya would be the first to abandon him. "You are innocent, Dido," she said vehemently. "We've got to fight this."

Kat looked up at her sister with hope.

Genya wasn't alone in her fighting spirit. A group of concerned citizens called a meeting at the church hall that very evening, and Kat was thrilled when hundreds of supporters gathered. In addition to people from the congregation, there were a number of students from St. Paul's and from Cawthra. There was a large contingent from the Vietnamese community, and even a number of complete strangers. Kat spied Ian's shaved and stitched head at the back of the hall, and so she darted down the aisle before the meeting started to greet her friend. He was not alone. Both Lisa and Michael were with him.

"Michael called me this morning when he read the newspapers," explained Ian. "We knew we had to do something."

"You guys called this meeting?" asked Kat in surprise, regarding her three true friends.

Lisa hooked her arm through Ian's and Michael clasped Kat's hand in his own. "We wouldn't exactly let you down," said Michael. "Whatever it takes, we're in this together."

That evening, after everyone else had gone to sleep, Kat went back downstairs to her beloved shattered *pysanka*. It was too late to put it back together, but perhaps it wasn't too late to make something out of the ruins. Slowly and painstakingly, she began to take the broken shards, and one by one and glue them onto a canvas in an intricate mosaic.

AUTHOR'S NOTE

As of April 12, 2001, there are three Canadians set to be deported and to be stripped of their citizenship. In each of these cases, accusations of Nazi war crimes were made, but no evidence was brought forth. There is no appeal. These cases are:

> Minister of Citizenship and Immigration v. Odynsky, 2001 FCT 138,
> Minister of Citizenship and Immigration and Katriuk, Docket: T-2409-96
> Minister of Citizenship and Immigration and Oberlander, Docket: T-866-95

In another case, accusations were made and testimony was brought forth, but once the trial was over and the Canadian was stripped of his citizenship, the people who testified against him admitted that they had lied under oath. Their testimony had been taken under the threat of torture by the former KGB. This case is:

> Minister of Citizenship and Immigration v. Kisluk, Docket: T-300-97

Mr. Kisluk died on May 21, 2001. To his dying breath, he maintained his innocence. His last testament can be read at: http://infoukes.com/uccla/issues/warcrimes/i_wrcrms_069.html

The notarized, witnessed confessions of those who bore false witness against him can also be read at the above link.

War criminals must be brought to justice, but our federal government's current approach is not working. If a person is accused of a horrible crime, justice demands that they be presumed innocent until proven guilty. That guilt can only be proven in a criminal court. Once a person is convicted of war crimes, then the government can punish accordingly.

Before beginning these proceedings, the government stated, "The key criterion in all these proceedings is the existence of some evidence of individual criminality. If that cannot be proven, no proceedings will be considered."

Unfortunately, the government is not following their own guidelines

RESOURCE LIST

Web resources

Teachers' resources can be found at the author's web site:
    http://www.calla.com
The infoukes.com web site is the most comprehensive and reliable Internet resource for all things Ukrainian. The main page can be found at:
    http://infoukes.com
World War II history can be found at:
    http://infoukes.com/history/
The issue of alleged war crimes can be found at:
    http://infoukes.com/uccla/issues/warcrimes/index-nuccla.html
The Ukrainian Insurgent Army (UPA) has published has published 32 volumes of chronicles in the Ukrainian language. There are English summaries of all volumes posted on the Internet at:
    http://infoukes.com/upa/
The government of Canada's report on the Deschenes Commission and war criminals can be found at:
    http://www.parl.gc.ca/information/library/PRBpubs/873-e.htm

Books

Thousands of Roads. Maria Savchyn Pyskir, translated by Ania Savage. McFarland & Co., 2001. ISBN 0-7864-0764-6.
The memoir of a young woman's life in the Ukrainian Underground during and after World War II.
Into Auschwitz, for Ukraine. Stefan Petelycky. Kashtan Press, 1999. ISBN 1-896354-16-5.
The memoir of a Ukrainian survivor of Auschwitz.

Film

Between Hitler and Stalin ... Ukraine in World War II. Ukrainian Canadian Research and Documentation Centre, 620 Spadina Ave., Suite 200 Toronto, ON CANADA, M5S 2H4, 416-966-1819 E-Mail: ucrdc@interlog.com

Acknowledgements

This novel is dedicated to my dear friend, Natalie Wasylyk.

It would not have been possible for me to write *Hope's War* had it not been for the people who allowed me to interview them about their own experiences or shared with me their expertise on a variety of topics.

The following people introduced me to primary documents dealing with Ukraine during World War II: Professor Peter Potichnyj, editor of *Litopys UPA: Chronicles of the Ukrainian Insurgent Army*; Dr. Lubomyr Luciuk, author of *Searching for Place*; Andrew Gregorovich, librarian extraordinaire at the Ukrainian Canadian Research and Documentation Centre; Oleh Romanyshyn PhD, editor of *Ukrainian Echo*; Wolodymyr Kosyk PhD, author of *The Third Reich and Ukraine*; Modest Ripeckyj MD, editor of "UPA Medical Services", volume 23 of *Litopys UPA*.

Many thanks to the following people who allowed me to interview them about their personal experiences: The Odynsky family and the late Serge Kisluk gave me details about what it was like to be considered a "sub-human" under Nazi terror, and also what it is like to be plunged into denaturalization and deportation proceedings here in Canada. I would also like to thank Eric Hafemann and Miriam Bauman for their insight on this matter from a legal perspective.

I would also like to thank Dr. John and Lidia Skrypuch, Stepha Wiwczaruk, Marika Szkambara, Marika Lopata, Victoria Tupeich, Natalie Wasylyk, George and Carol Mychailenko, Yevdokia Kovalchuk and others who shared with me their family stories of slave labour, terror, and everyday life under both Soviet and Nazi oppression.

Paul O'Mara, Dorothy Byers, Fabio Zanetti, Genya Palij Moore, Eugene Yakovitch, Aaron Campbell, Ian Smits, Marianne Bluger, Oksana Bashuk Hepburn, Janice Kulyk Keefer, Khanh Nguyen, Taras Podilsky, Ann Biscoe, Bill Hughes, Orysia Tracz, Iko Labunka, His Grace Bishop Yurij Kalistchuk, Father Sencio, Father Ozimko, Myroslav Yurkevich, Jean Paul Himka, Nell Nakoneczny and Marco Levytsky were all wonderful for giving me insight into specific aspects of the novel.

Readers, Orest Skrypuch, Cheryl Forchuk, Dorothy Forchuk, Polly Martin, Rosemarie Reichel, Janet McConnaughey, Merrill Cornish, Kate Coombs, Elizabeth Ferrall, Paulette MacQuarrie, Erinn Fitzpatrick, Steph Young, Lora McInnes, Olya Grod, Lubomyr Luciuk, Oleh Romanyshyn, Andrew Gregorovich, Myroslava Oleksiuk-Baker and Mike Beal all read through various drafts of the novel and helped me improve it.

The photos in *Hope's War* were borrowed from the private collections. Sincere thanks to Petro Sodol, Maria and Modest Ripeckyj, Mykola Kulyk, Andrew Gregorovich, Oleh Romanyshyn, Theophil Staruch, and Yevdokia Kovalchuk.

I am greatful to the Ukarainian Canadian Foundation of Taras Shevchenko for their support.

This novel would not have been possible without the wonderful feedback and encouragement from my agent, Dean Cooke, and Suzanne Brandreth. Also, sincere thanks to Barry Jowett, my editor at Dundurn.

Я дуже прошу Вас відповісти
на цей мій (Євгенії Петрівні). Вона
заслуговує цього. Хай береже її Бог
на багато ще років. Хай береже Вас,
благаю Бога і Вашого Татуся і рідних
Щоб прохати і побажати. Якщо будете
писати відповідь, то посилайте, будь ласка,
так, щоб мій не пропав. (Багато охо-
чих почитати, а відповідальності ніхто
не несе, така ще, на жаль, наша
Україна, хоч помаленьку ми приходимо
в Тяму).

Мій домашній телефон чин
нів: ли код з Києва до Ришкева
а домашній
тел. Євгенії Петрівни відповідно

З великою надією на
благополучний фінал Вашої
видавничої праці (і нашої
переписки).

Слава Ісусу!
Слава Україні!
О. Майбога